RETRIBUTION

LESSER GODS

As always, this book is dedicated to my amazing partner, who is always saving me from crazy situations and is always there for me.
Without you, I am lost.
Thank you for always pushing me to do the scary things and being my sounding board for all my creative endeavors.
<3

Also, thank you again to my amazing beta readers, editor, friends, and followers—even those I haven't met yet!
You make this journey memorable, fun, and worth every moment.
I hope Lesser Gods helps someone through these times as much as it has helped me through all these years.
Through community, art, and being ourselves, we will persevere.

Prologue

Why, our story has kicked off quite dramatically hasn't it?

I hope you enjoyed the little break before I continue.

Oh, yes, yes, I know what you're thinking. "What a cliffhanger!" Or maybe you're thinking, "What is even happening?" Or maybe even, "Are you crazy? You let that just happen?!"

All perfectly valid reactions! As I've said before, the universe is a complicated, tangled thing, and our story is no exception. Twists, turns, a few emotional catastrophes—yes, yes, all of that is ahead and more.

I'm sure you are chomping at the bit to get on with this story, aren't you? Good, good. I am glad.

However, before we begin, I would like to inform you of a few possibly sensitive subjects that will be mentioned in this part of our story.

Trigger Warning

This story contains some discussions and depictions of self-harm. These topics are important to the characters they concern, but *your well-being matters more*. If these subjects are difficult for you, I encourage you to skip those scenes.

You are not alone, and the world is better with you in it.

520 Years Ago, Nullhymm
On a Tuesday

Red and gold blood flowed between Lunette's fingers as they pressed their hand against the fresh wound at the base of their sternum. Warmth pooled beneath their palm, mingling with the icy chill of their metal armor and the curved bone dagger still lodged in their flesh.

The contrast made them shiver.

Their breath came in ragged gasps as what had just happened set into their mind; their skin started to feel cold and clammy. They had torn their way through the horde of reapers with the other Valdarr, fixated on the only thing that mattered—cutting down Thanatos. Their world depended on it. Clashing with the stag, they finally found an opening and struck. However, they had made one fatal miscalculation.

Lunette couldn't tear their eyes away from the blade; the light blue gem in its pommel caught the light of the alien sun that burned above. It was strangely beautiful. The battlefield that surrounded them faded into the background as the ringing in their ears overtook their senses—metal and bone clashing, distant screams, and Alastair's voice calling their name.

Their opposite hand released the hilt of their short sword, fingers aching from the strain of gripping it for the last hour. Glancing around their immediate area as they staggered back, the world felt as if it were spinning. Their peripheral vision caught the flash of white and gray fur as Alastair attempted to break through the chaos of battle towards them, his normally impassive face twisted with fear.

Don't be scared. We won... right? It's over. I got him.

A shadow fell across them.

The wounded stag loomed, impossibly tall, a gaping wound in his lower chest where Lunette's blade had struck true right before a reaper sunk their blade into them. The rage radiating from Thanatos' form could have steamed the cool air. His scythe lay forgotten on the ground. Golden blood ran from his chest, mouth, and nose down his jaw, dripping onto the ground.

Lunette staggered back, but he moved with them. His presence stretched like a storm cloud across the battlefield. The scythe lifted from the dirt into his waiting hand. Red energy pulsed at its peak, flooded down the blade of the scythe, mingling with the black death magic that flowed up its snath from the Creator's hand that gripped it, illuminating its edges and simultaneously cloaking it in shadow.

They held eye contact with the Creator's brightly glowing gaze, grim determination etched across their face. "You'll *never* take our world. Even after I'm gone."

The stag bared his teeth; his deep voice came in ragged breaths. "*Your world* etched its doom in the cosmos long ago. You can't stop what is to be!"

With a guttural roar, the Creator raised his scythe above his head with both hands.

Lunette simply closed their eyes.

I'm sorry.

A sharp gasp cut through the air.

Then—the wet, sickening sound of a weapon tearing through flesh.

Lunette's eyes snapped open.

The sunlight of this foreign realm reflected off the black and gold armor before them.

"Valdis!" Lunette's scream tore through the battlefield.

The black and silver jackal convulsed as the scythe sank into his chest, the red and black magic enveloping his body. His large, rounded ears and paws twitched as it drained what life remained, practically inhaling his soul into the blade. His sword slipped from his claws, its runes dimming pitifully when it struck the ground.

Then, stillness as he collapsed to the ground.

Lunette fell beside him. With trembling hands, they gripped his fur around the base of his neck and tugged, a childish effort to get him up.

"*Val!*" The cry tore from their throat, raw and broken, as they clutched at him, as if holding him tighter could bring him back.

Another familiar yell echoed through the chaos.

Alastair.

The gray wolf charged, axe raised, desperation etched into every line of his body. The stag sidestepped easily, grabbed Alastair by the braids, and dragged the ancient blade across the wolf's throat. Blood sprayed. Alastair dropped, twitching, gurgling, then fell silent.

Lunette screamed.

"You *bastard*!"

The stag smiled, cruel and deliberate. "Now," he breathed, wiping the red blood from his face, "seems you too have nothing left." He stepped forward. The ground trembled beneath his hooves. "You thought you could come *here?* Invade *my* world to save your own?" He laughed, a cold, echoing sound that caused the battle surrounding them to quiet and watch.

His hand lifted. The dagger buried in Lunette twisted deeper by an unseen force, causing them to gasp and fall back on their elbows. Agony burst through them, but it was a distant echo beneath the whirlwind of emotions tearing through their mind.

"They were right to imprison you and your little mortals—"

The monologue was cut short by Lunette's scream.

A surge of deep crimson energy tore from their open hand, sparking with the ferocity of a storm. The jackal's blade rose from the dirt, its edge now alive with the flickering red power. In a flash, it spun toward the Creator.

Thanatos barely dodged as the blade sliced across his chest through the already gaping wound, tearing it open further. Golden blood poured down his torso, over the bone armor and red robe he wore. His laughter died. He stumbled back, staring at Lunette in disbelief as he hit the ground.

Lunette's vision burned red; something rose inside their body, an energy that coursed so violently and untamed it dulled every single one of their senses. They shakily rose to their hooves, stumbling to step around their dead companions to stand over the Creator.

With another scream and strike of their hand—magic burst from their entire body, a wave of pure, raw destruction. The ground cracked beneath them. The sky darkened, recoiling from their fury. Energy, a red fire-like force, washed over the battlefield in all directions, like a tsunami. Consuming the reapers and what few were left of their small army.

Once a cacophony of clashing steel and bone, the landscape was now eerily quiet.

When the haze cleared, the two gods found themselves completely alone. Bodies lay in heaps and ash. No reapers, no Valdarr. Their vision focused, and with a shuddering breath their hocks became weak at the sight.

What have we *done? What have I done? I've killed them all... It was a mistake coming here.* Their heart pounded in their ears and tears welled in their eyes.

Thanatos writhed on the ground; hands pressed to the gushing wound on his chest. His eyes widened as he focused on the faun.

"*You...* What do you think you're *doing?*"

Lunette barely heard him. Red and golden ichor dripped from the dagger that was still embedded in them. Valdis' sword was somehow back in their hand, its runes revived with the energy of their fury. Their eyes shifted from the surrounding scene, to the sword, to the helpless-looking stag before them.

Lunette adjusted their grip on the sword, then took a shaky step towards the Creator.

A scream tore from their throat as they pointed the blade at his throat, mere inches from it.

They froze.

The stag did not fight. Instead, he watched the faun. His eyes widened for a moment and then... softened as he shifted his gaze to the sword's tip. Thanatos looked... disheveled. Numb. He did not fight; he simply held his wound with both hands.

Lunette stared back at the broken, hollow figure of the Creator beneath them.

Is he yearning for his last breath? What am I doing?

In his crimson, no longer blazing, eyes they could see their own reflection staring back at them. It looked mad. Their white hair and fur were soaked in ash and blood. The armor that encased them was far too clunky for their frame.

Lunette's arms felt weak; they started to tremble, their energy dissipating. *What am I doing?*

Suddenly, Thanatos' eyes shifted focus. The stag now looked past them. Rather, behind them.

Just as they turned to see what he was looking at, Lunette's world tilted, a force encapsulated them in one swift blow... and everything went dark.

Wednesday Morning, Present Day

Ash shot out of bed with a start. His whole body shook as he stumbled to his feet. Gasping for breath, he caught himself on a gilded vanity that was nearby.

His body felt raw. It felt as if there were a gaping hole in his chest. Ash's reflection more closely resembled a stranger than himself. Completely disheveled; his fur and hair were in all directions, the pink skin beneath the skull markings on his face felt extra raw. There was an overstimulating ache radiating through him; he swore he could feel his bones shifting beneath his skin, which was impressive, considering he was pretty sure most of them had already been broken at least once this week. His green eyes were bloodshot, and his throat was sore from the cold.

Yesterday, or whenever it was, came into his mind. What *he* had done. *He* brought Lunette there. *He* set Thanatos free. *He* fulfilled his purpose... for the *first* time.

"Ash! Fight back! Don't let him get away with this!"

Lunette's words rang in his ears like a bell at a funeral.

After learning that another Creator was hunting him for his knowledge about the Child of the Creators—rather, lack thereof— Leroy had suggested they go to Thanatos' prison. He suggested they reinforce the seals to stop anyone from potentially freeing the Corrupted One.

How foolish, how naïve...

Leroy had set them up. He knew Thanatos wanted Ash. He knew Lunette was the key to freeing him. These past nine years had been nothing but a *lie*. Then, when Leroy pressed Lunette's bloodied hand to the icy door. Ash simply sat there, watching it unfold, unable to move, *powerless*.

I failed them.

Ash and Lunette fled the icy cavern when the other Creator who had been pursuing them showed up just as the stag broke free. Thanatos battled the serpent, rendering him unconscious before he caught up to the duo.

Ash couldn't fight back. The stag opened a portal to an alien world, vowing Earth's destruction. Leroy dragged him, Lunette, and the unconscious Creator into this strange realm. Leroy ended up knocking Lunette out for their excessive yelling.

He recalled the burning cold sensation from the shadow tendrils that bound his body and dragged him along. The ache of broken bones beneath his skin from Leroy throwing him against the ice prison made him nauseous. However, through the pain and cold, he couldn't help but gawk at the foreign landscape—it was nothing like he'd ever seen.

They arrived at a decayed metropolis bathed in the glow of an unmoving ring in the sky that was this world's cold, orange sun. Broken carts littered its cobblestone streets, twisted iron fences, and red flames flickered in the remains of lanterns. Stone, towering gothic buildings and gray, exaggerated cat statues that wore robes and held staffs loomed over the streets of the extraterrestrial landscape. Their spires pierced the sky like jagged claws.

Specters of dead mortals of all different species hid around corners, watching from a distance as they were paraded through the streets towards a cathedral at the edge of the city. Its spire resembled the antlers on the stag's head; a red fire burned in the center of them.

Everything here appeared dead.

There was pounding in his ears. Was that his heart beating? Or an illusion he was alive?

When they approached the unstable drawbridge that led up to the cathedral, Ash's vision started to blur. The energy shifted as they crossed over the misty abyss below. Somehow it grew colder, and he couldn't see the bottom. His stomach lurched; the pain was too much. His legs buckled. He couldn't hear the snide comments Leroy made before his consciousness gave way.

It was all too much.

This can't be happening. It can't be real.

He blinked his dull green eyes a few times, attempting to focus on the present, which now made him realize that someone had changed his clothes from the coat and pants he wore before to a rough black and red robe. Also, they took his shoes. Whoever it was healed his wounds. The broken bones felt mended, as did the scratch on his face from earlier that week.

He crinkled his nose—*hopefully that wasn't Leroy who changed my clothes...*

Ash's ears swiveled to the pitter-patter of paws outside his door. With a *clink,* it creaked open. He turned fully, tail lashing behind him, ready to fight despite his exhaustion.

Standing in the cracked doorway was a small but stout, gray and brown lynx, wearing what resembled a priest's garb—except it was red and black. The way her judgmental yellow eyes scanned over his face made his stomach turn... or perhaps it was hunger from not eating for a day.

"Oh, *relax,*" she scoffed. "Attacking me won't get you far, anyway. Do you want food or not?"

"Food?" Ash croaked out, his voice hoarse.

"Yes, *food.* The thing living beings need to consume, though you are a god. Allegedly. Perhaps you don't actually need it." Her eyes scanned the length of his body, seeming unimpressed.

"I'm hungry," Ash responded quickly.

"That's what I thought. Come with me and don't try anything. I have permission to bind you if need be." She turned with purpose back the way she came and started down the hall. Ash hesitated a moment before trailing behind.

The empty halls were lined with doors to rooms like his; on the opposite side were red stained-glass windows that faced a baren, hilly, frost-laden landscape that seemed to drop off in the distance.

The walls and floor were made of stone, which only reinforced the ever-present chill of this realm. At the center of the long corridor, they turned down a short hall that opened to a room where a barren, tiered fountain stood tall. Three other hallways branched off each side around it. One hallway was blocked by a particularly large, carved wooden door.

"Just because it seems empty doesn't mean you're not being watched. Two of us are here to keep an eye on you," she said, eyeing his perplexed expression.

Ash barely got a glance at the rest of the odd sight before the lynx turned sharply down the hall to the right. The smell of earthy spices filled his nostrils as she pushed open a door to a large dining room. A lengthy, polished wooden table occupied most of the room, with enough seating capacity with its padded, carved chairs for more than two dozen individuals. However, despite being designed to accommodate many, the table was empty except for a single figure seated at its head.

Rasping a clawed hand on the edge of the table, the enormous stag's attention shifted to Ash. His red eyes, though no longer glowing with that violent, oppressive energy, made Ash stop dead in his tracks as they made eye contact.

"Ah, I've been waiting." Thanatos' voice rumbled. Even without the echo of the dank prison, his voice was smooth and deep. The candlelight in the room made his charcoal and pale gray fur shimmer, while his large ears were pointed toward Ash. Long, carefully brushed black hair outlined his upper body, with several loose braids falling around his face. A low-cut red robe replaced the ragged one he'd worn before. It was newer and less worn with sleeves so long they nearly covered his hands.

He looks almost... mortal.

"Yes, yes, I do clean up well." A chuckle rumbled from the stag's lips, making Ash furrow his brow in confusion. "Do not be alarmed, chosen one. I spoke in your mind before. Do not think that I cannot now that I am free. Come, sit."

His opposite clawed hand gestured to the chair directly to his right, where a plate of warm meat steamed in the cool air. The lynx gave Ash a nudge in the back, forcing his knees to unlock and step forward. He made his way around the table, not breaking eye contact with the stag, then sank into the seat next to him. A strong scent of myrrh filled his nostrils.

Thanatos tilted his head. "Why do you appear so nervous, Ash? I am not going to hurt you. You have been a good little errand boy." The rapping hand stopped only to grasp a silver goblet beside him. His thumb rubbed the strange pentagram-esque symbol on it before raising it to his lips. The motion causing his long sleeve to slip down his arm, revealing cleaner bandages around his forearm than before.

There wasn't a muscle in Ash's body that wasn't tense. The fur under his robe stood on all ends. His jaw felt fixated in a permanent clench. When Thanatos' eyes met his again, he looked away. *Should I be fighting back right now?*

"*Tch,* please," the stag snorted, "you did not fight before with backup, what makes you think that's a good idea *now?*" He gestured with a single, slender finger to the plate of steaming food. "Eat. You're starving."

Ash gritted his teeth but obliged by stiffly picking up the fork beside his plate. "Where—" He attempted to clear his throat. "Where is Lunette?"

A dark chuckle rumbled from Thanatos' chest as he finished another sip of what Ash assumed was red wine from the potent aroma. "Why am I not surprised that would be the first thing you would ask me? Your little faun is fine."

"But *where* are they? What are you going to do to them?"

"Can you *please* eat before your stomach's gurgling can be heard from the street?" The stag's eyes snapped to meet Ash's quickly, narrowing slightly.

Ash fumbled with his fork in his hand before quickly taking a bite of the proportionately cut and seasoned meat on his plate. It tasted of rosemary, thyme, and lemon. *I hope this isn't poisoned... or drugged.*

"It's *chicken*." Thanatos shook his head. "I would not poison you or drug you, my chosen one. That would be... counterproductive."

The lynx brought over another bottle of red wine and refilled Thanatos' goblet. "My lord, your forces have been properly deployed to the planet. They are gathering intel as we speak," she said firmly, not making eye contact with the stag.

"Excellent, Sih. We could have this over with by the end of the week then." Thanatos raised his glass with a small smile, then took a large gulp of the liquid.

Right... the end of the world. Ash looked up at the stag and chewed slowly before swallowing. "Why? Why are you doing this?"

"Didn't we already have this conversation? Don't you remember?" He swirled the goblet thoughtfully. Ash could just barely see the corner of his lip twitch as he responded, "It is my *destiny.*"

Ash's expression remained anxious. A growing sense of dread weighed on his chest. He forced down another mouthful; the flavors now dull on his tongue.

"Don't hurt yourself dwelling on it. There is much work that we will be accomplishing together." A smile crossed the stag's lips as he took another delicate sip.

Thanatos placed his goblet down with deliberate care. The sound of the metal clinking on the table made Ash flinch. Silence followed, broken only by the faint sounds of distant footsteps that seeped in through the stone walls and the ringing in Ash's ears. His gaze lingered on Ash while he finished his meal, a predator's patience in his posture, as if waiting for the right moment to pounce.

As he took the last bite of his meal, a soft "hmm" rumbled through the air. Ash suddenly felt the brush of claws against his cheek. The warmth of the Creator's fingers and the heavy scent of myrrh radiating from his fur caused him to recoil with a hiss. *Why is he warm?*

A small smile tugged at the Creator's lips. "Ash Darkscream..." he murmured, reaching again to brush a stray strand of Ash's black hair out of his face. "I must admit... seeing you in the flesh like this is much nicer than I anticipated it to be. You're different than I thought. Taller, as well."

From the corner of Ash's eye, he could see Sih crinkle her nose in disgust. She quickly grabbed Ash's plate from in front of him and placed the silverware on top of it with a *clang* before turning quickly to a room in the back that was presumably a kitchen.

"Pay her no mind. Some of the reapers are a bit... exasperated having a *living* lesser god in our midst. They will get over it."

I don't feel very alive right now.

With a scoff, Thanatos finished the last of his wine and placed it on the table before pushing himself up out of his chair. Ash couldn't help the widening of his eyes as he was reminded how outrageously tall he stood, antlers included. Thanatos' eyes caught his and a small, sly smile appeared at the corner of his mouth. "Come with me."

Even though his mind hesitated, begging him to do something else, Ash stood. His body continued to betray him. He followed Thanatos across the dining chamber into the fountain room with the other doors.

The stag's stride was unhurried, assured, and elegant. The echo of his hooves resonated with a steady authority that pressed Ash forward. They faced the door at the top of the room, which opened to reveal a blood-red curtain. Thanatos then drew the curtain aside so Ash could pass through.

A throne room.

They now stood by a wooden throne, carved with vines and antlers, backed by red stained glass, much like the rest of the building. It was perched above the rest of the room with stone stairs that led up to it. The rest of the chamber was vast, with towering stone columns that supported the cathedral. Looking up, Ash could see the red flame above through a hole in the ceiling, flickering endlessly and illuminating the hall. Scanning the room, he noted that it was... strangely empty. No pews, no chairs, just open stone floors and an old red carpet that led from the throne to the massive front doors. The cold was starting to make the tips of his ears go numb.

"In a few days' time we will be having a gathering. I've been thinking about it for quite some time during my... imprisonment. We can celebrate the start of another world falling.

Also, such an occasion would be good to present you as my chosen one." Thanatos did not make eye contact with him. His gaze stayed fixed on the empty room.

Ash hesitated by the curtain as Thanatos moved in front of his throne. The stag's silhouette against it nearly matched the antlers carved at its peak, his face illuminated by the red glow above.

"Look upon it," Thanatos murmured, motioning toward the ceiling. "The heart of Nullhymm. Once a symbol of hope, a beacon of power, it burns only for me now." His tone was softer, almost mournful.

Ash swallowed, unsure if he should speak, but the comment left his mouth before he could stop it. "You... don't sound very proud of that."

A low hum of amusement rippled from Thanatos' chest. "Pride is for those who still have choices." The stag turned to face him, his expression unreadable—neither divine wrath nor mercy, but something in between. "You'll come to understand in time, my chosen one. You may even come around to agree with what we are doing."

I really doubt that. Ash took an uncertain step forward, his ears flattened, tone firm. "I didn't choose this. I *don't* want to be here. I *don't* want this."

"I understand that is how you feel." Thanatos' voice gentled, the way one might address a trembling child. "But, as you very much know, destiny is rarely concerned with consent. It is only concerned with what we are *made* for. *You* were *made* for this."

His gaze lingered on Ash's angered expression, then turned to face the large doors at the end of the room, where the faint sounds of whipping wind could be heard. It almost sounded like voices echoing up from below. "You should rest. I feel you are still weak, and I want you rested for the others."

"The others?" Ash's tail flicked, uneasy.

"The gods of death from every plane of existence. They've been waiting to see the near-mortal who freed their sovereign." His crimson eyes glimmered like dying stars, watching the door, deep in thought. "Like I said. It will be... a celebration."

Something in the way he said it twisted Ash's stomach. He didn't answer.

"Until then," the stag commanded, turning back to face Ash, "your quarters are yours to use freely. The reapers will see to your needs." His voice grew colder now; command layered beneath politeness. "Do not leave this cathedral. Nullhymm has a way of devouring lost souls."

Ash's hands curled instinctively into fists, his claws biting into his palms. He wanted to shout, to demand answers, to run, but the words caught in his throat. Instead, he bowed his head, more out of exhaustion than obedience.

Thanatos regarded him for a long moment before lowering himself onto the throne and crossing his legs. "Good. Rest well, Ash Darkscream. You will need your strength for what's to come."

The door behind Ash opened, and the gruff lynx came in quietly, her eyes beckoning Ash to follow. With a final glance at the stag who watched him, he turned and followed Sih, the echo of their footsteps chasing them down the silent corridor as she led him back to his room at the end of the hall. The red light emitted from the hall's windows faded behind him as he entered his room, replaced by the dim flicker of a wall torch.

As she closed the door behind him, his body's tension finally released—unable to hold it any longer. The ache in his chest radiated through his entire body. *What the hell have I done? Where is Lunette? We need to get—can he hear me this far away?* Ash paused, cringing as he awaited a response. None came. *I'm far enough away then I guess...*

Ash glanced around the room. Everything was the same except that the bed had been made. A book and pen sat against his pillow. Narrowing his eyes at the objects, he walked over for a closer look. Picking it up and flipping through it with a single claw, he furrowed his brow at the blank pages. *A journal? Sketchbook?*

As he reached the back of the first page, he stared at a crudely drawn map that was sprawled across it. *What even is this?* Ash scanned over the drawing, squinting in the low light. *A map of this place?* There were some notes along the sides in terrible handwriting... *That handwriting is familiar.*

He flipped to the front of the first page. There he saw a note scribbled in the same terrible handwriting and blotchy pen.

Ash—

You're a nerd. Figured this would entertain you. See you soon!

Ash's stomach churned. There was no mistaking the handwriting. *Of course, it's Leroy. Where is he now? Probably plotting something again. That traitor...* He shook his head, unwilling to dwell on Leroy's betrayal any longer. He had bigger problems than that jerk.

With a sharp motion, Ash tore the page from the journal. Necromantic green fire flickered across his palms, the heat scorching the edges of the paper as he crumpled it and flung it away. The small act of defiance did little to ease the heaviness in his chest. His paws felt hot as he clutched the book tightly to himself and collapsed onto the bed, the mattress barely giving beneath his weight. A shaky sigh escaped him.

His lungs felt as if a boulder were crushing them, making each breath feel labored. He couldn't stop thinking about Lunette. Where they were. If they were alive. What they now thought of him. No matter how hard he tried, he could not banish the feeling of the stag's looming presence in the flesh. It was strange seeing him not encased in shadow.

"I freed him," he confessed quietly to the empty room. "And now I'm the one who's trapped."

Wednesday Evening, Present Day

The sound of rattling chains dragged Lunette to consciousness. Of course, that was the first thing they'd wake up to in a realm known for being an afterlife. Their head pounded viciously, each throb making their ears burn and their heartbeat thrum through their whole body like some cosmic drum determined to shake them apart.

They cracked their eyes open. A distant torch flickered somewhere beyond the bars, just bright enough to make them squint and reveal the cramped cell around them. What wasn't iron bars was stone, carved from dark, ancient rock. A frost-covered floor lay beneath them, clinging to their limp body. The metal bars themselves hummed with some kind of dark, ethereal magic. And, naturally, a neat pile of chains sat in the corner of their cell— thankfully not attached to them. Yet.

The sound appeared to originate from a cell opposite them.

There sat the serpent Creator from Antarctica.

His long, lavender hair was falling out of the ponytail on top of his head. His eyes, once radiant like the galaxies themselves, dulled. Previously, his presence was daunting—his battle with Thanatos had brought down the frozen cavern, and his inky minions had plagued the trio all week. Now, he sat hunched against the wall, the length of his snake-like body tucked beneath him, radiating an air of defeat. Large, carved chains encased his wrists. He stared at Lunette, unmoving. "So... you've finally decided to wake."

Lunette's brow furrowed, and they pushed themselves to sit up from lying flat on the frigid stone floor. "I was... unconscious," Lunette murmured, their voice hoarse from screaming the day before.

Yesterday... What happened? Wait—what happened to Ash?

Their ears perked as they looked at the serpent quickly. "Ash? Where is he?"

"How would *I* know where that betrayer is?" the naga scoffed, looking away. "I tried to warn him. Now look what he's done."

Lunette's eyes narrowed at the comment. "What? *Warn him?* You chased him all over Timbuktu trying to kill him! If it weren't for you, we wouldn't have done any of what we did in the first place! Besides, it wasn't his fault. Leroy was the one who *used me!*"

"Oh, it's *my* fault, is it?" a voice echoed down the hall. The tap of paw pads on stone echoed through the corridor of cells. Lunette's eyes met the piercing blue gaze of Leroy as he stopped to stand between them. The light reflected off his nose and ear piercings. His long tail swished playfully beneath his robe, which bore a striking resemblance to a priest's attire. Unlike traditional robes, though, its edges gleamed with gold fabric, while the belt and collar were a rich crimson that stood in sharp contrast to the blue streaks running through his hair. "It's so nice to finally see you two awake. Are you done screaming? I don't want to have to hit you over the head again."

"You *bastard.*" Lunette sneered, their ears flat back against their horns. "*You* did this. You *tricked* us!" They pulled themselves to their hooves with a wobble but nonetheless stood firm with their shoulders squared to the tall reaper.

"Well, *why* were you so easy to trick? Maybe you should pay more attention to your surroundings instead of swooning over cute boys. Better yet, learn to multi-task like I have."

"I do *not* swoon over cute boys!" they shouted, their voice cracking.

"Will the both of you *please,* for the love of all things, *shut up.*" The serpent groaned, leaning back against the wall of his cell. The sound of chains scraped across the floor as he shifted. "Lesser gods bickering about blame... as if it makes a difference. Typical."

Lunette turned their glare on him. "And what even are you, exactly?! What makes you so high and mighty?"

The serpent gave a slow, humorless smile. "I am Teramir, Creator of Worlds. An architect of space." His forked tongue flicked briefly between his sharp teeth. "However, I am currently posing as a trophy on a shelf for the so-called Creator I desperately want to annihilate."

Lunette's stomach tightened. The name hit something buried, an echo of memory that flickered like static. Then it was gone. "Well, I don't know you."

The naga tilted his head. "How typical. I see the spell is still in effect. You're too weak to overpower it, anyway."

Leroy chuckled from where he stood between them, digging in his pockets and pulling out a pack of cigarettes. "Don't you love irony? This is great, I love this."

Teramir's eyes narrowed, and for a moment, the air in the corridor thickened. A deep, cosmic energy pulsed faintly from the runes carved into his restraints. "Careful, reaper. You forget your place too easily."

"And *you* forget who put you in that cell in the first place," Leroy countered, his smile sharp. He turned back toward Lunette, eyes gleaming. "You should be so grateful I convinced Thanatos not to cast you outside the city to wander for eternity. He's in a generous mood these days."

Lunette's hands flexed against their sides. "You're lying."

"Oh, am I? Would you be able to tell?" Leroy tilted his head, his large ears flopping, grin widening. "Anyway, our precious Ashy-boy is doing great. Thanatos is hosting a gathering, some kind of celebration for Ash's arrival and being released, that kind of thing. All the cool gods will be there, *so sorry* you're not invited."

Lunette's teeth bared at the mention of Ash. They leaned forward so their nose nearly touched the bars. "If you so much as harm one hair on his head—"

"Oh, you are *so* feisty. Ash has a type."

The serpent exhaled sharply through his nose, interrupting the two lesser gods. "He's going to slaughter them."

"What?" Lunette turned their attention to the naga. "Who?"

"The death gods," he said, voice low. "All of them. He's said it before."

Leroy's grin faltered, just a flicker, gone before Lunette could read it. "You talk too much, snake."

Teramir's gaze glimmered faintly, and his chains rattled again, like something ancient stirring beneath the surface. "And you hide too much, *Leroy*. Tell me, do you still hear your brother's screams in the quiet hours?"

"*Enough!*" Leroy snarled, the air around him flaring. Cold, black tendrils of death magic rose around his feet. Frost crept up the metal bars between the cells. Baring teeth replaced his smile. "You'll keep that stupid forked tongue in your head or *I'll rip it out*."

"What is he talking about?! What is Thanatos planning? We should be *stopping* this."

Neither Leroy nor Teramir answered the faun. The silence that followed was thicker than the metal bars between them.

Leroy finally exhaled and straightened, brushing nonexistent dust off his robe and lighting his cigarette. The shadows receded. When he spoke again, his tone had returned to its usual sharp mockery. "You'll find out soon enough, *faun*. Everyone always does, in the end."

He turned to leave; a trail of smoke lingered in his wake as he climbed the stairs back to the cathedral. The torch extinguished, and the only sounds that remained were distant wind howls and the occasional rattle of Teramir's chains.

Lunette sank back against the wall, their arms wrapping around their shoulders. "Why does everyone here talk in riddles?" they muttered.

A long silence passed.

Memories of yesterday pressed on their mind. Who they were. What they *did. Why do I cause nothing but destruction?* The thought came unbidden from the depths of their mind, causing their chest to tighten.

Finally, Lunette broke the quiet. "Can he really do it? Kill the death gods? Kill our world?"

Teramir's eyes must have been closed. Lunette did not see them in the darkness. "He's Thanatos. He is death. If he can't, then it would mean he's pretty terrible at the one thing he's made for."

Lunette frowned softly and lay back down on the cold stone. *I hope Ash is ok. Why did I have to be the thing to cause this? This is my mess...*

For a long time, Lunette didn't speak. They stared at the bars between them, eyes adjusting to the dark until the faint glimmer of Teramir's scales took shape again, shimmering faintly like distant constellations.

"Are you still awake?" they whispered.

A pause. "Unfortunately."

Lunette drew their legs up to their chest, arms wrapped tight around them. "You've obviously tried to destroy Thanatos before. Why?"

A soft laugh, more bitter than amused. "Because that is how the *Great Plan* works. Evil versus good, neat little labels for a very messy universe. I am good. Thanatos is evil, obviously."

Lunette frowned into the darkness. "I don't know about that... You tried to kill Ash."

"It was for the greater good."

"Killing *anyone* doesn't seem like a greater good for *anything*. A wrong does not make a right. That doesn't make sense.

I feel like that's the bare minimum of morality, and yet here we are."

"That is funny coming from *you*," Teramir murmured.

"What do you mean?" Lunette said sharply. Their voice echoed off the stone walls, louder than they meant it to be.

The naga's chains shifted; the faint ringing of metal carried through the dark. "I find it amusing that your mother's spell has rendered you even more of a fool than before."

Lunette's stomach turned. "What are you even talking about?"

The serpent's voice lowered, a whisper now—almost intimate, almost kind. "Thanatos was made for ruin. You? You *chose* it. You'll remember eventually."

Lunette's breath hitched. A flicker, a sensation of heat, of screaming wind and burning light, flashed behind Lunette's eyes. Vanishing before they could grasp it. Their hand instinctively rubbed their sternum. "No," they muttered, "that's not... I would *never* do *anything* like him."

Have I? Their throat tightened at the thought. *I did... cause this.*

The sound of the serpent's movement filled the small corridor; his chains scraped as he leaned closer to the bars. His eyes glowed faintly now, twin fragments of nebula in the dark. "The soul never forgets, Lunette. Only the mind does. The spell over you may bury the truth, but it will claw its way back. You will remember that you are no better than the foe you face."

The words hit like a physical blow. Lunette's breath trembled, and they squeezed themselves, glaring in the direction of the serpent. "You're lying. You don't know me. You certainly don't know my mother."

"Oh, I know you," Teramir scoffed. "Apparently better than you know yourself."

For a moment, neither spoke. Lunette's heart thundered in their chest, their pulse echoing in their ears until they could hardly think. *He's lying... They're all lying to me. I don't even think I have a mother...*

Finally, Teramir's voice came again, barely audible now, like an echo through water. "When the gods gather above in a few days, listen closely to the silence that follows. Then you will know I speak only the truth."

Lunette didn't respond. Their throat had gone dry, and a cold sweat traced the back of their neck. They sat perfectly still, forcing their eyes to close while listening to the faint rattle of Teramir's chains until even that sound faded.

Replaced only by the slow, rhythmic beat of their own pulse.

Proof they were still alive. For now.

701 Years Ago, Astravir

Lunette winced as a brush pulled through their long, sleep-tangled, white hair.

"You really need to start braiding this before you go to sleep, Lunette."

They peeked out with squinted eyes into the vanity mirror in front of them. Behind them stood a tall, lean red fox who brushed their hair carefully, yet with the determination of someone cleaning up a crime scene. "You know I hate the feeling of it being braided. It makes it all... unevenly wavy. Valencia hates it as well."

"Well, our wonderful queen may have to just deal with that if it saves me from yanking you around like this every morning..." the fox murmured under her breath.

"Or, you know, you could just let me brush my own hair, Ava."

"And let you make yourself bald? I wouldn't be able to live with myself." Ava gave them a quick, fond smile before wrestling through the last knot. "Speaking of our lovely queen, she wishes to see you after a meeting this morning. She should be almost done."

"Wonderful..." Lunette mumbled, opening their eyes fully.

Ava dropped the brush onto the vanity with the air of someone who had just wrestled a wild animal and won. "There. You look marginally less like you were dragged backwards through a bush."

Lunette slid out of the chair and straightened their near sheer white dress that almost dragged onto the floor. From the corner of their eye, they could see Avas's disapproving gaze. "It's fine, Ava. I promise."

"I still think her highness should be dressing you more appropriately." The fox's tail gave an irritated flick as she moved to straighten the messy bed in the corner. "I do not like how much attention it draws. Especially from Wraven... she always stares at you like you're prey."

"She stares at everyone like that."

"Perhaps, but she especially stares at you."

Lunette shook their head, their large ears flopping with the quick movement. "It's *fine,* Ava. I promise. I will see you this evening for bedtime."

The fox rolled her eyes and sighed. "Yes, yes. Behave. Oh— and don't go bothering the stable hand today. He needs to tack a shoe on one of the horses before the queen rides this afternoon."

"Mm, no promises." Lunette grinned and quickly hopped out the door before the fox could scold them further.

Their hoof-clicks echoed along the marble floor of the palace corridor. *That's strange... I haven't seen it this empty in a while.*

No servants. No nobles. No guards pretending not to stare. Just the soft, distant hush of the city in the early morning outside the high windows and the rustle of banners shifting in the draft. Lunette slowed, ears swiveling. Morning at the palace was usually a blur of activity. Clinking dishes, hurried steps, quiet gossip outside the throne room while the citizens waited for an audience with the Queen for their morning blessings.

Maybe everyone's in a meeting with Valencia... Or maybe I finally slept through the entire morning, and they've given up on me. Though, they doubted it. Valencia didn't give up on anything she considered hers.

Lunette made their way down the long corridor toward the queen's wing, the hem of their dress whispering across the polished stone. As they approached the closed, carved oak doors of her chamber, faint voices seeped into the silence, muffled at first, then clearer.

One voice was unmistakable. Smooth, light, and absolutely drenched in proper cadence. "Our people deserve more than the scraps fate tosses them. They deserve preservation. Continuation. Perfection."

Lunette slowed, ears perked. *Preservation?*

A second voice answered, low, resonant, like distant thunder rolling across the earth. It carried an ancient gravity that made Lunette's bones hum. *Who is that?*

"Preservation is not granted without sacrifice."

Lunette froze. The fur along their arms stood on end. They edged closer, heart pounding, and pressed their back to the wall just beside the cracked door.

Valencia laughed, a silvery, cascading sound, so perfectly rehearsed that Lunette suddenly realized how rarely they'd heard her *actually* laugh. "Oh, please. I have already offered more than anyone else has. I don't just have a random group of worshipers for you." Her tone sharpened. "I built this kingdom from a dwindling priestess order. I brought them wealth, culture, and worship. They follow me because I give them a future. I will continue to do so."

"They bow because you demand to be adored."

Valencia scoffed lightly. "Every great ruler demands adoration. It keeps them in line."

A slow exhale, heavy enough that Lunette felt it vibrate through the wall. Hoofbeats paced the floor.

"If Astravir falls," Valencia continued, "I will not have my legacy buried with it. Give me eternity. Give *my people* eternity and in return..." Her voice softened, silky and dangerous, "my city will join your world and serve you."

Lunette's stomach twisted. *Eternity? Join... another world?*

The ancient voice steadily spoke again. "You wish for your entire kingdom to be spared when the rest of this world burns?"

"I *wish*," Valencia corrected, "for my people to ascend. To live beyond the breaking. To become part of your realm, untouched by time and ruin."

"You dream of a throne that outlives the universe," he murmured. "A queen crowned even when all other crowns have turned to dust."

"Is that not a benefit to what you offer? Immortality. Continuance. Purpose."

A long silence.

Lunette strained to hear every breath.

"You misunderstand my nature," the voice said, soft but unwavering. "I do not grant immortality as reward. I grant unending existence as *function*."

Valencia's tone held a hint of impatience, the slightest crack beneath her polish. "I have read the old prophecies. I know what your return means. They called you a purifier. A destroyer of worlds."

"A reset." He corrected calmly.

"*That*," Valencia replied triumphantly, "is why my people will survive. I offer you a kingdom already devoted. Already ordered. Already obedient. We will serve your cycle. We will serve your purpose. Fold us into your realm, your world, and you gain an entire nation ready to kneel."

Lunette clapped a hand over their mouth, breath catching. *Serve? Kneel? She's offering everyone? Without asking?*

"You are bold," the voice said. "Most mortals beg for a single life spared. You bargain for thousands."

"I am *not* most mortals," Valencia replied, her smile audible.

"Eternity is not glamour," he warned. "It is not beauty. It is not the preservation of your reflection. It is dark, unyielding, and unending."

"*I am* unyielding."

"Yes, quite." A long breath filled the space, an inhale deep enough to rattle the crystal vials on Valencia's vanity.

"Very well," he said at last. "When Astravir cracks, your city will be drawn into Nullhymm. Your people will remain. Your reign will continue. Know this," The temperature in the hallway seemed to drop, "eternity is not salvation."

Valencia hummed, unconcerned. "Rulership is always a cage. However... I will be proud to kneel to you, *Thanatos*."

Lunette's hocks nearly buckled. A chill crawled up their spine. *Thanatos*. A name only Valdis had whispered. He had been saying for months now that the city should be worried about his return, that there were rumors amongst the mages. They never believed his superstitions...

Inside the chamber, Valencia's voice lowered, yet stayed triumphant. "When you rise again, great one, call for me. I will be prepared."

"When I rise," Thanatos replied, "your world will end."

Silence. Then... hooves. Heavy. Drawing closer to the door.

Lunette clamped their hands over their mouth again, their back flattened against the wall so sharply it hurt, breath strangled.

The chamber door creaked as if nudged from within.

A cold draft slipped through the crack, brushing Lunette's legs like hands in winter. For a moment, they felt a presence, ancient and probing, sweeping across the corridor, searching.

Lunette held their breath until their lungs screamed.

The presence recoiled. The hoofbeats retreated deeper into the queen's room.

Lunette let out a ragged gasp. Then they sagged against the wall, hands trembling. *Valdis was right. Thanatos is real, and the queen... she's made a deal with him.* Lunette swallowed hard, throat tight. *I need to get out of here. I need to tell someone. Right now.*

They pushed themselves upright and ran, their garments billowing behind them. Their hooves thundered down the marble corridor, breath sharp, heartbeat thrumming in their ears. They rounded the corner toward the throne room... a sudden weightlessness enveloped them—

They clamored to regain their footing, but the marble rushed up to meet them.

Lunette hit the ground—

They lurched upright from the cold stone floor of their cell, so quickly that it nearly caused the hide on their arms to peel away. They swore they could see a couple of tufts of white fur in the frost. Their breath came in ragged gasps. *Too real.* Their body shook violently as they folded forward, hugging themselves.

Who was that... Thanatos... It all felt real. Did that happen?

Across the cell, in the dark, a pair of slightly glowing, slitted eyes opened. The serpent's voice slithered out of the shadows.

"You're remembering now," it hissed softly. *"Aren't you?"*

701 Years Ago, Val-Tirath

A warm sea breeze blew the long braid that draped over Ash's shoulder behind him. The waves lapped up against the cliff side that was merely inches from his paws. Ash always stood too close to the edge; it was the only place he felt like he could breathe. He inhaled the salty sea air and gazed at the sunset as it cast beautiful hues of orange and red over the ocean. It was a magnificent evening.

"Ash!" A high-pitched voice called, barely audible over the crashing waves.

He turned and looked behind him at the looming, dark homes behind him where a smaller figure stood. His little sister, Juniper, stood by the gate. Her paws cupped around her mouth as she shouted. "Mother says dinner is ready!"

"I'll be right there!" Ash shouted back. He turned and gazed at the sunset one last time before heading towards the wrought-iron fencing that surrounded the lush grounds of Darkscream Manor. Lanterns carved from bone and driftwood lined the winding path up to the gates, each flame a ghostly green that never dimmed, even in the wind. They glowed like watchful eyes along the way, guiding Ash up toward the manor that crowned island, the heart of his family's dominion.

The main building dominated the landscape with its imposing architecture. Constructed from dark timber and stone weathered with sea salt, it featured high, arched beams that accentuated its imposing structure. It rose several stories high, with expansive rooms that served not only as living quarters for his family but also as grand gathering spaces for the members of the commune. Despite its formidable, almost fortress-like appearance, it was a cathedral to death-itself as well as a home. He always thought it was beautiful.

Encircling the manor was a series of smaller cottages. These dwellings housed extended family members and close family friends, creating a tight-knit community nestled within the lush grounds surrounding the main estate. Smoke curled from chimneys and drifted into the sunset, mingling with the salty air.

He stepped through the wrought-iron gate and was met with the abundance of typical evening activity off the side of the manor. Black-robed figures crossed the cobbled paths, carrying jars of dust, bones, and saltwater, offerings for their evening rites by the courtyard fire. Laughter rang from a group of younger acolytes who sat polishing bone charms. The smell of incense, an earthy mixture he couldn't quite place, filled the air.

By the stairway to the manor, beneath the blood-orange sunset, Mercy stood waiting.

Her long fur sleek like wet black ink, her robes the color of dried blood trimmed with black thread. Everything about her posture was sharp, including the pieces of bone that held her bun in place on top of her head. Even her shadow seemed to obey her. "You kept us waiting," she said, her tone neither angry nor surprised.

"I lost track of time," Ash admitted.

Her eyes glinted. "Time," she repeated, almost amused. "A *god* should never lose track of something so precious."

Before Ash could answer, another figure appeared behind her—his father, Hawthorne. His green eyes were distracted but warm. His black robes were simple and nearly blended in with his equally dark fur; the fabric perpetually dusted with ashes and wood scraps from tending to all the homes' structures.

"There you are," Hawthorne said, smiling. "Your mother's been counting the seconds."

Mercy didn't look at him, her yellow eyes stayed fixated on Ash. "Gods of death must lead by example. If he cannot master punctuality, how will he master anything else?"

Hawthorne sighed, rubbing his wife's shoulders tenderly. "He's young. He will be all right. Besides, it's a rest day."

"I'm not that young," Ash muttered.

"You're twenty-four," Mercy said sharply. "A mere breath to eternity." She turned quickly, brushing past her husband to go up the steps to the manor. "Come along."

Inside the dining hall, fire flickered against banners depicting intricate double pentagrams. The air was thick with the scent of herb-crusted meat and bread. The long table was already set with food on six plates, but only two of his siblings sat waiting as they entered. Mercy took her spot at the head of the table, Hawthorne to her left, Juniper sat at her right, and Auburn across from her.

Juniper watched Ash as he approached his seat next to Auburn. Radiant and smug, the kit's sleek black fur and yellow eyes caught the light like polished amber. She smiled a perfect imitation of their mother's. "You're late again," she said sweetly. "Mother says lateness is a mortal habit."

Ash ignored her and took his seat beside his twin, who was hunched over, fingers tracing idle patterns on his rings made of bone. Bone jewelry hung around his neck, decorated his fingers, dangled from his ears, and pierced one of his nostrils. Despite his eccentric appearance, Ash's identical twin always seemed slightly dimmer than Ash, his expression perpetually tired.

"You okay?" Ash asked him quietly, hoping his mother wouldn't hear since she was talking to Hawthorne.

Auburn shrugged. "Mother says my aura's weak today. She made me reanimate mouse bones for five hours straight."

Ash frowned. "She shouldn't make you do that for that long."

"She said it'll make me stronger."

"It won't," Ash muttered. "It just hurts after a while."

"Then maybe I'm doing it right."

Ash looked at him, alarmed. Auburn's tone was flat, but there was something hollow beneath it—a resignation Ash hated.

Before he could reply, Oak entered through the side doors, the scent of salt clinging to him. His cloak was soaked, his emerald eyes bright with that restless wildness that always came after days at sea.

Mercy didn't even look at him. "You missed weekly ritual yesterday."

Oak scoffed softly as he plopped into the chair next to Juniper. "The sea doesn't cater to your prayers, Mother."

The table fell silent.

Even Hawthorne's hands froze on the tablecloth, the warmth fading from his face. Mercy's expression never changed, but her voice turned to ice.

"You forget yourself, son."

"I remember just fine," Oak said. "You're the ones forgetting we have free will. We don't have to play gods."

"*Free will*," she repeated, tasting the words as if they were foreign. "We are death incarnate, Oak. We do not ask permission to exist—we *continue* because *he* allows it and will continue to allow it so long as we are devout to him."

Oak only smiled, that same dashing smile that made her eyes flash. "Then maybe one day he'll allow me to drown in peace."

"Enough," Hawthorne said firmly, though the word carried no weight.

Mercy huffed and picked up her knife sharply. "We will speak of this later," she said coldly. "For now, we dine."

Dinner unfolded with typical ritualistic precision. No one lifted a fork until Mercy did. No one spoke above a whisper. Between courses, Mercy recited verses from a large leather-bound book decorated with intricate pentagrams.

Ash had memorized every word of that tome; now he only half-listened and recited by instinct. His thoughts drifted to the cliffs outside, to the sound of waves, to the sunset he wasn't supposed to watch.

Then, mid-recitation, a word caught his ear.

"Thanatos, the source of all endings..."

He froze.

He looked up, startled. *Has she said that before?*

Mercy's tone didn't waver. "To him we owe the gift of life and death. To him we return, all things that end. His shadow guides our hands."

Ash's pulse quickened. He didn't remember this prayer. They had always worshipped something, not a name, never a name. *Am I remembering this correctly?*

Am I... dreaming?

He turned to Auburn. "Did she say—"

"Shh," Auburn hissed, eyes wide. "Don't interrupt."

The rest of the table seemed unfazed, as if they'd been saying it their whole lives. Juniper's voice was loudest of all, her small form swaying in perfect rhythm.

Mercy lifted her chalice of red wine. "To the one who made us immortal in his image."

Ash's throat went dry.

"Mother?" he croaked out, his voice beginning to tremble.

She turned toward him with that same carved expression she always wore, only now it felt fake, an expression painted on a mask. "Yes, my son?"

"What are you talking about? I've never heard you speak of... of Thanatos."

The room fell silent, not naturally, but all at once, as if someone had commanded it. Every head turned toward Ash in perfect unison.

Mercy's smile did not reach her eyes. "Our lord. The first death. The god of endings. Why would you ask such a question?"

"But we never—"

"Of course we have," she said, too quickly. "You've spoken his name a thousand times."

"No," he insisted. "No, I-I'd remember."

Across the table, Oak leaned back, his expression amused... but stiff. "Seems your memory's as selective as your faith."

The room felt as if it were a ship in a storm, tilted. Ash stood up quickly. "This isn't *right*. This is *wrong*. We never spoke of Thanatos. Where am I?" He turned quickly, inspecting the room. His legs felt weak.

Auburn grabbed him, his grip too strong, too sudden. "*Sit down and pay attention.*"

With a yank from his twin, Ash fell back into the chair—

—and with a violent gasp, he bolted upright in bed. His head turned on a swivel, blackened eyes scanning every corner of the dark chamber he was assigned. Every muscle was tense. His paw pads slick with sweat. His ears pinned back against his head. His breath came in ragged gasps.

It was just a dream... it was just... a dream.

It can't be real... He was never there before...

Or was he?

Thursday Morning, Present Day

A knock sounded from outside Ash's door, causing him to jump. He pulled the rough robe tighter around his shoulders, still groggy from his fitful slumber. Before Ash could muster an answer or move a millimeter out of bed, the handle turned, and a familiar face stepped inside without waiting for permission.

Ash froze when he saw *him*. That smug, infuriating presence he'd come to associate with every single bad decision in his life for the last nine years.

Leroy filled the doorway, ears perked, calm, wearing that same arrogant grin he always had. He was dressed in a black, gold, and red priest-like robe Ash had never seen him wear. Twin bone daggers with bright blue gems encrusted in the pommels sat in sheaths attached to his belt on both of his hips.

For a moment, Ash could only stare. Then, he jumped to his feet, tail lashing, teeth bared. *"You."* The word came out low, hoarse, half snarl.

Leroy tilted his head, grin spreading. "Missed me?"

Ash crossed the room in nearly three steps, stopping only a couple of feet away from the caracal. "You *used me!* You used Lunette! You dragged us here—you—" His voice broke. "You let him out. This is *your* fault!"

Leroy's ears flicked lazily, as if the accusation bored him. "And look how well that turned out. You're fine. You're still breathing. You've fulfilled *something* in your boring life. You should be thanking me. So, you're *welcome.*"

Ash's tail lashed behind him. "You knocked Lunette out and—"

"—and saved them from getting killed," Leroy interrupted, stepping further into the room. "You're welcome for that, too."

"Don't," Ash took a step forward, claws unsheathed, canines flashing in the torchlight. "Don't you dare—"

"Careful," Leroy said softly, his hands raising in mock surrender. "You're a guest here, remember? Not a prisoner. There's a difference. I'm not here to do *anything.*"

Ash's laugh was humorless. "I don't see much of a difference."

The reaper's smirk faded a little. "Maybe not," he admitted. "However, *he* does see a difference."

"Thanatos? *Your* god?"

"So, you know his name, and you aren't brain-damaged yet." He snorted. "He's waiting for you."

Ash held his ground, every muscle rigid. "Again? Why—"

"He just is," Leroy said quickly, cutting him off. "Stop asking questions and don't keep him waiting. His patience is as bad as yours."

Leroy turned in a single motion and started down the hall before Ash could even blink. With a disgruntled huff, he jogged out of the room to follow.

"So, how are you enjoying your stay? Sorry for taking your shoes. We don't wear those here. Keeps us close to the realm and all." Leroy snickered softly, glancing over his shoulder. The daggers on his hips caught the red light; the curve of their blades made Ash shiver.

"I'm not. I want to go home." He looked away. It was hard to even look at him after what he had done.

"You know, I've got a feeling our landlord probably kicked us out. Rent was due yesterday."

Ash groaned and pinched the bridge of his nose with two claws. "*Yesterday?* You could have reminded me before we left—"

"Does it *really* matter now?" Leroy looked away. Leading him into the strange fountain room, he turned sharply into the dining hall.

Upon entering, Ash was welcomed with the same sight as yesterday: Thanatos sitting solitary at the head of the table, silver goblet in hand. The stag's ears perked slightly as they entered the room.

Ash's heart nearly stopped; images of his dream last night flashed into his mind. His mother's goblet in her hand while she recited prayer. Juniper swaying along. His twin snapping at him to pay attention. *It wasn't real... That never happened.*

"My lord, I bring you a singular Ash. He's quite feisty this morning, watch out." Leroy snickered as he led Ash to the same chair as before. This time, a small plate of eggs and toast steamed on the table in front of it, accompanied by a glass of milk. The same scent of myrrh filled the air around them.

Thanatos' head tilted as he watched Ash sit. "Are you? Was it a dream?"

Ash's eyes snapped to the stag's. "Why do you ask that?" *Because you were thinking about it, dipshit. He can read your mind, remember?*

A deep chuckle rumbled in his chest before he exhaled a sigh. "This realm has a tendency to do that. Bring up memories unbidden."

"It wasn't real. It was just a dream," Ash said firmly, picking up his fork, though his stomach felt nauseous.

"One would argue that dreams imitate, if not fully replicate, reality."

Ash looked down at his plate. The steam curling off the eggs and toast danced delicately in the frigid air. "They're just dreams," he said finally, his voice low. "They don't mean anything."

The stag tilted his head. "Then why do they trouble you?"

"They *don't*," Ash mumbled, an edge to his voice.

A faint *hmm* escaped Thanatos' throat—amusement, perhaps, or disbelief. "You wear your unease like you wear that robe, my chosen one. It is almost charming."

From where he leaned against the wall, Leroy snickered under his breath. "He's always so cute when he's nervous."

Ash shot him a glare. "Don't you have someone else to betray today?" He spat, tapping a claw on the table in irritation.

Leroy raised his hands once more in mock surrender, his grin sharper than the blades he wore. "There's more of the fire I was talking about. He's always so sassy. He *loves* to be snappy in the mornings. It's been a truly riveting nine years, my lord."

Thanatos didn't intervene, only watched them both—like a scientist observing an experiment. Finally, he set down his goblet.

"Sit," he told Leroy.

Leroy blinked, his smile wavered. "My lord?"

Thanatos gestured to one of the empty chairs. "You hover. It's distracting."

The reaper hesitated but obeyed, sliding into a seat several spaces down the table, across from Ash, resting one arm lazily across the backrest next to him. "As you wish."

Thanatos' attention returned to Ash. "Tell me what you dreamed."

Ash sipped his milk. "It was nothing."

"I am confident in my ability to be the judge of that."

Ash sighed. There was a pause of hesitation. "It was... my old home." Ash muttered through his teeth, pushing his food around with his fork before putting it down again.

"And?"

"*And* I don't want to talk about it. It was *nothing*."

Thanatos regarded him for a long, silent moment, his ears still perked in curiosity. The air in the room seemed to thicken—not cold, but heavy. Ash could feel something cold in his head, almost scraping his brain. Almost as soon as he noticed it, it was gone.

"Did you hear my name?" the stag asked softly.

Across the table, Leroy straightened slightly, his ears tilted in their direction.

"What? *No!*" Ash snapped, though the wavering tone in his voice immediately revealed his attempt to bluff.

Thanatos' tone remained calm, conversational. "In the dream. Did you hear my name?"

Ash's mouth opened, then closed. *He can tell when you're lying.* "Fine... I think so."

A faint smile curved the stag's lips. "Then it was not just a dream. You are remembering."

Ash shook his head quickly. "No. No, it was just... It's all mixed up. Things that never happened."

The stag's nostrils flared. He picked up his goblet again. "As I said before... You will see this place reveals what you hide; what you believe may not hold true here."

Ash didn't respond. What he wanted to say would possibly have gotten him tied up in those shadow tendrils again. *Leroy would probably love that...*

Thanatos watched him for a moment longer, studying him, then leaned back in his chair, swirling his wine. "Eat, Ash. I do not wish to see you starved in my home."

Reluctantly, Ash picked up his fork again. The food was still warm, buttery, and fragrant. Kind of like when Leroy cooked at home. It made his stomach turn. He took a small bite and then proceeded to eat slowly.

Leroy's playful smirk returned. "There. Progress. I knew you could do it. You love the 'Leroy Special.'" He fished around in his pocket, pulling out a nearly empty pack of cigarettes.

"Do you always have to talk so much?" Ash muttered.

"Only when I'm in good company."

"Then you must be very lonely."

Leroy chuckled lowly, resting his chin on one hand. "Touché."

Thanatos' chuckle joined his, deeper and smoother. "It is rare that I find myself in the company of lesser gods who are bold enough to bicker at my table."

Ash's whiskers twitched at the comment as he took another sip of milk, avoiding eye contact with the stag. Leroy simply smiled, proud of himself as always, and lit the cigarette. Thanatos watched him do so, his nostrils twitched at the smell.

"So... in other news. Your lover is doing just fine, even feistier than you, which is typical." Leroy leaned back in his seat and took a drag of the cigarette.

Ash's eyes snapped to meet his. *He'd better not be laying a claw on them.* He felt the stag's gaze upon him again.

"They were asking about you, you know," Leroy continued, nonchalantly looking over the claws on one of his paws. Ash's fur stood up on all ends. "I reassured them you're living your best life now without them, and that they should be proud you've actually done something with your—"

"That's *enough*." Thanatos' voice boomed, the rumble sending vibrations through Ash's bones. A wave of dense, oppressive energy washed over the room as the stag stared daggers into the reaper, who remained still. The smile on his lips still present, despite his ears turning back.

"Now you antagonize for its own sake. Put out that damned cigarette. Fetch me an update on the intel from Earth. I would like to get the end moving." Thanatos waved a clawed hand dismissively at Leroy.

Leroy's eyes narrowed slightly. "Yes, *Daddy,*" he replied through gritted teeth, putting the cigarette out on the edge of the table. He pushed his chair back, the legs of his chair scraping stone loudly, stood quickly, and strode out without looking back. The weight of the silence that followed could have broken bones.

Thanatos let out a breath before speaking, the echo of his power fading to a low hum. "He takes pleasure in friction. He knows I despise his vices."

Ash didn't look at him. "You said... the end. You're really doing this?"

"You freed me to fulfill my purpose. Why wouldn't I?"

The claws of Ash's free hand dug lightly into the table's edge. "And Lunette? Are they part of that 'purpose,' too?"

"Your *friend* is unharmed. Their role will reveal itself when the time is right."

"That's not an answer."

"It is the only one you will receive."

The stag rose, placing the unfinished goblet down. His shadow stretched long over the table. "In three days' time, when you stand beside me and the death gods gather, it will all make sense."

He pivoted on his hooves and proceeded toward the door, briefly pausing with his hand resting on the handle. Ash couldn't help but stare as the stag glanced back behind him.

"Do not let Leroy's tongue unsettle you. He provokes what he envies." He paused, rapping his claws on the handle. "I have decided you are free to wander through these halls and the courtyard out front. Do not stray over the bridge. Clear your mind."

The stag turned and left the hall. The door closed softly, leaving Ash alone with the remnants of food on his plate, a half-glass of milk, and eerie silence.

Three days is not enough time...

At the end of the barren throne room were heavy iron doors, carved with swirling patterns and cats in robes. They sat slightly ajar, letting in a chilling breeze. Pale red and orange light filtered through the cracks, beckoning Ash forward into the cold.

He padded up to the door, looking over the strange, intricate carvings. *What was this place before?* Ash ran a hand over it, the frigid metal burning his paw pads. Taking a deep breath, he grasped the thick, warped handle of the heavy, cracked door and opened it fully with a grunt of effort.

The chill of the outside world struck him immediately. Sharp and metallic, it burned his nose and face. He pulled his robe tighter around him, but it did little to shield him from the dry breeze that cut through the air. All his hair stood on end, a futile attempt to stay warm.

The courtyard stretched wide before him, a barren garden of gray cobblestone paths framed by towering arches of iron that led to the drawbridge he had seen before. No plants resided here, only the skeletal frozen remains of twigs scattered about. Frost spread across every surface like veins.

Beyond the drawbridge, the city of Nullhymm sprawled endlessly, shrouded in mist. The unmoving ring in the sky loomed above it all, its reddish light reflecting off the frost like dying embers. Towering buildings loomed over smaller abodes. From here he could see no one. If he hadn't been dragged through the city earlier, he would have thought it was abandoned.

Ash crossed the courtyard slowly, his breath fogging in front of him. The only sounds were the crunch of frost beneath his paw pads and the distant, mournful groan of wind against the cathedral.

He stopped near the edge of a broken half-wall with an iron railing where the drawbridge connected and the city was separated by a gaping abyss. The unstable drawbridge of rusted iron and blackened wood made him uneasy. The void below churned with fog so thick it looked alive; there was no bottom that he could see.

Leaning against the railing, gripping it loosely, Ash stared down into the depths. "This can't be real," he murmured to himself. *I hope Lunette is okay. Where are they? Where is he keeping them?*

Suddenly, a noise from the direction of the cathedral made his ears flick. Ash turned to face the massive structure; the red fire above was so bright it made him squint.

Quietly, he made his way over, just below one of the red stained-glass windows. He crept closer, paws silent on the frozen stone. The voices were muffled at first—then sharpened as he pressed himself close to the wall.

"...and they're appalled at how bad this one is," Leroy's voice came, smooth and casual as always.

Thanatos' voice followed. "Describe it."

"The reapers on the surface agree it's chaos. I *told* them it was really bad. Mortals tearing down other mortals, building weapons bigger than the ones that have already destroyed half their own lands. Half of them call it progress. The other half call it survival." Leroy laughed under his breath. "They can't tell the difference anymore. It's been like that since I showed up there, honestly. It's only gotten worse."

"They rot from within. They breed their own decay and call it civilization. They worship noise and hunger and the illusion of choice, while everything they supposedly honor is ripped out from under them. All the mortals of these worlds are the same."

There was a clink of a goblet being picked up in his claws, then the slow scrape of hooves pacing across stone. "They all squabble while their world dies. They drown in greed and call it ambition. They build temples of metal and stone and call it *faith*." His voice rose, cold and wrathful, the words vibrating through the walls. "All of it—*delusion*."

Ash shivered. Even from this distance, the stag's fury could be felt. The air itself seemed to pulse with his overwhelming energy, each word thrumming through the wall beneath his paws. It felt like the cave again.

Thanatos' tone dropped lower, quieter but no less dangerous. "Tell me, Arch-Reaper. Did your scouts find any?"

"Veins?" Leroy asked. "No, not yet. They exist, just like Teramir's design on the other worlds. Energy signatures match perfectly as usual. We just haven't found an exposed one yet. It's a big planet."

A pause followed by the scrape of claws against metal. "Have them find one then... Quickly. Then this world can be put down properly, like the others." There was a pause before Thanatos' voice returned. "They have proven they cannot coexist with their creation. So, their creation will be undone. Mercy, in its truest form."

Leroy scoffed softly. "Mercy. Right. The 'clean sweep' approach. Dramatic as always."

Ash could almost hear Thanatos turn toward him. "Do you mock me, Leroy?"

"*Never*," Leroy said quickly, though the edge of humor remained. "Just... appreciating your efficiency as always."

A low, dangerous hum filled the air, and when Thanatos spoke again, it was quiet but sharp like glass. "Efficiency would have been leaving them to suffer and do it themselves. I intend to erase them from existence as I have with all the other ungrateful mortals. The reapers will locate the best fracture point, a large vein that will lead directly to the heart of the planet. When the time comes, I will descend to Earth." There was a clink of the goblet being set down once more.

The Creator's next breath sounded almost like laughter, though there was nothing warm about it. "These ones call themselves advanced? Their progress breeds only war and isolation. They choke their own kin for scraps of power, blind to the truth that power means nothing once the light goes out. I could argue these worlds have only gotten worse in the last five hundred or so years."

"Mhm, yeah, understood," Leroy murmured, starting to sound annoyed.

"Inform the reapers," Thanatos continued. "Have the scouts mark any vein left exposed."

Ash's claws dug into the frozen stone. *He's serious.*

"Of course, my lord," Leroy said. "And your precious chosen one?"

Ash's breath caught.

Thanatos didn't answer immediately. When he did, his tone softened. "He will play his part. That is for me to be concerned about, not you."

Leroy let out *hmm*. "Alright. I'll be on my way then."

Ash pressed himself against the wall, eyes wide, until the sound of paw pads against stone faded into the cathedral's depths.

Then, from inside the room, hoofbeats traveled to stand by the window he was under. With a soft gasp, Ash ducked down and sat pressed up to the wall so tight he could have merged with it. His pulse thudded so loudly he was certain it would give him away. The wind bellowed through the courtyard, scattering frost over his paws like dust.

Ash held still. His breath came in shallow, quiet gasps. He squeezed his eyes shut, preparing for the inevitability of being discovered. For a heartbeat, he felt the cold brush his mind again, like a hand reaching. Then... nothing.

The hoofbeats receded deeper into the room and then faded entirely. Ash let out a shaky exhale.

I need to find Lunette... he thought, quietly rising to stand. He scurried his way back to the large iron doors. *Maybe that stupid map could actually help me...* The thought of using anything from Leroy—possibly useful or not—made his skin crawl. He still couldn't quite understand why Leroy had even given it to him in the first place.

Ash hurried inside the barren throne room, stopping by a stone pillar to catch his breath.

I'll just be careful.

Thursday Afternoon, Present Day

A flood of red light pooling down the stairs at the end of the hall interrupted Lunette's incessant pacing. Heavier, more deliberate hoofbeats descending the staircase replaced the sound of their hooves tapping against stone. The distinct aroma of myrrh rolled down the hall.

The stag Creator reached the bottom and locked eyes with the faun. The soft crimson glow of them stood out in the dark prison. Lunette gritted their teeth.

"*You.*"

A soft chuckle rumbled in Thanatos' chest. "You sound so pleased to see me, little warrior faun."

From across the hall, the serpent stirred, his slitted eyes glowing to life on hearing the stag's voice. "So, you've finally decided to join us."

Thanatos's hoofbeats resonated in the enclosed area, blending seamlessly with the soft swish of his robe. His antlers nearly brushed the bars of both cells as he looked between them, a satisfied smile playing at the corners of his mouth.

"I see you both have settled in well. You have not paced a trench yet, though I see your attempts." His clawed hand gestured to Lunette's cell, where scrapes along the wall could be seen along with a few slightly bent bars along the front. "You never have been one to do well in containment."

"What are you *doing* to him?" Lunette spat, squaring their shoulders, merely inches from the bars that separated them.

Thanatos tilted his head, smiling slightly. "Who?"

"You damn well know *who*. Ash. Where is he? What have you done to him?!"

"Ah, yes, your most recent fixation. How many do you have now?" The stag chuckled at Lunette's now flattened ears. "He is settling in well. Very obedient, I must say. More obedient than I thought he would be for someone who kept you as company."

"Let him *go*. He doesn't deserve this. He didn't ask for any of this."

Thanatos turned quickly, lowering himself to be eye-level with the faun, his eyes blazing in the dim light. "Did any of us *really* ask for this?"

"Oh, *enough* of your melancholy. Has anyone ever told you you're exhausting to be around? Even more so now... You haven't changed a bit since the day you stepped into existence." Teramir spat, his chains rattling as he gestured with his speech.

Thanatos held still, then slowly straightened. "You have yet to learn any manners since you slithered into existence either." He lifted a hand and curled a single finger to his palm. The chains that bound the serpent yanked him back, pinning him against the wall with a wince. "Perhaps we can take this time together to teach you some, *hmm?*"

"You *wish*—Teramir snarled, bracing against the chains that remained taut against the back wall. "You *wish* you were as powerful as I am. You were always the outcast of the four, too busy playing with your *creations* to actually *be a god!*"

With a soft *hmm*, Thanatos curled another finger. The chains slackened for a moment. Then—before Teramir could lunge at him—they tightened again, forcefully slamming Teramir into the stone. His head snapped back with a sharp *thwack!* The naga went limp, collapsing to the floor unconscious.

The stag returned his attention to Lunette, who stood with their ears pinned back. "It is so interesting to be preaching about ineptitude while being actively chained to a wall, isn't it?"

"What exactly is your plan here?" they spat.

"I figured I would see how you both were faring. Leroy has been giving me reports, but I was not fully confident in their accuracy. I see now that he was telling the truth."

"And what is the truth?"

The stag smiled more, a chuckle rumbling through his chest. He leaned down once more to be eye level with them. "That you are not nearly as mighty without a great, big sword in your hands."

The sword. Lunette's eyes widened slightly at the thought. They had completely forgotten about it. *The sword that could slay gods.*

Thanatos raised an eyebrow at them. "The seal on you remains strong. Nullhymm will break it soon enough. It will remind you of what you are. Much like Ash."

Lunette could feel the fur on the back of their neck rise. "What are you doing to him?!"

"*Doing?* I am not doing anything to him. Nullhymm is simply revealing what he's *truly* made for, who he *truly* is. Much like it will do to you, little warrior."

"Why do you keep him then? Why not throw him in a cell with us?"

"Now, throwing my chosen one in a cell wouldn't be very nice, would it?"

Lunette's brows knitted together in confusion. "Chosen one?"

The stag's head tilted curiously. "Yes. Did he not tell you?"

The faun opened their mouth to speak but paused, wracking their memory of anything in the last five hundred years that could have indicated that, other than Nikolas stating Ash was marked as some kind of sacrifice to Thanatos... Which didn't sound very 'chosen one-ish' to them.

"Um. No."

"*Very* interesting." The stag smiled more, his ears perked.

"He obviously wasn't aware of it. You must have made that up when you saw him, or you're using him, manipulating him for something!"

"Oh, I promise he has been well aware of that fact. At least... since Wednesday morning last week."

"Wednesday?" Lunette looked past the stag at Teramir, who lay limply on the floor, his forked tongue dangling from his lips. "That was when we were first attacked."

Thanatos continued to stare, unblinking.

"He said his *parents* told him about... about..." Their words trailed off. *About what I am... I caused this...*

"Yes, they did. However, your feline companion is quite... Derelict. He needed a bigger push for him to get in the right direction."

They shook their head, ears flopping as they did. "He... He never mentioned you like that. Ash only said his parents were looking for... for—"

"You."

Lunette's nostrils flared. "I guess. Even still... I never heard about you until we—"

"Met the vampire bat for the second time."

Lunette stared back, their mouth twitched, yet they remained silent. *How does he know all of this? Has he been watching us?*

"Does that concern you, little faun? That he had been hiding that he was seeing me, hearing me, *feeling* me, for a week... yet told you nothing?"

Lunette remained silent, their body stiff. *Why* didn't *he tell me?*

The stag searched their eyes, a satisfied *hmm* breathing out of his nose. "Do you wonder what else he may have hidden from you all these years?"

"I don't need to answer to you," they said firmly, their eyes narrowing.

"No. You do not." The stag straightened and rolled his shoulders, crossing his arms behind his back. "You will have to answer to yourself, though. You certainly have plenty of time to think down here. The memories will help."

Lunette gritted their teeth, leaning forward until their nose and chin graced the enchanted prison bars. Their breath fogged the frigid air. "I will get out of here... and when I do, you will regret everything you have done to us."

"How touching. Is that another one of your omens? You would take away Ash's freedom in pursuit of revenge?"

"*Freedom?* This is literally a prison!"

"Ash is not a prisoner. He knows that. I promised him that I would set us free. We will tear this universe down to the bone and rebuild our lives anew. He was *made* for this. *We* were made for this. Would you tear that from him in your unrelenting quest for revenge?"

Lunette's chest tightened, a familiar tug of defiance and... rage. Under their skin, they felt that raw, consuming power stir. It felt as though it nipped at the underside of their hide, beckoning them to set it free. "You don't offer freedom; you're forcing him into servitude."

The stag's eyes burned brighter as he studied them, intrigued. "We are *all* slaves to destiny. Even you, warrior faun, despite your rebellion."

Swallowing, Lunette forced the building rage in their chest down. *Now is not the time.* "I won't let you destroy our home either. You will *pay* for everything you've done."

"I will await your arrival with coin." The stag chuckled, turning on his heels and heading back to the stairs. The clicking of his hooves reverberated in Lunette's chest. "Until then, do enjoy your stay. I know I will be enjoying every moment with Ash."

Before Lunette could respond, he climbed the stairs, the door shutting behind him. The darkness returned.

A shaky breath escaped their lips. *"Damn it!"* they snapped, their fist collided with the glowing bars, bending them ever so slightly from the force, causing their knuckles to burn from the magic and frost.

I'm going to get out of here. I'm going to get that sword. I won't make Ash save me again. I will be there for him.

They turned swiftly and resumed their pacing, imagining ways to escape and pushing the familiar feeling of Thanatos' ever-glowing eyes out of their head.

701 Years Ago, Astravir

A scream broke through the pouring rain. Lunette turned quickly to block a bone blade that came down nearly inches from their head with their short sword. With a yell, they counterstruck, sending the feline reaper hurtling backward before it burst into dust. "There's too many of them!" Their heart hammered in their chest, head turning quickly as if it were on a swivel.

"We must push through to the temple!" A rough voice shouted. A tall, strong black and silver jackal appeared next to Lunette, brandishing a sword engraved with glowing runes. The red jewel in its hilt caught the light of the lightning above from the storm. "If we don't end this now, then it will mean the end of our world!" The jackal cut down another reaper effortlessly, his long black hair billowing in the wind as he did. Lunette could barely see his face. They could only stare at him, their eyes widening as they watched.

"Look out!" he shouted suddenly, shoving them behind him in one swift, fluid movement to block a reaper from bringing a blade down on their head.

Lunette gasped, slipping in the mud before catching their balance. They watched him from behind, blue eyes wide, muscles trembling underneath their black and gold armor. The sounds of battle and thunder assaulted them from every direction. *I was just sitting in a castle a few weeks ago... This is insane.*

The jackal looked over his shoulder at Lunette. His bright yellow eyes almost seemed to glow in the storm.

"This is the first temple; we must get to the top to call forth the first Creator!" He pushed forward, the other mortals clad in matching armor joined him, battling reapers as they advanced. Lunette followed suit, staying as close to him as possible.

The other members of the Valdarr formed a barrier around the stairs that led up to a tower that nearly touched the clouds. One, a tall gray wolf, the only one in silver instead of black armor—shouted, "We have this, Valdis! Just go!"

The abandoned temple was made of large, round stones. At the peak of the turret there was an open area Lunette couldn't see. Some sections had deteriorated after centuries of neglect. The outside was overgrown; vines and tall grass grew up the sides. Strange symbols were carved into the arched doorway in a language they couldn't decipher.

Valdis shoved his way through the partially broken doors with no hesitation. Lunette followed at his heels, gripping their sword to ground them.

Inside was no better than the outside. Moss and vines crept up the walls. Broken crates, chairs, and tables lay by the entryway. Weather-worn books littered the ground around the feet of bookshelves, and there was a very faint pulse of ancient magic that radiated within the walls. On the other side of the room, at what seemed like an altar, lay a dirty tapestry with what looked like black serpents. They couldn't decipher the main figure in the center. This whole place was a phantom of its former glory; Lunette could only imagine what it looked like when others would travel here to communicate with the Creator.

"Where to next?" They breathed, their chest heaving to keep up with their racing heart.

"We must get to the top and light the brazier. It will send a signal to the first Creator that we need him. It is the first of the three we must light." He spoke quickly, turning to stone stairs that spiraled up the temple's turret.

"Wait—" Lunette grabbed the jackal's free hand, stopping him in his tracks. "Are we... absolutely sure this is going to work?"

"I am certain of it." Valdis squeezed their hand. "Don't let doubts from those in your past cloud your mind. You saw their true colors, their defiance against our home. The fate of our world rests on us. Do you still trust me?"

Lunette's gaze softened as they stared into the jackal's eyes. "With my life. I chose you."

Valdis nodded once, smirking. "Good, because I don't think you can run back to the castle now. Come, we must hurry." With that, he gave Lunette's hand one more squeeze before starting up the steps.

The faun's eyes widened as they looked up at the seemingly hundreds of stairs that ascended the tower. Their ears flattened against their horns. *Why are there so many stairs?* With a shaky breath, Lunette followed.

After what felt like a millennium of climbing stairs, they finally reached the platform at the top. Lunette's heart was hammering in their eardrums. It felt as though every muscle was on fire. Valdis looked over his shoulder at the exhausted faun. "You're doing great, Lunette. We're almost there."

At the center of the platform stood a wide black brazier decorated with serpents curling around the iron columns that pointed up towards the sky. Lightning flashed overhead, its light bouncing off the brilliant purple gems set in the snakes' eyes. It was empty, cold-looking, as if nothing had burned in it for centuries.

Valdis moved to the brazier, sheathed his sword, then outstretched his paws towards it, dropping some items Lunette couldn't see into the brazier. As rain battered the stone beneath their hooves and wind sent strands of wet hair flying across their face, Lunette could not make out the incantations the jackal muttered quietly to himself. His eyes closed in concentration, and there was a shift in the air that made the surrounding area feel like static.

Lunette's eyes widened. *Is lightning going to strike here?*

Then... it all went silent. The rain stopped. The wind ceased.

A small flame flickered to life in the brazier. No bigger than a candle wick. Valdis opened his eyes and stared at it, his eyebrows furrowing together as he stared at it. "I thought there would be more—"

Boom!

A beam of light shot upwards from the flame into the sky, sending out a burst of energy at all angles, knocking the jackal back into Lunette, who grabbed at him to stop him from toppling off the side of the temple. The light shone a bright white, then settled into a deep purple, as it shot into the clouds above them.

As quickly as it began, it stopped.

The brazier lay barren again. The rain fell softly again, yet the clouds slowly cleared as the afternoon sun broke through from behind them.

Valdis looked at Lunette, his chest heaving from exertion from the ritual. "One down."

Lunette nodded once, still holding onto him, and listened. It sounded as if the battle had stopped below. "You did it," they breathed with a small giggle.

"*We* did it, my love." He reached a paw out and fixed some of the wet strands of hair that were plastered against Lunette's snout with a satisfied smirk. "We will find a spot to regroup, check the wounded, then we will press on to the next temple—

The air turned cold. Valdi's eyes widened, his muzzle curled into a snarl as he whipped around and drew his sword—three reapers appeared behind him. "Hold your ground!" he shouted to Lunette, who adjusted the grip on their sword and moved into a defensive stance, nervousness etched across their face.

The feline reapers lurched at them.

Valdis easily deflected two strikes, while Lunette stumbled as they blocked a reaper's attack, one hoof nearly slipping off the tower's edge. The reaper pressed in on them, swinging their blade at their torso, but Lunette parried it, their short sword locked with theirs.

The tall cat's eyes narrowed, his smile flashed into a wicked grin before using all of his strength to push forward, knocking Lunette back.

Sending them tumbling off the side of the tower with a scream.

"*Lunette!*" Valdis' voice cut through the wind rushing in their ears.

They twisted in the air, bracing themselves for inevitable impact with the ground below. The tower was rushing by them, the trees approaching quicker than they could register, until something cold snapped around their body—knocking the wind from their lungs—

76

Lunette drew a sharp breath as they rose abruptly from the stone floor of their cell. They coughed raggedly and looked around wild-eyed, unsure of where they were for a moment.

Alas... They were in the cell. Still in darkness.

Their heart thudded against their ribs. Their ears rang. The faun wrapped their arms around themselves, a futile attempt to ground them back to reality. They could just barely see the glowing eyes of Teramir boring into their small form tucked against the wall.

The screams still rang in their ears.

What are these horrible nightmares?

Who am I?

Thursday Evening, Present Day

The only sound Ash could hear, besides his own thoughts, was the sound of his paw pads slapping against the stone floors as he paced in front of the bed.

I just need to find Lunette. He ran a hand through his hair. *But if I go to them now... what then? I could make it worse. Thanatos could really hurt them.*

Ash clenched his fists, claws biting his palms as he did. With a huff, he looked over at the crumpled map on the floor. Swiping it up, he hastily uncrumpled the parchment and turned it over to the very poorly drawn map.

What the hell does "no" mean? Does he mean "no, don't go to my room" or "no, don't go down that hall?" Ash squinted at the scrawling in the torchlight and shook his head. "Well, this is practically useless." He mumbled to himself, tossing it onto the bed where it floated pitifully through the cold air onto the sheets. His nostrils flared as he took another glance at it, then at his room's door.

According to that, there should be something at the end of the hall... Maybe that other room I saw before. Ash's claws flexed once more, then he promptly turned to the door and opened it. He leaned just his head out the door, his ears flat against his head, tail lashing behind him, expecting someone to be there. Luckily, there was no one. The halls were bare. You would think a temple of death would be filled with reapers, no?

NO!!
YOU ARE HERE!!
MY ROOM
FOOD!!
NO!!
THRONE
EXIT

They must all be on Earth. The thought made Ash shiver. He could only imagine the mass panic amongst the mortals that was occurring below them. After all, there *is* a giant rift in the sky. That in itself should be causing pandemonium, never mind a bunch of creepy reapers wandering around. All Ash could picture was a bunch of Leroys wandering around, and that in itself was a horrifying thought.

Stepping out into the crimson-lit hallway, he stared down the empty corridor. He started walking quietly, though his footsteps sounded like a giant's in these barren halls. As he reached the center hallway to the fountain room, he stared down at where Leroy's room should be. Next to the caracal's room stood a large wooden door at the end of the hall. *That must be where he said "no" to.* Ash's whiskers twitched in thought. Did he really want to go down there and risk seeing Leroy's smug mug? No, of course not.

Let's see what's behind door number two, then. It makes more sense to be a prison. That was a lie. He just wanted to avoid Leroy. He turned down the short hall into the fountain room, then turned to the large, carved wooden doors that blocked off the "no" room. "Definitely a prison..." Ash breathed, grasping the handle and pulling the massive doors open.

In front of him was yet another small hallway that led to another set of humongous wooden doors. *Why does this place have so many damn hallways?* Ash shook his head before quietly striding up to the second set of doors.

As his paws rested on the door handle, he paused. His body froze in place. What if he did see them? What would he say? *Am I going to make it worse?* His ears flattened against his skull. Simply knowing where they were wouldn't hurt... Right? A flood of possibilities about what they might say rushed through his mind. How disappointed they were, how they didn't like him anymore, that he was a failure...

Like me anymore? Why would I care about that? Then the thought of their soft lips pressed against his in the safe house brushed his memory, their breath on his whiskers as they were so adamant that they would do this together.

Ash's paw fell from the door. He took a few steps back as his gaze fell to the floor. *No, I'll only make things worse.*

Turning away from the doors, he quickly started back towards the fountain, his hand covering his mouth, stifling a hitched breath as he did.

A squeaking hinge stopped him in his tracks as he reached the fountain. Ash turned around quickly on his heels to see the door at the end of the hall opened just slightly. Red light trickled from the crack onto the stone.

His brow furrowed. Ash made his way back and peeked inside. *This... is not a prison.*

It was a bedroom.

From where Ash stood, he could see an old canopy bed adorned with large red drapes. Enormous red windows covered the right wall, casting an eerie crimson glow across the room, much like the rest of the cathedral. There were a couple of tables and chairs, a fireplace that probably hadn't seen an actual fire in who-knows how long, and bookshelves that stood eerily empty.

Curiosity got the best of him.

Ash slipped fully inside, and the door eased shut behind him with a soft, breath-like click.

For a heartbeat, he didn't move. He stood there in the quiet, surrounded by red light, the whipping wind outside the windows, and the faint earthy scent of myrrh that clung to everything. His claws flexed anxiously as he took a tentative step forward, paws sinking into the old red carpet. It was uneven in places, worn down by centuries of pacing. Someone, or something, walked this room often.

This... must be his *room.*

Ash's eyes swept the space warily. The canopy bed looked as if it had been carelessly collapsed into constantly—its frame sagged, and the drapes were haphazardly pushed aside in a messy pile. The blankets were tangled and knotted. The worn, thin pillows were piled high at various angles. There were scrapes against the headboard that looked as if they were caused by antler points.

His ears tilted back.

For a being who supposedly created death, he seems remarkably bad at resting...

He stepped further in; each movement was like wading through mud. It felt... wrong to be here. Like he was peeling back the skin of something sacred or forbidden. Yet, curiosity tugged him forward. Would Thanatos care? Hurt him for being in here? Punish him? Ash didn't know. That was somehow worse.

The fireplace caught his eye. Dead cold, gray ash clung to the grate like dust in an abandoned home. It looked as if it hadn't been lit in years. Maybe centuries. Why would Thanatos need a fire? There were tools beside it, ordered neatly, as if someone had once used them often.

"What are you?" Ash murmured under his breath, running a claw lightly across the dusty, empty mantle.

Across the room, a small circular table was tucked against the windows, a worn, simple chair next to it. Its surface was cluttered. No, not cluttered. *Lived-in.* Objects scattered in no particular order: a cracked ceramic bowl, a pair of rusted scissors, half-filled vials of something herbal and metallic, rolls of cloth, a scrap of leather, safety pins, and... Ash's breath caught.

Is that blood?

Bandages sat in a small pile on the table. Old. Dried stiff. Coiled like snake skins across the table. Their dark gold stains stood out starkly against the pale cloth.

Ash stepped closer slowly, as if approaching a wild animal. His heart thudded in his chest. He reached out and lifted one cautiously, feeling the stiffness of the dried bandage. It was the same wrap he saw around Thanatos' forearms, but it never occurred to him that he could be injured.

Could he have been hurt by being imprisoned in the cave? How? By who? No one was in there with him. Did I do this?

Ash racked his brain trying to recall if he had actually fought back at some point, but the answer to that was no. He recalled the stag had them on even when he first saw him in the arctic.

He swallowed hard, a sting of pity rising before he shoved it down. *I shouldn't feel bad for him. He's a monster.* Ash placed the bandages down and backed away.

His instincts were screaming at him to leave. Immediately. Still, something tugged at his chest, a morbid curiosity, or maybe a new, sickening need to understand the creature that held him hostage.

Ash drifted closer to the bed now, fingertips brushing the tangled blankets. He imagined Thanatos lying here, enormous frame curled awkwardly into a bed too small, antlers catching the drapes and scraping the headboard, muttering in his sleep—wait, did Creators sleep? Dream?

"No, no," Ash murmured harshly, tearing his hand back. "Let's *not* do that."

He slumped onto a chair next to him, clutching his head in his hands as his breath trembled. He felt as if the room was pressing in on him. It was *too normal.*

"Why did you make me free you...?" His voice cracked as he whispered into the stillness. The question lingered there, unanswered, swallowed by the whipping wind outside.

Then... a soft creak echoed from the hall.

Ash froze. His ears shot up.

Footsteps—slow, heavy, steady—moved just outside the door, accompanied by the thumping of wood on the floor.

His heart lurched into his throat.

The hoofbeats paused right outside the room.
A shadow slid under the threshold.

Ash didn't move. Didn't blink. Didn't breathe. He forced his mind to be silent.

Just as he started to stand, the shadow drifted away down the hall, the hoofbeats growing faint as they traveled away. Only when they vanished entirely Ash exhaled, some tension leaving his body.

I need to get out of here. Now.

Turning quickly, he crossed the room in only a few steps, then slipped out. He closed the door as quietly as possible, but he couldn't help one last lingering glance at the bloodied cloth on the table.

Instead of fear or anger, the feeling that lingered... was confusion and a terrible, traitorous ache in his chest.

Ash turned on his heels and hurried through the small hallway, feet nearly silent against the worn stone despite the pounding heartbeat in his ears. The fountain room's frosted tiers glinted in the red light, and the air was thick with a faint but unmistakable trace of myrrh. It had to have been Thanatos outside the door. It was undeniable now.

He scanned the room again—corners, shadows, doorways—but found nothing. No towering figure. No glow of crimson eyes, just the whisper of a presence that vanished too quickly.

Swallowing hard, he forced his legs to move, retreating into the empty corridor that led back to his room. Every step felt strangely weightless, as though he hadn't returned from a bedroom but from a dream.

By the time he closed his door behind him, the adrenaline had ebbed, leaving him lightheaded. He stood there for a moment, back pressed against the wood, inhaling slow, shaky breaths.

What am I doing?

Ash pushed off the door and crossed the room, pacing again, his claws tapping softly at his sides. Every thought in his head collided with another: guilt for Lunette, fear of being caught, anger at Leroy, confusion about Thanatos, shame for feeling anything except terror.

"I shouldn't have gone in there," he muttered, voice cracking. "What the hell am I doing?"

He sank onto the edge of the bed, elbows on his thighs, staring at the floor as if an answer might appear there. The map still sat on the sheets beside him, its terrible handwriting mocking him with every crooked line.

I could find Lunette. However, if he goes after them now, he risks Thanatos' rage. After seeing what he did to that other Creator, there's no question that both of them would have no chance against him.

I could wait here. However, waiting meant doing nothing. Doing nothing was what got them both trapped in the first place.

Ash tilted his head. *I could ask Thanatos?* His gut twisted at the thought. *Are you crazy? Absolutely not.* He pressed his palms to his tired green eyes, exhaling a trembling sigh.

His voice came out barely above a whisper. "Why are you like this? Why am I like this?"

He lay back on the bed, the old mattress hardly giving beneath his weight, and stared up at the ceiling. The dim orange from the ever-burning torch on the wall flickered across the stone.

After a long moment, he whispered into the stillness, "I need to do *something.*"

701 Years Ago, Val-Tirath

The creaking wood floorboards of the upstairs hallway under Ash's paws made him cringe. Everyone in their family home was asleep, but Ash couldn't bring himself to rest.

These past few weeks his mother has been going on that it was "nearly time" for his "final ritual." What did that mean? He wasn't entirely sure. All his family members and extended family have been overly nice to him lately. It just felt weird; he hated all the attention. The new year *was* approaching, and while everyone tended to be extra friendly as the wheel of the year turned, Ash couldn't help this felt... different.

He rounded the corner of the second-story landing and stepped onto the first stair with care, pausing to listen for a creak. Nothing. Ash held his breath, then descended the stairs, stepping into the first-story foyer. No candles were lit, and the fireplace in the main family room was nearly burnt out. The stained wood walls and floors made the fortress-like home feel even darker. Just because he was on a floor below his parents' and siblings' rooms didn't mean he was free. He still had to tread carefully. He just wanted to see what they were planning. All week his mother had told him to stay out of the ritual room. Members of the commune have been going in and out of the house, bringing things in and taking things out, all under the guise of secrecy. Moreso than usual.

Keeping his tail tucked close to his body, he padded through the foyer into what seemed like an endless hall of rooms on either side. A nearly infinite enfilade of congregation rooms, magic-practicing rooms, supply rooms, and extra bedrooms for guests. At the very end of the hall stood two large, dark wooden doors that extended from the floor to the ceiling. Carved into each door were the double pentagram symbols Ash had seen his entire life.

Why can't I remember what those mean?

Ash approached the door slowly and rested his paw on the handle, gripping it. A familiar ache started in his chest. His hair stood on end. *What if I'm not meant to see what's in here? What if that ruins her plans?*

Ash's paw fell from the door. He took a few steps back as his gaze fell to the floor. *What am I doing? I'm just going to make it worse...*

Turning on his heels, he started back up the dark corridor when a cold breeze brushed his back. He stopped, ears flattening and tail twitching at the sudden chill. Ash turned his head to look back over his shoulder at the room. One door had opened ever so slightly.

He turned completely to face them again, hesitating for only a moment before proceeding back towards them with caution. He tried to shut it with his paw, but his growing curiosity made resisting difficult.

Well... it is open now.

Ash leaned around the door's edge to peek inside, but it was too dark to see anything. There were no windows.

Carefully, he slipped inside the cracked door, letting it ease shut behind him. He stood engulfed in darkness, then raised a hand so a small necromantic green flame appeared in his paw, illuminating the immediate area.

From where Ash stood, he could see a massive double pentagram carved in the wooden floor just down the short stairs in front of him in the sunken floor. Unlit candles surrounded the outermost part around the edges of the circle, then larger black candles sat perched at each star point. Past the top star point of the pentagram, perched at the top of the short stairs, Ash could faintly see the outline of the altar table in the green light.

This doesn't seem too abnormal.

He walked around the edge of the circular room, stepping over folded black cloaks that sat neatly at the edge of the sunken floor. The green light in his palm bounced off the dark wooden walls, casting an eerie glow over the empty cloaks around his feet.

He approached the ritual table cautiously, extending his hand out to illuminate the objects that lay before him. Ash's brow furrowed, looking at the table.

A large, leather-bound book.

Clumps of myrrh scattered about, as well as in jars as oil.

An antler painted black.

A sharpening stone.

And a piece of deer hide that was rolled up and tied closed.

What even is this? With his opposite hand, he reached out and pulled the slipknot that held the hide in its roll. Immediately it rolled open with the weight of its contents.

Ash's eyes widened as he stared back at his own reflection in the large, silver ceremonial knife that lay in front of him, illuminated by the viridescent light. The sharp light that bounced off the mirror-like edge reflected on his solid black fur, his green eyes wide, staring back at him. The skin on his face ached, staring at it.

"What the hell are they planning?" Ash breathed into the silence.

Thud.

Ash's eyes shot up. His entire body went rigid.

Silence.

He swore he had just heard something across the room. His fur bristled while he nervously gulped, flexing his claws. A heavy beat echoed from his chest as his heart raced.

Glancing back down at the altar table again, he caught a glimpse of himself in the knife, but also the shadow of something behind him.

Ash spun around, startled, holding up the green flame to illuminate his surroundings, but saw nothing. He turned back around and stared into the darkness past the pentagram.

Something was watching him.

"Mother?" He said softly, cringing at what the response would possibly be.

Nothing.

Ash paused, his ears flattened against his skull. "Father?" He spoke a little louder; his voice echoed off the rounded walls.

No response.

"Auburn? Juniper? Oak?"

Silence.

Ash's tail flicked subtly behind him.

"Is this some kind of joke? Come out, don't play in here."

The air was still, yet the flame in his palm flickered.

Ash swallowed, his heart continued to race, his claws flexed instinctively as he scanned the darkness.

"Ash Darkscream," a voice rumbled, low and resonant, vibrating through his very bones. It wasn't so much a sound as a presence, forcing itself into his head. The scent of myrrh from the table filled his nostrils.

Ash's breath caught in his throat. He searched the black expanse for its source. "Who are you? Who's in here with me? State your business!"

"My business?" The voice chuckled. From the corner of his eye, Ash swore he saw a shadow move out of view. "I am simply observing what might be *mine.*"

Ash's claws bit the palm of his free hand; he curled his lips, showing his canines. "Show yourself, spirit. I am the God of Necromancy. You have no power here." The fire in Ash's paws grew larger, brightening the immediate area, and for a moment he swore he saw red glowing eyes in the darkness.

"Spirit? Power? Necromancy? How adorable, how interesting... Death that produces life."

"I mean it." Ash spoke sternly, though his voice cracked.

"Intriguing that you would speak to me in such a way. Yet, I can taste the fear radiating from your skin. Do you know who I am, child?"

Ash took a step back, his head on a swivel, trying to decipher where the voice might be coming from. "I don't care who you are. This is a holy space—spirits are not welcome!"

"A *holy space?*" the voice said, amused. The air grew colder. The myrrh on the altar table was making Ash dizzy.

Then, from just outside Ash's right ear, it spoke. "There is *nothing* holy about *us*, Ash Darkscream."

With a gasp, Ash jumped away from the voice, stumbling on a folded robe on the ground and falling onto his back. The flame in his hand extinguished immediately, leaving him in complete darkness.

The voice chuckled lowly as Ash scrambled on the floor, fighting to get to his feet but stumbling and flailing as he did so.

Once he got to his feet, he reignited the green flame in his hand, just barely catching the silhouette of antlers and red eyes on the wall. Ash's whole body trembled. As quickly as he could, he wrapped the ceremonial knife back in its hide and half-heartedly tied it back together.

Gasping for breath, he sprinted around the edge of the room, feeling eyes on him as he did.

"You can't run from me forever. It is our destiny!"

Ash crashed into the double wooden doors and shoved them open, his paws slipping on the wood as he did, sending him hurtling towards the floor.

Friday Early Morning, Present Day

Ash was jarred from his sorry attempt at sleeping by footsteps at his door, light and quick, too deliberate to be the wind. His heart raced as his eyes focused. If it weren't for the torch on the wall, he would've assumed he was still in the dream.

He flipped around quickly, shaking the exhaustion off as he sat up on his elbow to stare at the wooden door with wide, blackened eyes, bracing to fight. Or to run.

A shadow lingered, then just before he could get up to investigate further... it vanished. His ears twitched sharply, following the soft patter of retreating paw pads on stone.

Paw pads. Not hooves. Probably not Thanatos.

There was a beat of silence in his thoughts.

But it is probably Leroy.

The thought made him huff.

Even here he's trying to spy on me.

Ash carefully swung his legs over and set his paws on the cool floor, the temperature eliciting a jolt that effectively jarred the tiredness from his body. With a grumble, he tugged his rough black-and-red robe tighter around his shoulders. He padded to the door and opened it a crack.

Nothing. The same long, empty hallway as it has been.

What is that bastard up to, anyway?

Ash dragged his claws along the doorframe in irritation, tail flicking once, twice.

Fine.

If Leroy wants to skulk around in the dark like some feral alley cat, then Ash could skulk right back. He deemed reciprocation was fair now—especially when he'd been kidnapped, emotionally terrorized, and betrayed in the span of a week.

He stepped out quietly, leaving his door slightly open, and started down the long corridor. Despite it being nighttime, or at least what he thought was nighttime, the same amount of light came in through the red stained-glass windows, casting his shadow against the doors he passed. The sun of Nullhymm burned at all hours like a funeral pyre.

Upon reaching the halfway point and passing the desolate fountain, he began to hear the sound of voices in the distance. His pulse thudded in his chest.

Is that Thanatos?

Ash slowed his pace so he could focus on the not-so hushed voices. From this distance it sounded like muddled words, but they began to make sense as he approached.

Not Thanatos.

"—and that is just part of it. The place you said you were living? Well, not living, none of us are alive, but—"

"Can you cut to the chase?" Leroy's familiar drawl sliced through the muffled air. He sounded sharp, impatient, yet there was a jittery, brittle edge beneath it, like cracked glass pretending to be smooth.

He was close enough that he could smell cigarettes now; Leroy's room was just four or five doors away from where he crept.

"Ah, yes, sorry, Arch-Reaper," the deep, squirrely voice stammered. "Anyways, that place you lived? About thirty-five miles away is a canal that the mortals dug out. It is pretty much a direct, wide-open vein below the water. They dug so deep they exposed a lot of it."

There was a pause, then a sharp exhale followed by a fresh gust of cigarette smell.

"So..." the other reaper continued nervously, "we should report immediately to our lord. He will be pleased we found it so soon."

"*Hm.* Yeah. Super-duper soon." There was a pause. Ash could just barely hear the embers on the cigarette crackle as Leroy inhaled. "Like, shockingly soon," Leroy went on as he exhaled, voice too light to be natural. "Much, much sooner than I expected."

"I know! I honestly think the others just want to... get it out of the way. Onto the next one, you know?"

Another drag of the cigarette.

Ash's nose curled at the smell.

"Yeah, yeah. I'm sure." Leroy's tone dipped, its playful edge fading, "except, you know... I think it's too soon."

There was a pause from the other reaper. "I-I'm sorry? Can you repeat that? I didn't quite hear you, Arch-Reaper."

"I *said*..." Ash could hear him force the words through his smile, "it's entirely too soon."

Ash flinched at the sudden *hissss* of a cigarette being put out.

He inched closer, his heart rate picking up the pace. The door was ever so slightly open, just enough for Ash to see the silhouette of the other big cat cast on the inside of the door. Leroy's shadow was nowhere to be seen; he must have been next to the torch rather than in front of it.

"T-too soon?" the big cat repeated, trembling. "Forgive me, Arch-Reaper, but our lord wanted this found immediately. He intends to... eliminate this world by the end of the week. I must insist we inform him at once." The big cat's voice cracked as he spoke, his tone dripping with uncertainty.

"Oh? Must you?" Leroy cleared his throat, smoothing his tone into something softer—too soft. "Tell me, who else knows about this?"

"Just me, Arch-Reaper."

"Oh, good. That's good. What a relief." Leroy let out a gentle laugh tinged with something dark.

Ash's skin prickled. Memories of the Antarctic cave, of Leroy's sudden, feral shift, flashed in his mind. His fur stood on all ends, his tail frozen in place.

"Arch-Reaper, I do not understand. I will just go ahead and report to our lord. You seem like you need rest."

"Oh, *please*," Leroy chirped. "There is no rest for the dead, and there is no need to trouble our lord. I'd be *delighted* to tell him myself." A shadow crossed in front of the big cat to the other side of the room. The tall, tufted ears were unmistakably Leroy's.

The visitor remained motionless, deliberately avoiding eye contact with the caracal. Somewhere in the room, Leroy could be heard rifling through a drawer, the sound muffled but distinct in the tense atmosphere. Ash inched forward, careful not to make a sound. From this new spot, Ash managed to get a glimpse of the tiger's black and red robe and the long, striped tail swaying slightly. Leroy's figure was obscured from view.

"Are you sure, Arch-Reaper? It seems like something is bothering you. I am happy to help—"

"Nonsense!" Leroy's voice rang out loudly. "Actually, I think you've helped *quite* enough!"

The tiger spun around, exposing Leroy to the side of him.

His ears were tall and rigid, eyes blazing with wild energy and a wide, crazed grin stretched across his face. An arm raised above his head as shadows shot up from the floor to twist around the tiger—

The glint of the bone blade's gem-encrusted pommel caught Ash's eye as his arm came down in a merciless swoop—

Ash slapped a hand over his mouth and whipped away from the door as the tiger let out a yell that was cut short—

The sickening squelch of blade tearing through flesh slashed through the frigid air. A surge of death-magic cracked through the air like a thunderclap, then vanished instantly as if someone snuffing a candle.

Ash's legs felt as though they might give out. He turned and risked another glance through the door.

Leroy stood relaxed. He held the bone dagger firmly in one hand, his other hand guiding black tendrils of magic that ebbed and swallowed the tiger's form whole.

The tendrils contracted once.

Twice.

Then collapsed inward.

Leaving nothing behind but a small, pathetic mound of ash.

Leroy dropped his hand and huffed, a satisfied smirk gracing his lips. He brushed the ashes under a nearby table.

"*Oops*. Sorry, pal, but I'll take it from here." Leroy let out a quiet laugh as he cleaned the bone blade against his black robe, even though it was spotless.

Ash's body trembled as he stared from his spot. His breath hitched violently. He thought he was going to vomit. He stifled another gag as he backed away slowly, his legs feeling as though they might give out from underneath him.

He killed them...

His feet carried him without thought, stumbling steps blurring together as the robe flowed behind him like a ghost.

Ash didn't fully register his own door until he crashed into it. Scrambling inside, slamming it shut, and pressing his back to the wood. His chest heaved with ragged, uneven breaths.

He killed them... He killed them... What is he doing?

701 Years Ago, Val-Tirath

"Again." A commanding voice rang out.

Ash grunted, flexing his sweat-covered paws until green necromantic energy glowed in his palms. His brows were knit in extreme concentration, his muscles ridged as he focused all of his energy on his hands, his mind stating his intentions for this energy on repeat. *Reanimate... Reanimate...* His green eyes blazed as they bored into the pile of bones in front of him.

With a swift flick of his wrists, he sent the energy forward into them, causing the bones to tremble as the magic infused within them. Ash's body remained taut, not daring to move until he saw the outcome.

The bones rose slowly, then picked up the pace as they assembled like a jigsaw puzzle into a small rodent. The amalgamation shuttered, tilted its head towards Ash as if waiting for orders. Ash lowered his arms, keeping eye contact with its eyeless skull.

"That is exceptional." His mother's voice called out again. She moved from the corner of the candlelit room to stand beside him.

The two felines watched the rodent as it shuddered again, convulsed, then spontaneously burst apart into a pile of remains once more.

Ash sighed heavily through his nose. He risked a glance at his mother, who stared at the mangled pile for the thirty-ninth time this afternoon. An exasperated sigh escaped her mouth as she pinched the bridge of her nose.

"Do you understand… how powerful you are?"

Ash looked away and wiped his palms on his black robe.

"I chose you over your brother because you are the strongest of your siblings. I can feel it under your skin. It burns strongly." Mercy turned to him and grabbed his shoulders roughly, forcing Ash to make eye contact with her.

"Perhaps Auburn would be better for this…" Ash mumbled, trying to look away.

"No. While his devotion is strong, his abilities pale before yours." She gave his shoulders a quick jerk when he looked away, so he would focus back on her blazing eyes. "I will hone your powers, your abilities. You will be powerful. You will be a god. You will kill for us to keep us alive. It is almost time for the final ritual, and you will be ready."

Ash's ears flattened. "Why do I have to kill anything? I am bringing back the dead. That is my purpose."

"How do you think something gets dead in the first place?" She snapped, dropping her hands from his shoulders. "However, you will do no such killing here. Only on your mission, when it is time. You must remain pure of killing for *him* until the time is right."

Ash's stomach twisted; he couldn't even picture what it meant to kill something, or *someone*.

"Yes, you can," his mother said suddenly, her tone uneasily monotone, making Ash's eyes snap to meet hers, his brow furrowed.

"What?"

"You *can* picture it. You know why? Because you already have. Don't you remember?"

Ash's eyes widened. His heart raced. *Back in the In-Between...* He recalled the slithering ink-esque serpent biting down on Lunette's leg. The rage. The sound as his magic enveloped it and crushed it out of existence. *But, wait...*

"That... hasn't happened yet."

Mercy smiled, a cruel smile with her ears folded back. "Do you feel remorse?"

Ash shot out of bed, gasping for breath, his heart racing. His whole body trembled. Unwelcome tears welled up in the corners of his eyes as his arms wrapped around him, claws digging into his shoulders. Images from earlier in the morning flashed in his head. That sickening sound of the tiger being struck down... Was it rage Leroy felt too? Or was he past that?

I'm no better than them... Am I?

Ash lay back down and pulled the blanket over his head. He continued to shake. He didn't dare close his eyes.

Friday Late Morning, Present Day

Ash didn't fall back asleep the rest of the morning. The trembling and initial panic had subsided, leaving a raw ache across his body as he lay huddled under the blankets. His eyes burned, head throbbed. The image of the bone blade coming down on the reaper stained his mind, more so *the sound it made*. It played on repeat like a bad song.

There was a harsh knock at the door that jarred his thoughts, though it was a welcome pull away from the constant replay happening in his head. *Leave me alone.*

The door creaked open, followed by a gruff, "Get up, it's time for your meal."

Ash immediately recognized the voice of Sih from the first night. "I'm fine. I'm not hungry," he croaked from under the blankets.

"That's great. However, your presence is still required in the dining hall whether you eat the food I made or not."

Ash sighed through his nose; his tail lashed under the blankets. Yet, despite the displeasure, he obeyed and got to his feet. The lynx squinted as he approached.

"Uh-uh. No. Brush your hair. You are not seeing my lord looking like that." She said harshly, pointing at the vanity.

Ash's brows furrowed. With a shake of his head, he turned to the vanity and straightened his hair to be less like a wild animal had made a nest in it. He turned back to the lynx and motioned to it, wordlessly saying, *is this better?*

"It will do," Sih rolled her eyes and turned away. Her stubby tail flicking behind her as she started down the hallway. Ash reluctantly, yet obediently, followed behind. He felt as if he were sleepwalking.

He couldn't help but get another wave of nausea in the halls as they walked. The lynx didn't seem to notice. *Stay focused. You can't think about this in front of him.* They approached the dining hall doors, and she led him inside, just the same as before.

Stepping into the ever-frigid room, Ash's eyes rose from the floor to see Thanatos in his chair. The stag's gaze lifted from his nearly empty goblet to meet his, a clawed hand tapping the arm of his chair impatiently. "You took longer to wake this morning. More memories?"

Ash simply shook his head and let himself collapse into the usual chair. There was a steaming plate of herbed chicken in front of him, the same meal as the first morning. Just looking at it made his stomach ache. "Can I have some milk?" he murmured. Maybe that would settle his stomach.

Thanatos flicked a finger at Sih, who rolled her eyes and walked off, then proceeded to stare at Ash.

"You look pathetic this morning."

Ash looked at him quickly, eyes narrowing. "What?"

A chuckle escaped the stag's lips. "Does that offend you?"

"Well, it's pretty rude..." Ash looked away, poking the food on his plate.

"Hm. Rude. I've been called many things in my existence... rude is a new one."

Ash opened his mouth to say something he would likely regret, but was interrupted by the slam of a door opening, followed by a glass being placed in front of him. Leroy stood entirely too close, a smug grin plastered across his face.

Ash's hair stood on all ends, his body ached, and nausea returned in full force. However, he strained every wrinkle in his brain to not think about what he saw last night this close to Thanatos.

"What even is this?" Leroy motioned to the chicken before Ash, a playful edge to his voice. "Our lord of darkness prefers eggs and milk in the morning! This is just blasphemy. I will have a chat with Sih myself."

Thanatos' gaze didn't waver. He swirled his wine absentmindedly. Ash couldn't help but eye the bandages around his forearms. The ache in his chest was not helping his stomach. He reached for his milk and took a small sip.

"Do you have an update for me? I felt a reaper return last night."

"Yeah, one did. He left, though." Leroy moved away from Ash to stand by Thanatos, arms behind his back.

The stag's head tilted slightly, watching Ash's shoulders tense up merely an inch. "What did he report?"

"He said they were struggling to find a spot. This planet is a little more difficult, it seems."

Ash's abdomen clenched. He felt dizzy.

"I have a suggestion," Leroy continued, "if you don't mind."

Thanatos looked at the reaper and raised an eyebrow. "Speak, then."

"My suggestion is to call all the reapers back to Nullhymm."

"*Tch,*" the stag scoffed. "Why do you suggest such a thing?"

"Well, my lord, we have our gathering in two days now. Sih and I are fantastic decorators, as you know. However, I believe this occasion will need, as the mortals say: *all hands-on deck.*"

Thanatos took another sip of wine, his ears swiveling while his eyes became unfocused in thought. Ash mimicked the movement by sipping his milk too, mostly to avoid making any expressions that might give away his thoughts... Or lack thereof.

"Originally I planned for them to come back Sunday." Thanatos spoke slowly, still considering the reaper's words. "A day earlier will delay our investigation of Earth."

"Yes, I understand. But... *someone* needs to keep an eye on our adorable guest." Leroy gestured to Ash, making Ash's ears flatten. "If both Sih and I are going to be preoccupied, there will be no one to make our little lord's food correctly. You know the other reapers aren't nearly as experienced with the needs of the living as we are."

Thanatos rasped his claws on the table before shifting his gaze to Ash—who had just finished the last sip of his milk, then proceeded to wipe the residue from his lips away with the back of his hand. A sigh escaped the stag's nostrils. "Fine. Call them back."

Leroy's grin widened. He dipped his head in a small bow. "Yes, Daddy. Right away."

The reaper turned quickly and marched out the door, a bit more exaggerated than usual. He fished a cigarette out of his pocket and lit it as he did. Ash turned his head to look at the stag, who seemed to still be deep in thought. His goblet was empty, yet he still swirled it in his hand.

Ash cleared his throat, which seemed to get Thanatos' attention. "What... can I expect on Sunday?"

"What can you expect?" The stag repeated, placing his goblet down with a soft *clink*. "As I said before, I am presenting you as my chosen one."

"Yes, but what does that entail?"

A small smile spread across Thanatos' face. "What is wrong? Do you not care for the unexpected?"

"No." Ash's whiskers twitched. "I'm not really a fan of surprises."

"I suppose that is to be expected given the events of this week. Very well..." Thanatos folded his hands in his lap, causing his sleeves to fall over his hands. "You can expect to be announced as my champion. Lots of wine. No food though. I know a lot of death gods eat, but I find it unnecessary for these types of gatherings."

Great, so I'm not going to eat? Not that Ash was feeling peckish, but it was the point.

"Nonsense, there will be food for you in the kitchen if you should need it. You are the honored one, remember? You can expect at least a hundred gods. Including your parents, of course."

Ash went rigid. "My parents?"

Thanatos watched Ash with a hint of enjoyment. "Yes, of course. They *are* gods of death. At least they try to be." An amused snicker escaped his lips as he traced the edge of the goblet with one of his claws.

Ash's mind was going a mile a minute. He hadn't seen his parents *in the flesh* for over *five hundred years*. What will they say? What will they do when they see him? Would his siblings be there?

Will they be proud of me? The thought was involuntary, but nonetheless came through louder than he wanted.

The stag's ears perked. "Does that matter to you?"

"Does what matter?" Ash said quickly, pushing the food around on his plate.

"If they are *proud* of you?"

Ash paused. His mother's words echoed in his head. *Weak.* "I don't know." He breathed out.

"Your parents are nothing." Thanatos said quickly, a little too quickly.

Ash looked at him, his brows knitted together with a mixture of offense and confusion.

The Creator nonchalantly waved his hand. "They do not matter. While I am grateful for their *sacrifice* of their son to me, their opinions of you and what you have done with your life do not matter. You are beyond them now. The 'zombie apocalypse' is also beyond you."

The zombie apocalypse... That was all it was meant to be. Somehow that seemed easier than whatever was happening now. Ash shook his head. "I don't understand..."

"The opinions of others serve no one but the ones spewing them." The stag pushed himself out of his chair slowly, rising to his hooves with usual elegance. "Even then, it is debatable... The more time you waste trying to 'correct' the opinions of others, the less time you have to focus on what *matters*—which is what lies ahead."

He adjusted his robe and a few dark, stray braids that fell out of place with the motion of standing. Ash couldn't help but stare up at him, his expression still mixed between confused and slighted. Thanatos brought his attention back to him, a smug smile playing at the corners of his lips.

"As I stated, you are above them now. What I say is law here."

Ash let out an involuntary scoff, causing the stag to raise an eyebrow.

"You laugh at me?"

"I can't picture being... above my parents. Also," Ash shook his head, placing his fork down. "You... sounded like Lunette just now."

The stag paused, his expression perplexed yet still amused. "Did I, now? *Hm*." He tapped a claw on his chin. "That must be attractive to you then."

With that, he turned with a small laugh, his robe fluttering in the cold air as he crossed the room. Ash sat there agog, trying to wrap his head around what had just happened.

"Attract—attractive? I don't—I'm not—we're not—I don't like Lunette that way! I don't think anyone is—I don't know what you're talking about."

"Mhm." The stag stopped in the doorframe. "Do finish your food. You need to eat *something*." With another satisfied snicker, he left the room. His hoofbeats echoing across the hall, leaving Ash to sit there still agog, a hundred different thoughts racing through his head.

Does he... want me to think he's attractive? What the hell was that?

A few moments passed, and he decided that he'd had enough excitement for one morning. Pushing himself from the table with an awful scraping of his chair, he rose to his feet. Sih came into the room with purpose, her ears flat.

"Come on. Let's go. Back to your room. I'm not letting you leave for the rest of the day; I have too much shit to do," she mumbled under her breath.

"I thought I wasn't a prisoner?" Ash's eyes narrowed.

"No, but you *are* a disruption. You will distract the reapers as they prepare. I need you to stay away so that they can focus. Entertain yourself or," she waved her hand in thought, "take a nap."

Ash sighed and followed her to his room, memories from that morning resurfacing as they walked down the hall. He couldn't be free from them forever.

Do you feel remorse?

Yes.

I do.

Friday Evening, Present Day

Lunette's eyes felt heavy, but they didn't dare allow themselves to rest. Sleeping on the frigid stone floor was not doing them any favors, and their usual cozy maroon turtleneck was tattered and torn from everything that had happened. However, it wasn't just the cold that kept them fighting to stay awake.

The dreams. Were they dreams? Lunette was not entirely sure. Regardless of what they were, the feelings they elicited from deep within their chest were not pleasant. No matter how much Lunette attempted to shove them down, they couldn't help but keep asking what it all meant and if it was real.

They felt hollow.

Hollow from the ache of missing and worrying about Ash. Hollow from Leroy's betrayal. Hollow from the words the two Creators had said to them. Hollow from the cold. Hollow from the overbearing feeling of being trapped in a literal cage, unable to do anything.

This was probably the longest Lunette had ever physically sat still. They were always traveling, always on the move, always looking for something to do. Now, here they sat with nothing but their own thoughts and an asshole of a Creator within yards of them.

Speaking of which, the rattling of chains jarred from their circling thoughts Lunette in the dark. *Great, he's awake again.*

"I feel your gaze. It's annoying me." The serpent mumbled, his voice gruff from the cold.

"I'm not even looking at you," Lunette groaned, pulling their legs closer to their chest from where they sat against the back wall of their cell.

"Don't lie. I can feel your eyes on me. I can feel everything."

"That's... Don't say that. That's weird."

"You are the one who is being 'weird' just staring at me."

"I literally can't even see you. It's pitch black in here."

From across the narrow hallway, Lunette saw a small purple orb flick to life in the Creator's palm. It illuminated the immediate area around them. They could see Teramir's hand straining to keep it alive. His brows were knit in concentration, his iridescent lavender hair trembled ever so slightly with his shoulders, the cuffs around his wrists glowed softly, attempting to snuff his power.

Alas, it was successful, and the orb extinguished within moments of being lit. "Damn it," Teramir cursed under his breath. He sounded as if he were breathing heavily from the effort.

"Where did he even get those cuffs? How can they repress even a Creator's power?"

"They were originally designed to hold *him*. He was in this prison once, long ago, long before you were even a speck in this universe."

"Weird." They replied, simply, exhaustion was starting to take over them again in the darkness. Lunette rested their head back against the cool stone, letting the sharp coldness keep them awake.

"You do not look like you have slept," the serpent said quietly.

"I don't want to sleep anymore."

"That is childish. Weren't you all about being 'strong' and 'facing the darkness,' or whatever it was?" he scoffed.

Lunette gritted their teeth. As they opened their mouth to make a snappy comment back at the pompous Creator, a red light was cast down to the prison from the top of the stairs, causing them to squint. Heavy, deliberate hoofbeats descended the stairs. The heavy aroma of myrrh followed suit.

Thanatos reached the bottom and looked between the two as he positioned himself between them, the same way as before. "My, my. You both look worse for wear." Lunette's ears went back, and they rose to their hooves, despite the fatigue that caused their muscles to ache.

"What do you want?" They spat, not taking their eyes off the enormous stag.

"It would be rude of me not to visit my guests occasionally. Also, I figured you would want an update on how well my chosen one is doing." A sly smile crossed his lips, causing the hair on Lunette's neck to stand up. "He is doing well overall; however, he seemed a bit rattled this morning. He is having dreams like yours, remembering what was lost. However... you look... worse."

Lunette bared their teeth. "What are you *doing* to us?"

"You are a *coward!*" the naga interjected with a hiss. "You're a *weak-minded*, manipulative—"

Thanatos raised his hand, the chains tightened just a bit on the serpent, and he went silent. "Do I have to knock you out again? Because I will. And I *will* enjoy it."

Teramir's eyes narrowed. He sat up straight and lifted his chin, just below eye level of the stag. His nostrils flared. "Fuck. You. You, *parasite*."

With a flick of Thanatos' wrist, he flung the naga back into the stone wall where he slumped to the ground.

"We will humble him yet," the stag sighed. "I thought keeping him near you would make him *think* just a little bit. Making him listen to your self-righteous, motivational speeches would do him a sliver of good."

Lunette gritted their teeth. "What the hell do you want now?"

"I wonder where you got all that motivational speaking from. Was it from Valdis? I could picture him doing that. He was always overconfident and holier-than-thou."

Valdis. Lunette stiffened at the name, a prickle of recognition threading through their mind. Something about it tugged insistently at the edges of their memory, elusive and tantalizingly familiar. *The dreams... Are they actually real?* Thanatos watched their reaction closely, amusement flickering in his eyes as if he relished the discomfort.

"Ah, yes, Valdis," Thanatos mused, voice curling with a kind of dark nostalgia. "Always so sure of himself, always believing he could inspire those around him. Leading everyone into the unknown for a 'heroic cause' that was well over his handsome head. Yet, he never acknowledged how he, himself, was just as much of a manipulator did he?"

Lunette's jaw clenched. Images of the armor-clad jackal filled their mind. The way his hair whipped around his snout in the storm, the sword gripped in his claws as he reduced reapers to ash, the way he said: *"my love."* They shook their head.

"You talk about him like I know what you're talking about. But all you do is twist the truth. What do you really want? What are you doing to us?"

Thanatos' eyebrows raised, a playful smile across his lips as he leaned down to be eye level with the faun. "Little warrior, I have not lied to you *once*. I speak only the truth."

Lunette glared, stifling a trembling breath. "I don't believe that's true."

Thanatos tilted his head, his antlers nearly brushing the cell bars. "You can believe what you want. Everyone cherry-picks their truth, anyways. They all like to believe what suits their narratives."

"Quit avoiding the question and *answer* me! What are you *doing* to us?"

"I am *doing* nothing. As I said before, Nullhymm has a way of plucking at the memories buried deep within the mind. If I could stop it, I would." The smile on his lips faltered ever so slightly at the last words, but he straightened to hide it. "Besides, I think it is a good thing for you and Ash to remember who you are. What you were made to be."

"I am not made to do anything. I make my own path." Lunette gritted their teeth, moving to be closer to the bars.

"Hm. Your naivety is wasted here, faun."

"What do you even want? Why are you down here again?"

Thanatos paused, his gaze searching Lunette's face, studying their visible exhaustion. "I told you, I wanted to visit my guests and see how you were both faring, and you are faring as I expected. I find it interesting that you are fighting so hard to avoid the memories that are arising. Why is that? Do you fear the truth?" He folded his hands behind his back and tilted his head.

"I don't fear anything. Especially you."

"Very cute, but we both know that is a lie. Has Teramir been getting into your head, perhaps?"

Lunette simply glared at the stag, their ears pinned back, and their small bushy tail flicked in irritation, earning a deep *hmm* from the Creator. "Interesting. I thought you did not let others get to you."

Their glare remained steady, but uncertainty flickered across their face. Silence lingered before they spoke again, voice low and strained. "You keep talking like you know us better than we know ourselves. Maybe that's what you want—control over our thoughts, our choices. You're trying to manipulate us, manipulate Ash."

Thanatos let out a quiet laugh that echoed in the cold chamber. "Ash is already so heavily manipulated by others; I only seek to set him free. To free both of us from this... hellscape of a universe that condemns us and fulfill our destinies. I observe and speak the truth, Lunette. I do not need to manipulate when you do it to yourself just fine."

For a moment, the only sound was the echo of their breathing mingling with the perpetual chill. Lunette's fists clenched at their sides. "If you observe so much, then you already know I'm not interested in destiny. Ash will stand up for himself. I just know it. He doesn't need to be forced into what you want him to be."

"I am not forcing my chosen one to do anything. He is not chained or locked away like you are. He wanders this place freely, and yet he has not made any attempt to leave... That speaks for something, doesn't it?" The stag's eyes glinted with pride, he leaned down again to be eye level with the faun, his antlers brushing the bars and peeking between them ever so slightly. "Does it make you jealous that he chooses to stick close to me when he leaves you every single time?"

In a quick motion, Lunette's hand shot up from their side, grasping the tip of Thanatos' antler that peeked in and yanked it toward them, bashing the stag's forehead into the metal bars with a loud *thud!* He gasped and stood up quickly with a stumble, rubbing his head and growling angrily. Lunette watched with a satisfied smirk and crossed their arms.

"*You*, I will have you put in *chains*!" Thanatos hissed, rubbing his head with his hand, feeling his antler over to make sure it didn't break. "You think yourself mighty in strength and 'freewill' but mark my words, you are just as enslaved as the rest of us!" He shouted, turning quickly on his heels and marching back up the stairs. Slamming the door before Lunette could say another word.

As the echo of the slamming door faded into the icy silence, Lunette let their smirk drop, replaced by a sigh of exhaustion as they slid back against the freezing stone, sinking to the ground. Their chest heaved with adrenaline, but the satisfaction from the encounter with Thanatos was short-lived. They still felt exhausted. *I can't fall asleep.* Yet their eyes felt heavy.

"That was a good one," Teramir's hoarse voice broke the silence.

Lunette pressed a hand to their temple, glancing toward the shadowed corner where Teramir was. The darkness was back, and they couldn't see him but could feel his sly smile. "Don't start," Lunette muttered, voice rough.

"I am not starting anything." There was a pause. "You've got guts, you've got fight. I'll give you that. Even if you are no better than he is, you at least call him out on his idiocy. He thinks he is so clever."

Despite Teramir's words echoing with a note of rare, twisted approval, Lunette didn't reply. Instead, they pulled their legs close as the bitter chill seeped through their clothes and pressed into their bones. Exhaustion was weighing heavier on their shoulders.

Before they could stop themselves, their eyes drifted shut. Despite the fight, their body had given in... for once.

701 Years Ago, Astravir

Lunette sat with their legs pressed together, elbows pinned sharp against their ribs. Their hands were folded in their lap so tightly that if they clenched any harder, something was going to crack... bone or sanity, whichever gave first.

"Oh, quit looking so stiff." Valencia hummed from her throne beside Lunette, waving her hand nonchalantly in their direction. The maned wolf queen lounged as if the world existed solely for her comfort. The morning sun cut through the open balcony behind her, reflecting off her amber fur and highlighting her lithe features. Brightly colored jewels dripped from her throat and wrists, each gem catching reflections so brightly it made Lunette squint occasionally. Her long limbs draped over the throne with casual elegance, every inch of her posture radiating command.

"You look like a carved gargoyle, darling. Try... breathing."

Lunette inhaled, though it sounded more like a gasp than the calm breath Valencia wanted. Their near-sheer white dress rustled as they adjusted.

"That's a little better, I suppose," the wolf hummed. "It's just like any other day, baby." Her hand reached and touched the top of Lunette's head just between their horns, giving them a couple scritches with her claws. "I do not understand why you are being so... off. Just don't think about whatever it is that is bothering you."

Lunette nodded softly under her hand. *Yeah, like that has ever worked for anyone...*

At the base of the stairs that led to the throne, citizens of the capital gathered in eager rows. Claws clicked. Hooves shifted. Wings rustled. All eyes were lifted toward Lunette, faces bright with devotion and expectation.

"Now then," Valencia murmured, moving to tap her claw against the arm of her throne. "Smile for our people."

Lunette attempted something that might have been a smile on a stronger, braver day. Today it looked more like a grimace of dental pain.

Valencia's lips twitched. "Close enough."

The guards by the end of the stairs raised their intricate, gold-spiraled staves. One spoke out to the crowd. "Our blessed oracle will speak now!"

Lunette's stomach twisted. *Blessed oracle.* They grew to hate that title. The queen loved it. The crowd adored it. They recalled as a child they would feel so honored, their little hooves swaying against the chair they currently sat in, smiling at strangers, giving them hope for things they didn't understand. Hearing later how it came true in some way or another and receiving their thanks.

Lunette swallowed, throat tight as the crowd leaned forward. The queen brushed a lazy hand along Lunette's arm, a touch that to anyone else looked affectionate.

"Go on," Valencia whispered, voice honeyed. "Just... tell them something nice. Something hopeful. Just a broad statement today, that's fine. They always admire that."

Like what? That I saw you this morning?

Lunette's fingers trembled in their lap.

The memory of the conversation slammed into them so forcibly their breath hitched. The cold voice behind the door. The words: *when Astravir falls.* The promise of "survival." They couldn't even make it to Alastair to tell him what happened. No one else knew.

I need to get out of here.

Their wide eyes stared at the crowd. A thousand faces stared back. Waiting.

Lunette opened their mouth. Nothing came out.

The pressure in their chest swelled until they thought they might break. The throne room blurred at the edges. Their inner vision stuttered between past and present, between Valencia's soft voice coaxing them forward and the cold voice of Thanatos promising to save only what she gave him.

"*My dear,*" Valencia's voice slid into their ear, velvet and venom, jarring them from their obsessive thoughts. "You are trembling. You know how they get when you hesitate."

Indeed, the crowd was shifting uneasily. Worriedly waiting for their daily blessing.

"Oracle?" someone from the crowd called gently. "Is something wrong?"

They wanted to scream—*yes, actually, we're all going to die!*

Granted, that was not... the smartest thing to shout to a crowd who was there for good news and blessings.

Lunette's eyes scanned the crowd once more, then locked onto a familiar pair of bright yellow eyes in the crowd. A black jackal stared back, his brows knit in confusion and concern. He tilted his head as they focused on him. Lunette watched him mouth the words, "What's wrong?"

Everything! Everything is wrong right now. I hate to admit you were right, but...

Instead, Lunette forced themselves to breathe. To lift their chin. To say something, anything, to satisfy the queen and the crowd so they could get out of here.

"Ah... Today..." Lunette whispered, voice wavering so faintly.

Valencia's ears twitched in annoyance. "Speak up, child."

Lunette cleared their throat. "Sorry. Ah... Today will bring clarity."

The crowd murmured amongst themselves, seemingly trying to decipher who that applied to.

Valencia's hand tapped the arm of the throne again, beckoning them to keep going.

"And," Lunette continued, pushing through the tight ache in their chest, "you should... cherish one another. You may need each other sooner than you think."

A strange hush fell.

Lunette noticed the jackal's gaze sharpen, more concern than confusion now.

Valencia's claws tightened on her throne.

Lunette swallowed, dread bubbling. *I should have... worded that better.*

The wolf's gaze sharpened. "Such poetry in your omens," she said sweetly, though her eyes burned. "Our oracle is gifted, are they not?"

The crowd applauded, pleasant but with an air of awkwardness. Lunette's pulse pounded so loud they barely heard it.

As the guards quickly dismissed the people, Valencia leaned toward them, voice low. "We will talk later about your... choice of phrasing."

Lunette stiffened. "I didn't mean—"

"Oh, I know." Her smile was a knife's edge. "You've been a bit off lately. I hope you're not hanging around that *jackal* lately. You know how I feel about his kind. You worry me, baby." Her hand reached up and petted their hair again. It made Lunette's skin hurt. "Why don't you return to your room? Have a nice bath and calm down. I will have your meals brought to you instead of the dining hall so you can relax the rest of the day."

"Yes, my Queen," Lunette murmured, looking back at the exiting crowd. They caught the jackal's eyes again, who lingered behind.

He gave a look that Lunette grew to learn meant "meet me later."

I will, they thought, pushing themselves out of their seat.

Valencia motioned for one of the guards to accompany them. They made their way toward the hall that led to the chambers. Halfway down, they stopped to look behind them. From her throne, Valencia watched them. Her expression puzzled, trying to decipher Lunette's words assumedly.

They turned back around. A sudden intense dizziness took over their vision. Lunette raised a hand to their face and closed their eyes.

Then opened them quickly to find themselves lying on the ground of the frigid cell. They could hear their heartbeat in their ears.

What's happening to me? What does any of this mean?

700 Years Ago, Val-Tirath

The candlelight on the vanity reflected off Ash's solid black fur. He stared at himself in the mirror, meticulously braiding his hair. The short parts still hung in his face, but they weren't long enough to cover the worry that resided in his eyes.

A knock at the door caused him to jump, then sigh in frustration. "Yes, I am getting ready now. I will be down in a minute."

The door opened, anyway. Ash watched the reflection in the mirror as Oak slipped in and closed the door behind him. "Hey."

"What do you want?" Ash said, his worried expression replaced with annoyance. He redirected his attention to finishing the braid.

"I just wanted to see you before the ritual. I leave in an hour to go back out to sea."

"Ok. Bye." Ash used a small piece of leather to tie off his braid, then adjusted his bangs, keeping his gaze focused on what he was doing.

Oak sighed through his nose. "Ash. Today is important."

"Yeah, I know. That's what Mother keeps telling me, and yet you're leaving."

"Ash," Oak spoke firmly, "this is... different. It's going to change everything. It's not too late to leave."

Ash rolled his eyes and turned to face his older brother. "I'm not like you. I won't just run away from my family whenever they annoy me a little bit. Mother says I was made for this. I have to believe all of this is for *something*."

Oak's ears turned back, his eyes narrowed. "I choose to be free from all this nonsense. There is a difference."

"It's not nonsense to me, then." Ash turned to his bed, where a long black robe lay. With one swift movement, he grabbed it and pulled it over him.

"Ash, I'm serious. This just seems... wrong. I've seen her preparing this week. It's not the same as her average rituals."

"Goodbye, Oak. Don't drown in the ocean or something."

Without another word, he pushed past Oak, the tension between them hanging in the air as their shoulders made contact. The door swung open, and Ash strode into the hall that led to the landing, his footsteps carrying a mixture of uncertainty and determination.

As he walked, his senses became acutely aware of every detail—the aged wallpaper, the paintings of family hanging on the walls, the creak of the old floorboards beneath his paws, and the closed doors that marked each sibling's and parents' rooms. So painfully normal on this abnormal day. Ash couldn't ignore the twisting feeling in his gut.

Reaching the landing, he hesitated, resting his hand lightly on the railing as he leaned over. From where he stood above, he could see the steady stream of commune members filing into their home. The line of dark-robed, black felines snaked its way through the foyer and toward the ritual room at the end of the hall, everyone moving with an air of purpose and anticipation. The rhythmic thud of their footsteps reverberated off the high walls, rising up to where Ash stood watching.

Everyone's going to be there, I guess.

"Good luck, brother," a soft voice murmured from next to him. Ash turned to see his identical brother Auburn there, who did not attempt to hide the visible disappointment in his expression.

"I'm sorry that it isn't you." Ash sighed. "I know how much you wanted it to be."

"It's alright, Ash. Our lord deemed it wasn't meant to be, I guess. I will keep practicing and participating, then maybe someday I will be able to join you and do the ritual myself another time."

Ash nodded softly. "Honestly, I don't even know what to expect or even what they're going to be doing to me."

"I think it's some sort of baptism or dedication to our lord for all the training you did and how much natural power you possess." Auburn looked away from Ash, watching the last of the members who came in through the door. "A great honor. Truly."

"Will you be joining us?"

"No, mother said the siblings aren't allowed to. We're staying up here for the day and we'll have dinner after."

Ash's whiskers twitched as he frowned. "I see. I was hoping you would at least be there, but I understand."

"It will all be good though, and we'll see you at dinner." Auburn offered a small smile to his brother, who looked at him and nodded.

"Yes, you will." Ash patted his back. "I should head down there; mother wanted me in there as soon as I was dressed. See you at dinner." Auburn gave him a single nod before he proceeded down the stairs, feeling his brother's eyes on him the whole way.

The foyer was empty now. All the guests who were piling in must have made it to the ritual room already. Ash took a brief look around, then proceeded to the hallway that led to the ritual room.

It's just another family ritual. I don't understand why everyone is so up in arms about it...

Ash turned down the long hallway and stared down at the large wooden doors. Something tugged at his chest, stopping him in his tracks. His whiskers twitched, and the tip of his tail flicked slowly.

What if they're right? What if this really does change everything?

There's no way.

The thought came quickly, shoving the doubt to the side.

The rituals from before were just prayer and necromancy rites of passage, and they all said the same things.

He took a step forward, then proceeded down the long corridor, his black robe flowing around his feet. Ash stopped right before the door, staring at the carved handles before curling his paw around it.

Alright. Here we go.

With a deep breath and a swift pull, he opened the door. The candlelight from the hallway pooled into the room, casting an orange stretch of light over the center of the room, over the double pentagram, and to the altar table where Mercy stood tall. Her eyes glanced up at Ash as her chin raised. Her face was marked with white paint in the shape of triangles in the corners of her cheeks.

"He has arrived."

From around the room, robed figures that filled the entire space turned to look at Ash in unison, their black fur and features incomprehensible in the shadows, except for the white symbolic paint on the corners of their faces. Their eyes reflected in the darkness.

Ash tensed up.

They aren't in full face paint...?

"It is time," Mercy's voice commanded.

Ash took a step into the room and the door closed behind him.

Saturday Morning, Present Day

Movement in the halls awakened Ash. Not just one this time, but many footsteps pattering down the hallway. Doors were opening and closing, there was conversation and shouting that made him think there was a mob outside his door. His heart raced. Images of the robed figures in his dream flooded his thoughts.

No... No, I'm not there. I'm still here.

He rose to his feet and padded to the door, creaking it open just a crack to see down the hallway.

Yes. Still here. What is going on?

For the first time, the halls of the cathedral were full. Spectral, bone-armored felines stood at every corner, armed with ethereal bone blades and spears. Robed feline reapers, much like Leroy and Sih, quickly moved through the halls. Carrying bundles of red curtains, tablecloths, and other aged décor fit for a party.

I didn't think there were this many.

A few of them caught Ash's eyes and stopped to stare before moving again. His hair stood on end. He shut the door again.

He didn't need the attention. He's had enough for one week.

From behind him, there was a rapid, musical knock on the door. It caused him to jump, but he knew that rhythm anywhere. Ash whipped open the door to stare up at Leroy, who stood there with his ever-present grin.

"Good morning, sunshine. How are you liking the activity? It's like living at home again!"

Home... Not Val-Tirath...

"New Bedford was never this busy right outside our door..."

"Maybe not to this extent, but hey tourist season sucked ass in the bad way."

Ash thoughtfully nodded with a *hmm* before looking past him at the other reapers. He could barely look at the caracal still. The soft echoes of the tiger reaper continued to linger at the edge of his thoughts.

"Ready for your typical 'Leroy Special' breakfast?" The arch-reaper moved to be in his focus again, causing Ash's ears to flatten.

Ash sighed. He knew the drill now. "Lead on."

"With pleasure." He snickered, pulling a cigarette out of his pocket and lighting it.

"How do you even manage to find those here? Don't you run out?" Ash groaned, using his paw to wave some of the smoke that drifted past him away.

"I keep a hefty supply on me. I hoarded all the ones you would bring home from work when I asked for them." He took a drag of the cigarette before speaking again. "It's part of my charm; I can't let it get tossed to the wayside just because I'm home!"

Ash shook his head and waved the smoke away again. They wove through the tens of reapers, many of which stopped to stare.

The armored ones didn't budge, but their eyes followed Leroy and Ash as they walked down the hall.

"Don't let the big ones scare you. They're just guards and they don't talk. Some of the other reapers are shitty fighters, so the big man keeps them around to accompany those ones and keep the other spirits on their best behavior. They won't bother you as much as the others will." Leroy scoffed, nearly brushing against one of the spectral guards as he rounded the corner.

They approached the fountain room, which now had the door to the throne room open wide, where reapers were bringing things in and out of it, then into the dining room.

However, this time the dining hall was empty, save for two plates of food.

"Where is Thanatos?" Ash asked flatly, trying to avoid the strange, empty feeling he felt seeing his chair barren.

"Our lord is a bit preoccupied this morning. So, you'll be eating with me. Just like old times!" Leroy clapped Ash on the back before moving to sit directly in Thanatos' chair while finishing his cigarette, where the second plate of food sat.

Ash couldn't stifle his growl from the cold slap, and his eyes narrowed watching Leroy sit in the stag's place.

Why do you care?

The buttery eggs that sat before him with a glass of milk looked somewhat appetizing. His stomach wasn't in as many knots as yesterday, yet his body still felt raw. Leroy's presence didn't help.

Leroy started digging into his plate, eating quickly, almost ravenously. Ash crinkled his nose, watching, shaking his head.

"Why do you even eat?" he asked, pushing his food around. "It makes no sense."

"It's simple, Ashy. I like food; therefore, I eat it." He shrugged, an amused smile on his face.

"I guess I just never gave it much thought," Ash gestured at him, "the fact that you're technically dead."

Leroy's grip on his fork tightened. His smile looked a little more forced. "Never mind." Ash said quickly before taking a bite of his food, not wanting to bring out whatever unstable side Leroy seemed to have.

Leroy didn't respond for once. He simply kept eating until his plate was spotless. Ash hadn't even gotten a quarter of his eaten by the time he finished.

He stared down at his plate, pushing eggs in slow circles with the side of his fork. Next to him, Leroy wiped his mouth with the back of his hand in the least polite fashion possible, sighed loudly, and leaned back in Thanatos' chair like he owned it.

"Well," the caracal said, tapping his claws against the armrest, "you're still a miserable bundle of storm clouds, even here."

Ash glared at him. "A lot has happened, no thanks to you."

"Oh, sure." Leroy made a loose, dismissive gesture. "I get it. Your entire worldview shattered. Your cult family's god is real. Your beloved planet is next on the chopping block. You had a bad dream. My condolences."

Ash's tail lashed. "You say that like it's a normal week for you."

Leroy grinned, quickly lighting another cigarette and letting it dangle from one corner of his mouth. "You're just jumpy. More than usual."

"I wonder why." *Maybe because I saw you kill someone.*

"Oh, I can answer that for you, actually." Leroy leaned forward, elbows on the table, grin sharpening. "It's because you're the new favorite... and *you like it.*"

Ash blinked and shook his head vigorously. "What?"

"The favorite," Leroy repeated slowly, as if explaining math to a toddler. "You know. Golden child. Pet project. Chosen snack for the Creator of death itself. Congratulations, really. Major promotion. Not above me, yet, though. I can see the way you two look at each other. You're liking all the attention from Daddy-O."

Ash stiffened, his lips curled back slightly to flash his canines. "I'm *not* his favorite, and I *certainly* don't like anything that's happening."

Leroy's grin widened. "Oh, Ash. Sweet, clueless Ash. He literally calls you *his chosen one.* He hasn't breathed down someone's neck like this since, well, since me, technically. I see the way you look at him, how you listen to him, you're *fascinated* by him." His ears flicked. "I must admit it feels weird having all this free time now. Like retirement, but with fewer margaritas."

"You're joking," he growled.

"Always," Leroy said breezily. "Except when I'm not."

Ash hated when he said things like that. He hated it even more that he couldn't tell which he actually meant.

Leroy flicked ash from his cigarette directly onto the old tablecloth. "You should admit it to yourself and enjoy the attention while it lasts. He gets... fixated on the shiny ones."

"I'm not shiny... If anything, I could use a shower."

"You're endearingly sassy and new," Leroy corrected. "It's close enough."

Ash set his fork down with a sharp clink. "Can we talk about something else?"

"Of course!" Leroy snapped his fingers. "Let's talk about your lover."

Ash nearly choked. "They're not—Lunette is not—"

"Fine, fine, whatever you want to call them—your *friend* who just so happened to smack lips with you." Leroy rolled his eyes. "Anyway. They're alive. Mostly. A little irritated with life, but who isn't these days?"

Ash's heart leaped painfully. "Where are they?"

"In a cell. Being dramatic. You know how they get." A sly smirk crossed his face. "Feistier than you, honestly. I think they actually tried to bite me yesterday. You like the lively ones."

Ash's fur bristled. "I need to see them."

"You *need* to stay put," Leroy said flatly. "Daddy-dearest will be pissed if he finds out you went and saw them."

That's funny coming from you. "I don't care."

"Well, I do," Leroy huffed, leaning back again and taking a drag of his cigarette. "Last thing I need is scraping you off the stone floors, or even worse… Getting our lord all agitated. You do *not* want to see him when he's huffy."

Ash glared. "You don't actually care."

"Oh, you wound me." Leroy pressed his hand to his chest. "Of course I care. If you die, or vanish, or wander off, Thanatos will be hovering over me again like an overbearing mother hen with antlers."

Ash rolled his eyes. "And that matters why? Why does he hover over you? I thought you said your god hated you."

"Well, *yeah,* he hates me," Leroy announced, a little too loudly. "Now he's busy hovering over *you*. Which means I can finally breathe, smoke indoors again, do my work in peace—"

Ash's ears flicked back, and before he could stop himself, he blurted out. "You killed someone yesterday."

Leroy snorted, shaking his head, grinning. "You saw that? Look at you being sneaky. That was work-related." Leroy waved it off with a flick of his wrist, taking another drag of his cigarette. "Don't worry your handsome little head about it."

Ash's stomach twisted. He didn't know if he felt disgusted, nauseous, or both. Probably both. "Why did you do it? What is your plan here? They didn't do anything—"

"Drop it, Darkscream." He flicked more ash from his cigarette onto the table.

"But—"

"I *said*… Drop. It." Leroy watched him silently for a moment, something unreadable, almost sharp, behind his eyes. Then he smirked again, light and breezy.

"Just relax, Ashy-boy. Keep being complacent. You'll see Lunette soon enough. Whether you want to or not."

"That's not comforting."

"It wasn't meant to be."

Ash swallowed hard. "Leroy... what are you actually doing? Helping me? Hurting me? Both?"

"Why choose?" Leroy snickered, rising from the chair and stretching lazily. "The universe is complicated, reapers even more so. Try not to think too hard. It'll make the brain-soup spill out your ears."

Ash didn't laugh. Leroy didn't expect him to.

The caracal took one last drag off his cigarette and flicked the butt into a nearby empty goblet with perfect accuracy.

Then he turned to the doorway, tail swaying behind him like a lazy pendulum.

"Oh, Ash?"

Ash looked up warily.

"Try eating your breakfast before it gets cold. Then I suggest staying in your room the rest of the day like good ol' Sih wanted."

"For what? What is happening today?"

Leroy grinned without warmth. "You saw all of those peons running around. You distract them. Best stay in your room, play with that book I brought you."

Ash's whiskers twitched irritated. "Fine." *I don't want to be around them, anyways.*

"Attaboy." Leroy winked, then slipped out of the room. Leaving Ash alone at the empty table.

Where even is Thanatos?

Saturday Morning, Present Day

Thanatos' hooves clicked down the stone stairs to the prison, causing Lunette to look up from where they stood with their back against the freezing wall—another futile attempt at keeping themselves awake. However, the constant movement from above was doing a good job at that already. The red glow from the open door illuminated the prison enough that Lunette could see Teramir stir from his slumber. His forked tongue flicked out lazily as he squinted and groaned, pulling himself off the frigid floor.

The stag stopped between the two cells, the same as always, and craned his neck to look at Lunette, careful to keep his antlers away from the bars this time. "I told Leroy I wanted you in chains."

Lunette's eyes narrowed as they crossed their arms. "Yeah, I'd love it if he opened that door to come in here."

"*Hm,*" the corner of the Creator's lip twitched. "Touché."

"What the hell do you want now?" Teramir hissed from his spot, causing Thanatos' ears to flick back in his direction.

"How many times do I have to tell you that it would be rude to not visit my guests," Thanatos straightened and adjusted a braid that fell out of place, "this will be the last time for a little bit, I'm afraid."

beings besides us in this universe, and you *cursed us* with
!"

"*Her* artistry *cursed us with life!*" Thanatos slammed his fist
ard against the magic bars they bent under the pressure. The
sent Teramir flying back with so much power the stone
ked upon impact. As the serpent slid down it, golden blood
ked the stone.

The stag's chest heaved with shaky breaths. He turned his
slightly to look over his shoulder at the faun, his eyes
inuing to burn bright. Lunette swallowed, staring with wide
at the Creator as he turned to face them completely, bracing
nselves for the inevitability of also being thrown into a wall.

"We were created to amuse that sorry excuse of a maker in
image, by her design. I believe this was meant to happen, I
destined for this. I was doomed from the start to be betrayed
ny creator. For why else would this have happened?" Thanatos
ghed, a dark, sarcastic laugh as he ran a hand over his face and
d the red robe that hung loosely on his body. "We all have a
pose that was planned from our birth. I am simply living up to
of their expectations."

"You don't have to do this," Lunette interjected, holding
ir ground. Every muscle was taut, waiting for impact. "We are
what others force us to be. We can choose differently."

A half-hearted chuckle erupted from Thanatos' chest, yet
expression remained deadpan. "You are so painfully naïve. If
u hadn't had someone constantly saving you, you would have
en dead long ago."

Lunette pushed themselves off the wall and
the bars, staring up at Thanatos with gritted teeth.
mean by that? What are you planning?"

The stag clapped his clawed hands togethe
them, a smile playing at the corners of his mouth. "
probably know, I am hosting a gathering. I have no
Leroy has opened his big mouth about that. So, tha
will not be down here at all tomorrow and most likel
after so I can focus my attention on removing that p
existence."

Lunette opened their mouth to shout but was
shut off by Teramir's hiss that cut through the air. "Y
what do you think this will even solve?! Destroying e\
fix the damage *you* caused! Only your *elimination* wil

Thanatos' ear twitched irritably before his lips
snarl. He whipped around to face the serpent Creator
slammed his fist into the bars, his eyes blazing a crim
it illuminated the serpent's face. "I'm getting really tir
When will you learn *I* didn't do this? My *maker* forced
our *Creator* betrayed us!"

"*Our* Creator created us in *her* image! We are e
her will and artistry!"

"Why don't you ask yourself, *brother,* if I am the
evil, what does that mean if I was conceived within *her*

The naga opened his mouth. A stutter escaped I
sharp teeth before his nostrils flared and his forked tong
After a moment of thought, he leaned forward, pulling ag
chains to be inches away from the stag, his bright purple
with his. "You were a blot. A mistake. There should have

Lunette's eyes narrowed, a growl escaped their lips, yet they couldn't deny the pain in their chest the statement caused. "I don't—"

"Save your breath," Thanatos waved his hand dismissively, then turned back towards the stairs. "The next time I see you, Earth will be in its final stages of life, and the next 'end' will be upon us."

Lunette stared at the stag, their hands balled into fists at their sides. "I will get out of here and I will stop you again. I will get Ash and I out of here."

The stag glanced at them out of the corner of his eye, staying facing the stairs. "Did you really stop me before? Or did you just prolong the inevitable?"

Lunette didn't have an answer. Their mouth twitched at its corners. They could feel tears welling in the corners of their vision. Thanatos said no more. He only walked back up the stairs. Lunette listened to the door close behind him, encasing them in darkness once more, then his hoofbeats faded into the depths of the cathedral. They breathed in shakily and wiped their eyes with their sleeve.

Ash, I hope you're ok. I won't leave this mess for you to clean up again. I will save us both. They thought loudly, secretly hoping maybe somehow Ash could hear it. All they wanted was to see him again, to hug him and be out of this mess.

"Teramir?" They breathed into the dark.

No response.

Please don't be dead.

They sank to the floor and pulled their legs to their chest. The faun ran their hands through their dirty white hair, gripping their skull as they did. A soft, unbidden sob escaped their lips.

Why did I have to be like this? I didn't want this either...

Their hushed sobs softly echoed in the prison until exhaustion finally took over, and the frigid stone prison fell into silence with their slumber.

700 Years Ago, Astravir

"Keep going!" Valdis' voice cut through the harsh clanging of weapons colliding.

Lunette dodged a reaper's blade that slashed through the air, their teeth gritted as they plunged their sword into the bone armor-covered reaper, causing it to dissolve immediately into dust.

"We need to hurry once we get up there! I don't think we can take another wave if they respawn!" Alastair, the tall gray wolf in silver armor, shouted as he cut down two more reapers with a single swing of his axe.

They had entered the underbelly of the city of Astravir to avoid the queen's attention. Valdis had gotten word about the queen commencing a hunt for the Valdarr, so he determined if they used the abandoned underground tunnels in the cover of night, they would be able to make it to the final temple that lay just within the city walls by the castle.

"How did they even know where we would be?" Lunette shouted, knocking down another reaper as they made their way to Valdis at the front of the large party.

"I do not know," the jackal replied, adjusting his grip on the glowing sword in his grasp.

"Valdis!" Alastair shouted over the group as the sounds of blades crashing suddenly ceased. "They've retreated!"

Lunette and Valdis glanced back at their companions, realizing the reapers had disappeared. The group now found themselves alone in the dim underground tunnel as Valdis' expression tightened in concern.

"What's happening? Why did they vanish?" Lunette said through heaving breaths.

"They must be planning something. *Move!*"

At Valdis' command, he broke into a run down the earthen tunnel, his engraved sword casting a glow ahead. Lunette and the rest of the Valdarr hurried after him. Soon, they reached a ladder set into the packed dirt wall. "This way—up!" Valdis called, wedging his sword between his teeth as he swiftly climbed and pushed aside an iron grate at the top.

Lunette lingered, keeping a careful eye as each of the Valdarr climbed the ladder ahead, ensuring everyone reached the top safely, just as Lunette reached for the first rung, all the fur on the back of their neck stood up. It felt as if they were being watched. Frozen in place, Lunette turned and peered into the depths of the dark tunnel behind. For an instant, it seemed as if a pair of bright blue eyes were staring back at them from the darkness.

"Come on!" Alastair shouted from the surface.

Breathing heavily, Lunette slid their sword back into its sheath and climbed the ladder with measured care. Emerging into the cool night air, they paused atop the grate, scanning the cityscape that sprawled before them. The streets of Astravir, bathed in the glow of the full moon, revealed rows of stately marble and stone buildings. Their silhouettes stood proud and unyielding, a familiar sight that stirred something deep within Lunette. Not far off, the grand palace dominated the skyline—a vision of splendor, its marble pillars crowned with gleaming gold accents that caught the moonlight and scattered it in shimmering patterns across the rooftops. For an instant, Lunette felt a longing ache for the old life they had left behind.

What I am doing is more important. This is bigger than all of us. I have a new family now. I chose this.

"Lunette!" Valdis' voice snapped them back to the present.

He and the others were already moving swiftly and quietly toward a small, forgotten temple nestled at the end of the narrow street. Lunette hurried after, heart pounding, the sound of their hoofbeats echoed on the cracked paving stones that led them back to the group, their eyes never stopped scanning everything around them. They couldn't shake the feeling that something was watching them. The air was thick with the scent of moss and night-blooming flowers, and every shadow seemed to shift with hidden threats.

Approaching the temple, Lunette's eyes traced the intricate patterns of vines woven across ancient white marble walls. The copper details had weathered to a pale green, and the overgrown courtyard bristled with trees whose branches arched overhead, swallowing the courtyard in shadow. Only slender beams of moonlight filtered through, dancing on the cracked marble steps where the entrance lay.

Valdis and the rest of the Valdarr had already slipped through the wrought-iron gate, their movements swift and silent. Swallowing their nerves, Lunette moved to join them, pushing through the overgrowth and iron that clawed at their matching black and gold armor.

At the door, Valdis motioned for Lunette to come help him. Together they began cutting the thick vines that barred the way. The silence pressed in, broken only by their labored breathing and snapping of the vines.

And then, without warning, a shout rang out.

Lunette whirled as familiar palace guards in shining armor charged down the street, their spears poised, white and gold flashing in the moonlight. The stillness shattered in an instant. The Valdarr braced for battle, moving into an arched formation around the front steps. The thunder of pursuit echoed off the walls of the buildings and city.

"*Lunette,*" Valdis spoke urgently, grabbing them by their shoulders and forcing them to face him. "I need you to go in there and light the brazier."

"What! Without you! My power, it's unstable—I don't know what I'm doing I—"

"There is no time. We have trained your magic well, and this one requires that. We will hold off the guards. I told you from the start your abilities will be needed on our journey. Now is that time. There is no ritual for this Creator. Now, *go!*"

Valdis shoved Lunette through the cleared doors into the temple. The door slammed shut behind them. The air vibrated with the shouts of the Valdarr, and the thunder of a starting battle reverberated through the stone. Lunette's breaths came in small gasps as they attempted to get their bearings in the pitch-black room.

Near the door, a torch blazed to light with a red flame. Lunette watched as dust danced in the torchlight. With a shaky sigh, they focused their attention ahead.

I can do this. I can do this for Valdis. For Alastair. For Astravir.

Their hoofbeats echoed throughout the empty room as they marched forward. Crimson torches on columns that lined the path straight into the room came to life as they walked. Ahead of them, at the center of a circular dip in the stone floor, a lone brazier sat.

Unlike the other braziers they encountered, this one was very… Plain. No intricate iron designs, no paint, no indication of who it represented. The only possible indications were dusted over embellishments on the surrounding floor in red paint, it seemed to be a spiral that started from under the brazier and spanned out to the edges of the circular dip and stopped just before the tall white columns that encircled the area.

"Ok, ok." Lunette breathed shakily, their heart racing.

I can control it. I am in command of it. I don't have to be afraid of it.

Stretching their hands out over the iron structure, and closed their eyes. They strained in concentration, feeling the familiar energy at the pit of their stomach stir. It nipped at their hide as it rose, causing a familiar burn at the pit of their stomach. They envisioned the flame in their hand, sparking the fire in front of them. The scent of myrrh filled their nostrils as they focused.

"Do you *really* think that will work?" a deep, velvet-like voice rumbled in the dark.

Lunette's eyes flew open, their breath hitched in their throat. In the darkness beyond the circle bright, red, blazing eyes stared back at them. The floor vibrated with hoofbeats as the entity stepped forward to the edge of the illuminated area. A stag whose antlers nearly brushed the columns came into view. His long jet-black hair framed his face and shoulders. The few thin braids around his face swayed as he came to a stop at the edge of the circle. In his hand he held a scythe whose blade was made entirely of bone. At the back of the blade, a red orb flared to life, illuminating his imposing presence further by reflecting off his red robes and ash-colored fur.

Thanatos.

A cunning smile played across his lips as he took in their surprised expression. "I've heard so much about you, little warrior faun. You and your omens are quite the attraction, or so your Queen tells me."

Lunette blinked, and the stag appeared at another pillar in the circle, causing them to gasp. With a quick yank, they unsheathed their sword. "Don't come any closer." They growled through gritted teeth.

"My, my, you are quite ferocious. From a queen's pet to a full-fledged warrior, misguided by a *vermin* who decided it would be more fun to try to become something like a god. He *blinded* you with the illusion of choice." He chuckled darkly before vanishing and reappearing on the opposite side.

Lunette thrust the tip of their sword in his direction, eyes narrowing. "You don't know me."

The stag's antlers caught the flickering red light as he tilted his head, grinning wider. "Oh, but I do know you, Lunette. Don't think I haven't watched your little rebellion unfold, step by reckless step. You have been led so blindly into the darkness."

Lunette snarled, their lips curling to bare their teeth. "You will *never* get away with this! You will never take our world!"

"Oh, but it's already begun. Can't you hear it?"

Lunette's ears flicked back to the sounds of battle outside. The high-pitched whistling of blades cutting air and colliding with armor pierced their eardrums, even from all the way in here. Their heart thundered in their rib cage. They adjusted the grip on their sword and glanced at the brazier before raising their free hand in its direction. "I will put an end to this."

"Well, then let us see..." With a sweep of his scythe, the circle of torches extinguished, "how well you truly do in the dark."

The grip on their blade tightened, their knuckles pale beneath their snowy fur. Their heart drummed faster in the darkness. They felt movement behind them and whipped around, swinging their sword wildly, just catching a glimpse of the scythe's glowing orb as it vanished once more.

Focus. Just focus.

A blur of red light came towards them swiftly. Lunette flinched back and dodged it effortlessly.

"Impressive," the stag whispered in their ear.

They whipped around, cutting the air with their sword and holding pressure as it collided with the snath of Thanatos' scythe. It blazed to life upon impact, illuminating the wild smile on his face as he pushed back against them.

In a flash, he vanished, causing them to stumble forward from the release of pressure. A rush of air came from behind them. Lunette pivoted on one hoof to dodge another swing of the bone blade that illuminated the darkness. Lunette swung their sword at the stag, who parried the blow, causing him to stumble back slightly and vanish in the darkness.

Lunette could feel the pressure mounting in their chest, each rapid heartbeat fueling a surge of energy that rose from within. The warmth of it seeped through the cold, black-and-gold armor clinging tightly to their frame. They let out a yell as they swung their blade once more in the darkness, just quick enough to parry the scythe once more before vanishing again.

You can control it.

The scythe flared, casting sharp light as it descended directly toward Lunette. Reacting instantly, they gripped their sword with both hands, holding it horizontally above their face to intercept the blow. The force drove them downward until their spines met the marble floor, every muscle straining to keep the deadly blade from coming any closer. Just inches separated the scythe's point from Lunette's nose as Thanatos loomed above, his features twisted with effort as he pressed down, determined to break through their defense.

The sword's blade bit into their palm, red and gold blood streaming down their forearm. Clenching their jaw, they let out a guttural roar, unleashing a surge of crimson magic that erupted from their grasp. The force hurled Thanatos across the chamber, slamming him into a pillar and splintering it with the impact.

Lunette jumped to their hooves. Their breath came in ragged gasps. The red chaos energy overtook their palms, their normally bright blue eyes glowed a bright light red with the energy that raged through their entire being.

The fire. I need to light the fire. I can do this.

They looked at the brazier beside them and dropped their sword, channeling their energy into the iron structure.

Lunette poured their energy into the brazier, but a sudden flash from the bone blade streaked toward them, forcing them to act on instinct. In a fluid motion, they spun around, narrowly avoiding the scythe and catching its handle mid-air. Thanatos' eyes blazed as he pulled against the pressure of Lunette's strength. Their hands burned as they gripped the snath, the freezing death energy radiating from it singed their palms.

"You follow *foolishly!* You diverge from your purpose and look where it has landed you!"

Lunette's teeth gritted, their eyes blazed brighter as they pulled on the carved handle harder.

Suddenly, the crimson blaze from the brazier surged downward, spilling through the heart of the iron frame and igniting the red markings on the floor. The fire roared to life, racing swiftly in a spiral around Lunette's hooves.

A brilliant shaft of light shot up from the brazier, smashing through the ceiling and sending shards of glass cascading onto both cervidaes below.

Locking eyes with Thanatos, Lunette unleashed a powerful shout, forcing him back with a torrent of magic. The blast ripped the scythe from his grip and sent him sprawling into the ring of fire. Lunette loomed above him, clutching the scythe, breath ragged, red and gold ichor streaming down their hands.

"This is my purpose; seeing that you don't make it any farther!"

The red orb on the stag's scythe blazed, filling the chamber with a pulse of heat as they raised it above their head. The Creator stared up at them with widened eyes. He raised an arm in front of his face in defense as Lunette squeezed their eyes closed... and brought the blade down on him.

However, a force stopped the blade mid-strike.

Lunette's eyes flew open to see a purple-scaled hand hovering just above where their hand was on the scythe. Their eyes met bright, twin galaxies that bore into them, and before they could fully register what was happening, they found themselves being hurdled through the air, through the wooden doors to outside, and landing on the ground with a force so hard it knocked the wind from their lungs and a *crack* filled their ears.

Their vision was swimming, blurred from the pain in their torso, and their ears rang. Lunette gasped for breath; through the ringing, they could hear muted shouting.

"Take them to the prison outside the city! These *traitors* will pay for the sins they've committed against the crown, including manipulating our prophet!"

Lunette tried to force their vision into focus, but everything remained a haze, the pain threatening to overwhelm them. Suddenly, they were trapped, immobilized, unable to draw breath. As an unbearable pressure clamped down on their chest, they gasped for air, but something solid invaded their lungs, and a wave of panic crashed over them—

Saturday Evening, Present Day

"Get *up*," a voice echoed, jarring Lunette from their slumber on the frost-covered floor. Their eyes snapped open as quickly as their body sat up, meeting familiar bright blue eyes staring down at them from outside the cell.

"How fast can you run?" Leroy asked, voice low, while his long tail flicked subtly under his robe. His usual smile was absent, replaced with an expression one could only describe as... deadly serious. The room was dark, save for a sliver of red light coming down the stairs from the cracked door. Lunette could just barely see the caracal in front of them.

Their hair stood on end, their eyes narrowed. "Why are you asking me that? Are you threatening me?"

"Shut *up* and *answer* my question." He didn't blink. His posture was stiff. His hands were shoved in his pockets.

This is strange...

"I—I don't know? Pretty fast?" Lunette stammered out, pulling themselves to their hooves. "What is wrong with you?! Where is Ash? What the hell are you planning?!"

Leroy dug in his pocket and held up a single, softly glowing key. The magic on the cell's bars glowed softly in response. Despite Leroy blocking their view, Lunette could feel the serpent Creator staring.

"You afraid of heights?" he asked calmly.

"Heights? I—"

"*Yes*, yes, come on! I don't have all day."

"No, no, I'm not afraid of heights. Well... maybe a little. Actually—"

"I am going to unlock this door. The second I do every reaper in this cathedral will be on your ass. Thanatos included. Go through the center of the city. Run as far as you can . At the edge, there's the portal. Jump through it."

"*Why* are you doing this? *What* are you planning?" Lunette asked, their breath hitching on the last word.

"Does it really matter?" He spun the key once on his finger before inserting it into the keyhole in front of them. Every muscle in Lunette's body tensed. They looked up at Leroy and met his eyes.

"Now..." A quick grin flashed across Leroy's lips before uttering a single word. "*Run.*"

The door flew open, and with a slip on the frost—Lunette bolted out the door and up the nearby stairs. Their breaths came in ragged gasps as they reached the top, shoving the door open, and the red light emitted from the stained glass of the cathedral nearly blinded them. They were at the end of a hall; there was an opening towards the center. Armor-clad guards whipped their heads to look at them, unsheathing their weapons. Without a second thought, they ran, their hooves hammering the unfamiliar stone floor as they did.

In front of them, several feline reapers rushed out of rooms. The guards stepped up to them, swinging their swords and knives as they did, but Lunette effortlessly dodged them.

At the end of the hall, they heard hammering on a door and shouting.

After dodging a few more swings from the armored guards, they turned sharply down the center, into a fountain room. There was no time for hesitation.

In a snap decision, they hopped over the fountain's edge, running through it, then hopping out the other side. Bolting through the doors at the front of the room, throwing a curtain aside, they found themselves overlooking a decorated throne room. There were tables and barrels of wine everywhere, with fanciful goblets and glasses.

"*After them!*" voices shouted from behind. They could hear the clamoring footfalls of reapers.

No time.

They jumped the stairs and bolted through the room to the iron doors, out into the frigid air. The surrounding landscape was littered with stones, dead grass, and frost. The wind whipped their hair around their face.

There was the sound of glass shattering behind them, and for a brief moment they glanced to see Thanatos leaning out of a broken window. His arm outstretched, shadows rapidly traveling the ground towards them. "You can't run from me! I *will* find you!" He shouted as the shadows stretched beyond them to the drawbridge that now started to pull up.

Acting on pure instinct, Lunette turned towards the bridge, avoiding the shadows that twisted and tried to grab at their legs. Their hooves slamming as they dug into the ground and ran at the ascending bridge.

They ran up its increasing axis, and just as they reached the top, without any hesitation...

They leaped from it.

Time seemed to slow as Lunette soared through the chilling air, over the misty abyss that divided the cathedral and city, their hooves stretched out desperately for the other side.

"Lunette!" a familiar voice cut through the air from behind them. It wasn't Thanatos. It wasn't a reaper. For an instant, suspended above the abyss, Lunette felt a surge of déjà vu—a flicker of warmth blooming in their chest despite the biting cold. Maybe the sound came from within their head?

Has this happened before?

They didn't dare look back. With a bone-jarring jolt, their hooves met the frozen ground at the city's edge, causing them to tumble forward in a somersault. Then, catching enough momentum to jump to their feet, they stumbled forward, sprinting into the labyrinth of ghostly streets.

Darting past towering structures, vaulting over shattered carriages, and weaving between ghostly mortals they couldn't spare a second to consider, Lunette powered forward. A rush of oppressive energy surrounded each side . *Reapers.*

They ignored them and pressed on. They leaped over shadow tendrils, dodged grabbing claws of the armor-clad felines that were chasing them, and pressed on. It felt like an eternity of endless sprints, dodging what felt like a hundred grabbing hands. As they neared the edge of the city, that's when they saw it: *a portal.*

Just past the last scattered buildings on the edge of the land, just before where it dropped back down into a misty abyss, stood a portal. Jagged and pulsing with dark power, it loomed, beckoning them forward. From just beyond the portal, in the sky shrouded by the fog, they could see the rift that looked down at Earth.

They homed in on it, and with even more vigor they dug their hooves into the frozen soil and stone to push faster.

Sliding to a stop at the portal, they hesitated. Looking behind them, they saw the reapers catching up. They swallowed. Their heart couldn't beat any faster.

They stepped back a few paces before launching themselves into the portal. A startled cry escaped their lips as they flailed for a moment, suspended between worlds, then they saw the snow-covered ground racing up to meet them. They slammed into the frozen earth and tumbled head over hooves. Breathless, they hauled themselves upright, shaking the snow from their ears and horns. They found themselves in Antarctica, just outside the collapsed prison from before.

Disoriented but determined, Lunette scanned their surroundings, bracing for whatever might emerge from the swirling frigid air or the portal behind them. The snow had covered any trace of what happened only days ago. As if the world had already forgotten. Lunette tilted their head to the sky. The rift to Nullhymm was shrouded by clouds, barely visible to the eye.

Back on Earth. Where it all started... Or, rather, ended. Each breath burned with the cold. Their sides ached from the quick escape. No reapers in sight, the only sounds came from the echo of their own frantic heartbeat and the hum of the dark portal behind them.

With a grunt of effort, they pulled themselves up to stand.

I have to make it back to New York.

I need that sword back.

I will free us, Ash.

I swear.

Sunday Morning, Present Day

A clawed hand ran down Ash's cheek.

His eyes were unfocused. Warmth enveloped his whole body, accompanied by a pressure that resided behind his back and under his legs. The ringing in his ears muffled the sound of classical music.

"Ash… *Ash,"* a deep, familiar voice whispered through the tinnitus.

He inhaled sharply, his senses overwhelmed abruptly by the earthy scent of myrrh. It pulled him from the haze, beckoning him to reality. His eyes opened fully and adjusted to the sight before him.

Thanatos.

Inches from his face the stag sat with a sly smile and his ears perked. His red, glowing eyes were fixated on him. Ash realized the pressure he felt was from his lap, which he was perched on, not unlike a prized concubine, with a warm arm wrapped around him.

Every muscle went rigid. His ears flattened against his head. The breath in his throat caught so abruptly that he nearly started to choke. The stag's eyes glinted with amusement; his grip tightened on him.

"My chosen one. Welcome to your new life."

Ash's eyes followed his other arm that extended to the throne room around them. A mass of feline death gods stood at the base of the throne, including his parents at the front. The edges of the room were lined with spectral feline reapers illuminated by candlelight. All eyes were on him.

His body disobeyed him. His muscles trembled as he stared back at the gazes that bored into him. His breath became ragged and uneven, his heart raced, his paw pads sweated. He tried to shove himself away from the Creator, toppling off his lap, falling—

Ash woke with a start to the faint hum of distant commotion—a low sound that seemed to vibrate through the walls. For a moment, he assumed he was still dreaming. Sitting up, he tightened his robe and watched his breath fog the air as he attempted to shake off the dream and focus.

What are the reapers doing now?

Suddenly, he recalled the chaos that had unfolded the previous night. *What happened?*

Ash rose to his feet and headed toward the door. As he got closer, his gaze lingered on the faint scratches marring the wood. Scrapes and dents remained from when he'd pounded on it the night before, desperate for answers after hearing all the shouting. Someone had trapped him inside. No matter how loudly he called out or how hard he banged on the door, nobody ever responded.

Now, he wrapped his fingers around the handle and gave it a tentative shake, testing whether it was still locked.

Weird... it's unlocked now. He cracked it open to peek out.

Empty, save for a couple spectral guards who remained unmoving as usual. The overlapping voices were louder out here, that was certain. At a glance, it looked as though nothing had happened at all.

Slipping out of his room, he made his way to the fountain area, feeling the guards' eyes on him as he went. The sound was coming from the throne room. The door was open ever so slightly. Ash peeked in and could see just beyond the curtain. Thanatos stood before a crowd of at least fifty reapers who all talked amongst themselves, Leroy and Sih at his side.

"All of our focus needs to be on today, regardless of what happened. Do you all understand the task at hand?" The stag boomed, causing the crowd of reapers to go silent.

Ash could see some nodding along, others looked confused, others looked... angry?

"You will not act until the time is right. I will give the signal." Thanatos clapped his hands together. "Enjoy it. For a new age will be upon us. Then we will resume our task of the planet below."

Ash could see Leroy's ears swivel back as he listened, yet he still held a toothless grin. Sih appeared stoic as usual, her expression nothing less than grim determination.

What is he planning?

Thanatos' head snapped to look at Ash. "Ah. My chosen one. So good of you to join us. Come here." He motioned for Ash to get closer.

Ash's ears flattened, his claws unconsciously flexed at his sides, yet he obeyed and moved to stand by Thanatos. The stag laid a hand between Ash's shoulder blades.

Why is he warm?

For a brief moment his dream from last night flicked into his mind, but he shoved it down before he could risk Thanatos hearing *that* thought. The stag watched him, a small, amused smile on his lips.

"Remember this evening is about our honored guest, who will be a guest no longer. A permanent addition to our cathedral."

The reapers looked at Ash, who tensed up under their gaze. He felt Thanatos' thumb gently, almost tenderly, rub his back while he watched the reapers' reactions. It only furthered his discomfort, but he couldn't deny the warmth was... slightly nice in the frigid environment.

Why is he the only warm thing here? Is he... alive?

Thanatos suddenly dropped his hand from Ash's back but didn't look at him. "Now, everyone, back to your duties. I expect this to be an extraordinary evening."

The reapers bowed their heads in agreement, then began dispersing. Thanatos turned to Ash with his hands folded together.

"You must get ready as well. When was the last time you bathed?"

Ash flexed his claws involuntarily in thought. *Actually, the last time I showered was when I first saw him...*

"Uhm... last week."

Thanatos shook his head quickly, his ears flopping against his antlers as he did. "Absolutely not, that is far too long a wait. Sih will draw you a bath immediately. You will bathe and you will be given a better outfit to wear."

Ash shivered at the thought of bathing in this freezing realm. Thanatos scoffed at him.

"We have *fire*. It will not be freezing."

"It will be when I get out of the water."

Thanatos sighed through his nose and shook his head once more. "I will have a fire lit for you then." He motioned to Sih to get a move on, which she did, but not without rolling her eyes.

The stag smiled at Ash, making his ears flatten against his head. "You may wait in your room. She will not be long."

Ash glanced at Leroy, who wasn't looking at Ash. Instead, he fidgeted in his pocket, presumably messing with an unlit cigarette. Ash brought his attention back to Thanatos and left without another word. However, he didn't make it three steps inside the fountain room before a voice hissed at his side.

"Look at you," Leroy drawled. "Freshly introduced to everyone. Freshly scolded for your hygiene. Truly, you're living the dream."

Ash nearly jumped out of his hide. "Can you *not* sneak up on me? Shouldn't you be doing your job or something?"

"I didn't sneak," Leroy said, falling into step beside him and lighting a cigarette. "You're just rattled. Like a chihuahua in a snowstorm."

Ash glared. "I'm fine. I'm not a chihuahua."

"Mhm. So. How does it feel?"

"How does what feel?"

"To be paraded for all to see tonight, just for Daddy." The words dripped with amusement and venom. He took a drag of the cigarette.

Ash's stomach dropped, his nose crinkled at the smell. "I'm not—"

"Oh, *quit* with the 'I'm not' game! It's getting exhausting." Leroy leaned in, voice dropping to a whisper. "He barely looked at me today. Do you know how *rare* that is when there's this much commotion? Normally he's breathing down my neck about everything. 'Leroy, don't do that,' 'Leroy, stop smoking inside,' 'Leroy, go do this.' But now?" He gestured with his cigarette hand exaggeratedly. "Now I get almost a whole eight hours without feeling like I'm in a performance review." He clapped Ash's shoulder hard enough to make him wince. "Truly, Ash. You are doing a spectacular thing here. You're going to fit right in."

Ash rubbed his shoulder. "I'm not *doing* anything."

"Yeah, *exactly*. I need you to keep doing that."

"Thanatos is just—"

"Obsessed?" Leroy replied sweetly. "Fixated? Clingy? Possessive? Enamored, am I close?"

Ash's ears flushed hot. "He's not—it's not like that."

"Oh? Did you miss the part where he practically purred over you in front of fifty reapers?" Leroy took another drag of his cigarette, continuing to walk alongside Ash. They were almost at his room. "Trust me, Ashy. We *noticed*. I still think you're liking it."

Ash grimaced, glancing back down the hall they had just come from. "I just don't understand him."

"Nobody does." Leroy shrugged. "He's a creative type. Very dramatic. Very, 'I alone bear the weight of the living, all will fall at my hand,' et cetera, et cetera. I'm sure you've noticed." His tail flicked behind him. "Anyway, enjoy being the shiny toy today."

Ash hesitated. "Leroy... what's actually happening tonight? You all keep preparing like it's some kind of... coronation."

"Oh, nothing so boring," Leroy said lightly. "Just a *small gathering* to celebrate the return of our esteemed Creator. Drinks, conversation, ritual slaughter. Very typical workplace culture."

Ash's fur bristled. "Ritual what?"

"Kidding!" Leroy sang. Then, after a beat: "...sort of."

He stepped closer, lowering his voice. "If I were you, I'd focus on not tripping over your robe. All eyes will be on you. Like I said yesterday and today, keep doing what you're doing."

A cold weight sank in Ash's stomach. "What about Lunette? I still haven't seen them and—"

"Ah yes, yes, your partner in crime." Leroy clicked his tongue. "They're fine. Still feisty. Still breathing. Still very much in the 'scream at everyone' stage of imprisonment. Adorable, really."

"Well, what happened last night? I swore I heard their name and my door was locked—"

"What are you even talking about?" Leroy scoffed. "Are you having dreams about them now? Or are you having trouble telling the difference between what's real and fake? How meta."

Ash's chest tightened, his lips curled into a hiss. "I want to see them."

"I bet you do." Leroy flicked the remainder of his cigarette away, then leaned in until Ash could smell smoke on his breath. "Stay in your lane. Do as I say if you really want all of this to end."

Ash stiffened, baring his canines at the caracal. "Is that a threat?"

"Me? Threaten you?" Leroy pressed a dramatic hand to his chest. "I would never."

Ash opened his mouth to argue—only for Thanatos' voice to echo down the hall again. It sounded like he was looking for Leroy.

Leroy's smile faltered. Barely. His ears angled back in something that looked more like annoyance than listening, then he smoothed his expression with a more relaxed grin.

"Well. Duty calls." He flicked Ash's chin with a claw. "Try not to have a meltdown before the banquet, okay?"

Before Ash could swat him away, Leroy sauntered off.

Ash stood frozen in the hallway, heart pounding, his ears pressed as far back as they could go. He pinched the bridge of his nose with his claws before running a hand down the skull-like markings on his face with an exhale.

Something is wrong.

Something is very, very wrong.

Ash paced his room for what felt like an eternity until the door swung open. Sih stood in the doorway. Her robe looked extra pressed and perfect today. Her red belt was tied tightly around her waist, a short bone fist weapon rested on her hip.

"Bath time." She said flatly. "Follow me."

With usual reluctant obedience, Ash followed behind. The halls were a little emptier now. They all must be in the throne room preparing.

She took a sharp turn into the fountain room. Ash slowed his pace, but still followed.

Was there a bathroom here that I missed?

Sih turned again to the large carved doors at the left of the fountain. Ash's stomach dropped.

Why are you taking me to Thanatos' room?

With a single swoop she tossed the doors open and strode down the hall to the bedroom. Ash hesitated but followed.

Please don't be in there...

He crossed the threshold into the stag's room. There, by the once barren fireplace that now boasted an impressive flame, was a wooden tub filled with water. The room was... warm. It immediately caused Ash's fur to be less bristled under his robe. But... the room was darker. He turned his attention to the windows, where one was boarded up now.

What happened there?

Sih walked further into the room and pointed at the bed. "Put these on when you're done. No snooping around. I'll be able to tell."

On the stag's bed, a black robe sat neatly folded. Golden thread adorned its edges. Its large sleeves had velvet cuffs. A silver pendant lay on top of it, carved with the same pentagram Ash had seen forever.

The lynx moved back to the door.

"No funny business. I'm not going to sit here and babysit a grown-ass man. I sure as hell don't want to see you naked." She curled her lips in disgust. "Just don't be too long."

She shut the door behind her, leaving Ash standing there awkwardly in the pleasantly warm room.

He eyed the robe and the bath, then went over and dipped a paw into the warm, steaming liquid. The fire cast an orange glow over it that made the water look like it was dancing with the flames. If he wasn't about to bathe in the Creator of Death's bedroom is a foreign frozen hellscape, this would actually be quite relaxing.

Glancing at the door one last time, he heard Leroy's words echo in his head.

"Stay in your lane."

That bastard is planning something.

Sunday Morning, Present Day

After navigating the frozen wasteland, guided only by the ethereal magic that radiated from the portal in the distance that they had all originally taken to get there just days ago, Lunette finally found their way and stumbled through it. Falling to the ground as they did, sending the snow that clung to their tattered pants flying at all angles in the dank portal room.

With an annoyed huff, they pushed themselves up onto their hooves and looked around. The black stone arch loomed behind them. The sigils still burned brightly just as they had before. The room's torches flared to life upon their arrival. Still, no reapers followed. The only energy they could feel was the unstable magic that radiated off the portal incessantly. Lunette shivered, remembering Leroy's magic activating it while those inky creatures gained on them.

I shouldn't linger here.

Turning towards the door, they left the room behind and made their way down the long hallway, watching the torches come to life as they approached them. Once they reached the end, they climbed the ladder and pushed open the hatch from before. Thankfully, it wasn't sealed.

Lunette stepped outside. They took a deep breath; the air was cool but not nearly as frigid as Nullhymm. Compared to there, it might as well be summer in New Bedford. Scanning the surrounding area, they noticed the car that they had taken over here originally was still in the parking lot.

If I had the keys, that would be helpful. At least I know the way… I need to hurry.

Despite desperately wanting to take a moment to relish being home, to rest their aching muscles from sprinting and take a breather from the chaos they had just endured to get here, they instead turned and quickly started walking in the direction of Ash's home. There had to be something there that could help them.

Lunette approached the rundown, single story, Cape-style house that Ash had been living in. There was a new, tattered "for rent" sign on the lawn.

They figured, since they were here in New Bedford, they might as well see if Ash had any supplies that they could snag to bring back to him to help. They needed all the help they could get to stop Thanatos, so maybe Ash had some secret powerful-necromancy-thingies in his basement.

He's always so secretive. He's bound to have something helpful.

Approaching the front door, they touched the handle to open it, but as they did, the door drifted open. Lunette's brows knit in confusion, then the feeling was quickly replaced with panic.

What if there's a reaper in here?

They steeled themselves, taking in a big breath, cracking their knuckles, then proceeded to whip open the door.

Silence.

The kitchen was empty, and from where they stood, they could see the living room was just as bare, with the same furniture as before. The house still reeked of cigarette smoke.

Lunette stepped in cautiously, their ears perked in alert to anything—or anyone—who might jump out at them. They peered into Ash's room. It was completely vacant, save for some blankets on the bed and trash bags. Then they leaned to peer down the hall into Leroy's room. It was just as barren.

It's all cleaned out now. What about the basement? They thought, turning their attention to the old door that led to the cellar.

It was slightly ajar.

The hair on Lunette's neck stood up.

They moved slowly to the door, cringing at the creaking of the floor under their hooves, and opened it slowly. The hinges squeaked loudly as it creaked open, revealing the dimly lit basement.

Why are the lights on?

Cautiously, they stepped down the stairs, watching over the railing as they descended into the small cellar that appeared empty. Ash's candles, jars, bones, books, and all had vanished. It was all cleaned out. They reached the bottom step and moved fully into the room, their shoulders slumping in defeat, staring at the empty shelves.

"Are you looking for Ash?" A deep, husky voice rang out from behind Lunette.

They whipped around, raising their hands in defense as they did. They made eye contact with a tall, burly, black cat in a long, sea-weathered coat. His green eyes glinted in the dim light of the cellar.

"Oak?" Lunette breathed, lowering their hands.

The stoic cat nodded once. His eyes looked tired, his fur had a slight tinge of red sun-bleaching to it. "You're the one I saw before, when Ash summoned me. Is he where I think he is?"

"Where do you think he is?"

"With Thanatos." Oak looked away, hiding the tinge of pain behind his eyes.

Lunette's lips pursed, their ears turned back. "Yeah, you're right. How do you know about Thanatos? You never mentioned him when you spoke to us. Only about Nikolas."

Oak let out a low sigh, the tip of his tail flicking. "I know *all* about Thanatos," he said quietly, voice dipped with regret. "I wasn't a hundred percent sure when I saw him that he had gotten in contact with him, but that cut on his cheek made me suspicious." He stepped further into the room, boots thudding softly on the bare floor. "What he described was hunting him sounded more like a disgruntled death god than death-itself. That's why I didn't say anything. Also... I didn't want to put that back on Ash."

"Put what back on Ash?" Lunette's brows knit together in confusion, not entirely sure still if they should trust him or not.

The tall cat's ears swiveled back; his eyes fell to the floor. "Our whole family was obsessed with Thanatos. After Ash woke up from the ritual, he couldn't remember a lot of things. Weirdly enough, he couldn't remember anything about Thanatos most of all. My parents thought it was some kind of… divine intervention. That maybe Ash would learn about him on his own and be drawn to him because of the ritual. They stopped calling him Thanatos around him, only the *Corrupted One*."

"None of that… makes sense." Lunette shook their head, their ears flopping as they did. A hundred questions ran through their mind, their chest felt heavy.

"Nothing my parents did made sense. Why are you here?"

"I escaped from Thanatos. I came here looking for anything that might help us defeat him. I have to get back to Nikolas in New York."

"Why? Think he'll help you again?"

"Ash and I brought him some sword that was said to be 'forged by the Creators.' We got it for him in exchange for information about who was chasing us. I need it back. If it can kill gods, then it can kill Thanatos."

Oak nodded slowly. "I'll go with you."

"Oh, you don't have to do that."

"Nikolas may be more likely to help if I'm there. I've known him since I came to Earth a few years ago, plus… I can't help but feel some responsibility for what Ash has… been through. I guess." He looked away, shrugging his shoulders a bit. Lunette couldn't help but note the similarity between his and Ash's mannerisms.

"Fine. We need a way to get there, though. You know, I made a portal back in New York. I can't help but feel like I used to be able to do that more."

"I could... help you. I used to help Ash practice magic. So, I know a thing or two. What magic are you versed in?"

Lunette tilted their head from side to side. "I... don't really know."

"Well, show me. Perhaps I can decipher it."

They looked at the cat skeptically. "Ah, I can try? I don't like how it makes me feel." They brought their hands up in front of them, holding them a few inches apart, and focused. A few seconds passed, and a crackle of red energy flickered between them, slowly forming a bright red ball that depicted as soon as they dropped their hands. Their skin tingled. Something tugged from within. "I don't want to do more if I don't have to. It feels wrong." Lunette put their ears back and looked at Oak, whose brows were knit together.

"Chaos. I haven't seen that in ages. Only back home, I met a handful of spell-swords who wielded it. It's a nearly forgotten practice. Where did you learn it?"

Lunette simply shrugged. "Is that... a bad thing?"

"No, no magic is inherently bad. It is how you use it that matters." Oak rolled his shoulders back and adjusted his posture. "So, portals. Portals aren't typically that hard. A lot of magic users use them. Especially lesser gods. Close your eyes and imagine where you want to go."

They raised an eyebrow, then closed their eyes. "Now what?"

"Put your hands together, the same was as before, then imagine the place you're trying to go as vividly as you can."

Lunette did just that, though a hint of doubt was visible in their expression. "This is kind of weird."

"Stay focused." Oak commanded. "Now imagine that vivid image moving from your mind, down your arms, into your hands while you summon your strength."

Lunette squeezed their eyes shut more, picturing the towering buildings, the busy streets, and the old apartment complex. They pictured the shape of the door handle, Colby going ahead of them, Ash following suit, and Leroy staying behind. They pictured the staring eyes as they appeared in the middle of the street, stopping cars, the exhaustion that overtook them when they teleported everyone there, Ash's arms catching them as they collapsed.

"That's it. Now imagine that magic enveloping us and bringing us there." Oak's voice rang in their ears. He had moved closer to stand by them.

A quick blast of heat and light shone through their closed eyes, causing them to gasp and look around. Their hide tingled, a wave of exhaustion coming over their body. The sound of cars filled their ears; the smell of gasoline and food filled the air.

No longer in the dank basement, Oak and Lunette now stood on the sidewalk outside Nikolas's apartment building. The sun was still rising, casting a yellow-gold glow over all the buildings that made dark shadows in the streets.

Lunette looked at Oak with wide eyes. Their breath came in gasps. *I can't believe I did that.* The black cat simply nodded, though a small smile pulled at the corner of his lips.

"Let's get in there." They said, stumbling forward. Oak grabbed their arm quickly to stabilize them.

"Careful now. It's exhausting to use that amount of power at once. It will get easier with time."

Lunette nodded, steadying their breathing as they leaned on Oak for a moment, feeling the lingering buzz of magic fading from their fingertips. The city buzzed around them, oblivious to their sudden arrival. A few passing pedestrians gave them curious glances, but most hurried along, caught up in their morning routines.

The apartment building loomed above, its bricks warm in the rising sunlight. Oak gave Lunette an encouraging look. "Ready?"

Lunette mustered a small smile and nodded. "Thank you."

Almost there.

Sunday Afternoon, Present Day

It was time.

Ash stood off to the side, behind the curtain. He was just out of sight of the masses of feline death gods who gathered in the open space, filling the gaps between the stone pillars and mingling with one another. There were dozens of tables, lit by black candles, all covered with aged red tablecloths and fanciful drinkware. Red wine was everywhere; Ash could smell it from where he stood.

Who knew there were this many death gods...

"They are from all different worlds," a low, amused voice rolled into his head like fog.

Get out of my head.

"I was simply answering your question, my chosen one."

I didn't ask for your input.

"I am only trying to be helpful. It is quite the sight, is it not?"

Ash peeked around the curtain and scanned the crowd again. Wine glasses balanced in claws, some were scraggly, some were composed, many were adorned in various symbols of death Ash had never seen. They chatted softly, politely, loudly. Like this was some divine gala. A few stood alone, watching everything. Taking it all in. He didn't see his parents from this angle.

"They are all here for you, you know."

Don't lie. They are here because they all worship you.

"Hm, true," Thanatos hummed, *"however, they know the occasion... And that occasion is you being here with me, my chosen one."*

That occasion *is that they just want to save their own asses...*

A dark chuckle filled his head. *"How right you are."*

From behind Ash, Thanatos entered the throne room, Leroy on his heels. They both slipped past him to go to the throne, leaving Ash behind the curtain to gawk at their different attire.

Leroy wore his usual black, red, and gold priest garb; however, this time a silver pendant hung around his neck with the dual pentagram symbol carved into it. It glinted under the red light above. The twin bone blades rested on his hips.

The stag wore fitted, carved bone armor that went over his usual robe. It looked like a spine down his back, a ribcage around his chest, and shoulder mantles that curled upwards, radiating red death magic. In one hand he gripped his tall, ever-threatening bone scythe. The strong glow of the red orb within it illuminated the intricate vines and carvings.

The crowd immediately quieted, their attention undivided on the stag, before erupting into cheers. Thanatos was not looking at them though; his eyes lingered on Ash, who still stayed out of sight. Ash couldn't help but stare back.

Where did that come from?

"Ceremonial, my chosen one. Only brought out for special occasions."

Thanatos shifted his attention to the crowd before him and raised his free hand, silencing them. "Thank you all for your presence this fine evening. It feels... refreshing to be among you again after so long. During my imprisonment, I had a lot of time to think to myself about how we would proceed. I am pleased to say that the Great Plan is underway once more. However, before we begin, and I delve into more detail, I must introduce the one who made tonight possible."

The stag looked over at Ash, a smile tugged at his lips. "Come now."

Ash took a shaky breath before stepping out fully. Immediately, he was met with gasps, murmurs, and small claps, as well as one loud gasp he immediately recognized as his father's.

Just where Ash couldn't see before stood his parents, Mercy and Hawthorne. Mercy, rigid as usual, however there was a smile across her face that Ash didn't recognize. It was full of pride. Hawthorne looked the same, grinning and holding his wife's shoulders, waving at Ash as he moved to stand beside Thanatos.

Their faces hadn't changed much—lines etched deeper, eyes still sharp. His hands curled into fists at his sides as he stared at them, then slackened. His stomach churned, a mix of something bitter and something he couldn't name. Even from here he could smell the faint, almost-forgotten scent of home that lingered on them. He swallowed, tasting the bitter tang of memories he hadn't wanted to remember.

"I present to you Ash Darkscream, a lesser god of necromancy who freed me from my prison. He alone brought the key, allowing me to step out once more to resume my plan for changing the state of the universe."

From Thanatos' other side, Ash could see Leroy's lip twitch and his eyes narrow slightly, yet his smile did not waver.

"Ash comes from the Darkscream family of Val-Tirath, a small island on the First Planet, just off the southern side of the city of Astravir. His family dedicated Ash to me, offered him as my chosen one many moons ago, and after being set free I have decided to humbly accept him as such."

From the corner of Ash's eye, he could see his parents receiving congratulations from other nearby gods, which Mercy accepted with a satisfied smirk. Other gods rolled their eyes and murmured amongst themselves.

"Pay them no mind. They are jealous."

I wasn't. They all look... annoying.

A soft chuckle filled Ash's head. *"How right you are again."*

Thanatos' attention went back to the crowd as he clasped his hands together. "Shall we celebrate with drink? Then we will discuss later in the evening what our plans will be moving forward."

Sih came up the stairs to the throne and placed Thanatos' usual silver goblet in his hand. The potent liquid filled it to the rim. Thanatos raised the goblet, and in turn the gods who had glasses raised theirs back, and the crowd erupted in a cheer.

Taking a sip, he backed up and relaxed into his throne. Ash shuffled awkwardly, not really sure what to do with himself now.

The stag motioned to his parents. "I believe they would like a word with you. You have my permission to mingle."

Yeah, but I don't really want to.

Ash glanced at his parents, who seemed to be patiently waiting at the bottom of the stairs.

"I believe you should. You might not see them again after tonight."

Ash glanced at Thanatos, who was sipping his wine, watching him with an amused glint in his eye.

You just want to be entertained.

"Is that a crime?"

Ash rolled his eyes and descended the steps to his parents.

"Ash." His father reached him first.

Hawthorne's hands clasped Ash's shoulders, firm and warm in a way Ash didn't remember. His green eyes shone as if he might cry. Hawthorne, who never truly raised his voice, who never interfered with Mercy's authority, who always smelled faintly of wood smoke and sea-salt. Ash felt his throat close.

"My boy," Hawthorne whispered, voice trembling, "look at you... Look at what you've done. We—your mother and I—we're so proud."

The word hit like a physical blow.

Proud?

Ash blinked, struggling to breathe through the tightness in his chest. "Father, I—" he managed, but Mercy stepped in before he could finish.

She pulled him into a sudden, fierce embrace.

For a heartbeat, Ash froze. His mother's arms around him felt wrong in a way he couldn't name, familiar and foreign at once. *Was it the last time she embraced me when I was born?*

"My son." Mercy cupped his face, her touch gentle in a way he didn't trust. Her yellow eyes shimmered with pride so intense it bordered on hunger. "You did it. After all this time, you finally stepped into what you were meant to become. You saved us. We will live forever under the reign of the true Creator."

The words sharpened like glass in his chest.

Ash swallowed hard. "Mother, I didn't. This isn't—"

"Oh, hush," Mercy shook her head softly, running a thumb across his cheek like she used to when he was small. Yet tonight it felt wrong. "Tonight is your moment. Thanatos sees your worth now. The universe will soon follow. We will all prosper in a brighter future."

His stomach twisted.

Hawthorne squeezed the back of Ash's arm, grounding but hesitant, as if sensing the storm beneath Ash's skin but not knowing how to reach him. "It means something," he murmured, "that he accepted you."

"If... you say so," Ash whispered. It felt forced.

"You should mingle," Mercy breathed, glancing back at the other gods who were still watching them. Her smile sharpened. "Let them see you stand tall. Let them see who you belong to."

Ash stiffened. A cold, invisible hand brushed the edge of his mind—Thanatos again, listening, amused.

"You know she is only doing this for show," the stag murmured in his thoughts, warm as velvet and cold as bone. *"Remember what I told you. They made you to be like this. It doesn't matter what they think."*

Ash's pulse quickened.

Mercy touched Ash's chin, turning his face back toward her. "Why do you look worried? Are you overwhelmed? It's natural. This is a big night. Remember when you gave your first passage reading at home?" She snickered, shaking her head. "Always so stressed."

Ash forced a swallow. "I didn't expect to... see you both again."

Mercy laughed softly. "Oh, darling. You say that like we wouldn't come for one of the most important nights in the history of death."

Something wasn't right.

Hawthorne rubbed his arm again, more tightly this time. "Everything's going to change, Ash. We'll finally take our rightful place. All of us. And you... you'll be at the center of it. You helped us. We knew you would."

Ash stepped back before he could stop himself. "I didn't... ask for that."

Mercy's smile faltered—only slightly, but enough for Ash to see the crack beneath it.

"Oh, speaking your truth now?" The stag hummed in his head.

Ash shook it off.

"Ash," she said, voice dipping into something quieter, firmer. "This is bigger than what you want. You've always known that. I made you powerful for us, for *him*. Though... I would have liked it if you actually did your job on Earth."

Never satisfied, even here. Typical. Her words rang in his head, just like that night in the basement. *I made you powerful.* He'd spent his entire immortal life crushed under that knowledge. But hearing it again—here, now—made the cold in his chest spread.

Hawthorne looked as if he wanted to say something else, something gentler, but Mercy laid a hand on his arm to silence him.

"Ash, sweetheart," she said softly, almost lovingly, "don't ruin this with doubt. Tonight is a celebration. Tonight... destiny catches up."

Ash forced a breath through clenched teeth. His claws flexed involuntarily.

Where is Lunette? I need them.

Instead, he whispered, "I... need a moment."

Mercy opened her mouth, but nothing came out.

Hawthorne touched Ash's arm one last time. "We'll be around. Don't stray too far."

Ash nodded once, then slipped away from them, heart hammering as he disappeared into the throng of death gods.

In the back of his mind, Thanatos whispered. *"Beautiful, isn't it? The way even your Creator's love can be conditional."*

Ash's breath caught. This was supposed to be some kind of celebration.

So why did it feel like a funeral?

Sunday Afternoon, Present Day

The elevator ride was quiet, save for the groaning and occasional rumbling of the old elevator. Lunette recalled Ash's nervousness while they rode up, though he hid it well. They could always tell when he was feeling a bit unsure. They, too, felt nervous heading up to the unfamiliar god's domain. So much was unknown at the time, but they felt intent on what they were doing here.

The uncomfortable weight of the sigils began to press in. Lunette saw Oak visibly stiffen. "They're protective wards. No need to be afraid."

"I am *not* afraid. I do not feel fear."

"I see where Ash gets that from…" Lunette smirked playfully, trying to lighten the mood.

With a *ding,* the elevator doors rattled open. The familiar long hallway, emblazoned with sigils, lay before them. It felt heavier than before, and Lunette swore there had to be more sigils on the walls than last time. They looked at Oak, who stared down the hallway with confusion on his face. "Was this not here when you saw Nikolas last?"

"No. It was not."

Oak stepped out in front of them and made his way down the narrow hall, stopping just short of the door. Just as he raised his hand to knock, a familiar voice rang out from behind it.

"Who's there? What do you want?"

"This is Oak Darkscream."

There was a pause. "Darkscream?"

The sound of several locks unlocking sounded, and the door creaked open. Peeking at them was the familiar face of Joey, looking confused as ever at Oak. "You're not Ash." He shifted his gaze to Lunette. "Wait, I know you from last week. You're Lunette. Where the hell is Ash?"

"That's exactly why we're here." Lunette said, pushing to be more in view. "We need to speak to Nikolas. It's urgent. Please."

Joey paused, his face twisted in thought. "You did save our asses back in Spain. Fine." He turned his attention to Oak. "I don't know you, so I'm keeping an eye on you."

"Likewise," Oak grunted under his breath.

The young bat opened the door all the way and stepped to the side. Entering the space, they were met with the familiar soft glow of the fireplace and intense aroma of spices. Oak inspected the very outdated room, eyeing the wallpaper and paintings on the walls. "He hasn't changed anything in here."

"Yeah, my dad isn't one for redecorating," Joey said before going to stand in front of Lunette. "So, what's going on with Ash? Why isn't he here?"

"He's imprisoned. We need to talk to your dad; I need that sword back."

"Whoa, whoa. Now? Haven't you heard there are reapers prowling the streets? We need that sword for protection ourselves. We think Thanatos is going to come to Earth."

Lunette's ears flattened against their horns, their expression turned solemn. "Yeah... he is. Unless I stop him."

"You? Look, what you did in Spain was badass, I'm not gonna lie, but we're talking about *Thanatos*. Not those gross goo monsters." Joey shook his head quickly, folding his arms and tucking his wings as he did. "Besides, what does your stopping him have to do with freeing Ash from wherever he is?"

"Because he is in Thanatos' grasp," a smooth voice grumbled from the hallway.

The three of them looked to the voice to see the tall, imposing, eyeless vampire bat standing just in the entryway of the hallway that led to his office. His clawed fingers were rested in the grooves of the wall, wing taught under his outstretched arm. His long black hair was not slicked back as it had been before. It hung around the edges of his face. A purple velvet vest hugged his torso as last time, yet today the buttons were slightly askew. His square, pointed nose twitched in their direction. "I can only assume that is why you are here."

"You're right," Oak said simply, with a nod.

"It has been a long time, Oak Darkscream. I knew it was you; you do not reek of death nearly as much as your younger brother."

Lunette stepped around Joey to go to Nikolas, stopping only a few feet from him. "I need that sword back. I need to stop this. Thanatos has Ash, and he's planning on destroying our world."

The bat tilted his head down in their direction, as if to stare at them. "Weren't you the one who said you didn't understand why a sword was practical in 2023? What makes you qualified, then? Clearly, something triggered the failure of your attempt to prevent this at its source. How did you both fail and release him? Or did someone beat you to his prison with the child?"

Lunette stiffened, their eyes falling to the floor with the word 'failure.' Nikolas tilted his head the other way, waiting for an answer.

"It... was me. I did this. It was all my fault." They admitted softly. They could feel Oak's eyes drilling holes in the back of their head.

"*What?* You failed to mention that before. How could you—" Oak spoke quickly, taking a step forward.

Nikolas raised the hand that was not holding the wall, silencing the cat. "Why do you say that?" He spoke quietly, his voice vibrated through their bones, reinforcing the ache in their chest.

"I... was the key to releasing him. I'm the child of a Creator... apparently," Lunette whispered. The eyeless bat's eyebrows raised, his ears perked curiously. "Leroy was with us and... And it was his idea to go to the prison to reinforce the seals on it with Ash's magic, but when we got there he attacked Ash and me. He... used me to open the prison." Lunette paused to inhale, then exhaled, "Thanatos imprisoned us in Nullhymm."

"Then how did you escape and not Ash?" Oak pressed on them, causing them to turn their head away from both of them. Their bushy tail drooped behind them.

"Leroy set me free. I don't know why. I don't understand any of this."

"Well then, how do we know this isn't a trap? You didn't mention any of this before. What if he let you go to do something much worse, like... like... kill Ash or something?"

"I *don't know!*" Lunette shouted, their shoulders heaving with their breath. "All I knew was I needed to get here so I could get that sword back so I can put an end to this once and for all. I won't wait for Ash to clean up my mess. Not again."

Silence hung thick between them, broken only by the faint sound of Nikolas's claws tapping rhythmically against the wall. Lunette's confession rippled through the room like a chill, but before anyone could speak, Nikolas's features softened imperceptibly. "Regret will not close what's been opened," he said, voice low and certain. "Whether he has a plan or not, it won't matter. What matters is what you do next."

"That's why I came here for the sword."

Nikolas regarded Lunette with a soft *hmm*, his expression unreadable. "If the sword is what you need, then you must be certain of your abilities to kill him. So, I will ask you again, what makes you qualified?"

Oak shifted uneasily, tail flicking behind him subtly, but held his tongue as Lunette clenched their fists and lifted their chin to meet the bat's eyeless gaze. "Because I feel like I've done it before. Back on my homeworld... I can just barely see it in my head. I feel like this is not the first, or the second, time I have faced Thanatos. I know that sword could stop him and free Ash; you said it yourself that it was forged by the Creators to kill gods."

"You *feel* like you've done it before?" Nikolas repeated, tilting his head again.

"They do wield chaos magic. Very powerful chaos magic." Oak interrupted, his voice softening with his posture.

"And... I saw them use the sword," Joey added with a nod. "They looked like they knew how to handle it."

Lunette looked back at them both and gave them a small, thankful nod, then turned back to Nikolas, searching his face for a sign, any sign, that would reassure them. "I may not remember everything," Lunette said quietly, "but I know what I feel. And right now, what I feel is that I must try. If I run, if I hide, if I don't fight back, Thanatos wins before the fight even begins. These memories I've seen of facing him... They can't all be dreams."

Nikolas regarded them for a long moment and tapped his claws on the wall in thought. "Alright. Do you remember what I told Ash when he asked for something from me?"

Lunette's brow furrowed, thinking back to last week. *That feels like a year ago...*

"I told him that I do not give anything away for free. What are you willing to offer me for the sword?"

Lunette blinked confusedly, then opened their mouth to speak, then closed it again to think more.

I literally have nothing... Is the world not ending good enough?

"I don't know. What do you want?"

The tall bat turned his head towards his son, then Oak, then back at Lunette. "Let us step into my office. Just us, please." With unnatural grace he spun around, swapping hands to keep his fingers in the grooves on the wall, and proceeded down the hall to his office. Lunette's ears turned back nervously as they looked at Oak—who motioned for them to just go.

So that is what they did. Lunette rolled their shoulders back and followed the imposing bat as he rounded the corner into his office. They watched as he ran his hand across the desk as he rounded it to sit in his chair. "Close the door, please." He said simply, gesturing behind them. Lunette closed the door behind themselves and stepped just in front of the desk.

"Why are we in here?"

"I would prefer to keep this between us. It is... quite private." He laced his clawed fingers together on his lap and leaned back in his chair, tilting his head towards the window that cast a golden glow across the room. "You have seen Nullhymm then. Is it true that the souls of those Thanatos has killed wander its streets?"

"I think that's who they were. I didn't get a good glimpse while I was running. I was imprisoned under the cathedral until I escaped."

"It is interesting to have confirmation that the legends are true, that it is something of an 'afterlife.' Can I assume that it is not pleasant?"

"Oh, yeah, it's awful. Freezing cold, everything is dead, the sky is all weird, there's frost everywhere, the city looks practically abandoned from what I could tell when I ran through it... Why do you ask?"

Nikolas paused and tilted his head down. He turned his chair to fully face Lunette. "My... brother was murdered many, many years ago. I always had a feeling he was condemned to Nullhymm like the others." His ears drooped slightly; he fidgeted with his fingers in his lap before tilting his head away from Lunette. "I can only imagine his suffering in that place. I will give you the sword if you can guarantee my brother's soul is freed from that place. When you kill Thanatos, it should, in theory, free all the souls."

Lunette watched the somber bat, their ears drooped. "I'm sorry for your loss. I promise that I will stop him, that I'll free your brother and Ash, no matter what it takes."

He nodded once. "Thank you. While I'll continue to live with the burden of his death, it will bring me some peace to know that he is not suffering anymore because of me. You may take the sword." Nikolas felt the desk over, then ran his hands underneath it. There was a soft *click*. The top of the desk seemed to pop up slightly. He lifted it up a bit more and pulled out the sword from the compartment that was hidden within the top. It glowed in the sunlight. The metal reflected the golden rays; the red gem in the center of the hilt glinted as he turned the handle towards Lunette for them to take it.

Lunette stared at it; something tugged at their mind. They could see Valdis striking with the sword. The glow of its edges as it cut down the reapers. They wrapped their hand around the handle. The runes began to glow as they tightened their grasp around it.

"Thank you." They breathed, pulling it close to them. "I promise to do right by you, by everyone."

"I don't doubt it, but I can feel your exhaustion. Rest here for a bit; get some food in your body. You will need your strength to face him. You can't expect to go toe-to-toe with death when you are that tired," Nikolas hummed, tilting his head to them.

Lunette wanted to argue. They wanted to keep moving, but he was right. Every muscle ached still. "Thank you." They breathed. He gave a simple nod and gestured at the door.

"Rest well, warrior faun."

Sunday Evening, Present Day

"So, what is he *really* like?" A bone- and feather-decorated snow leopard asked, leaning a little too close for Ash's comfort.

Ash had been searching—in vain—for a quiet corner, some sliver of shadow to disappear into. Instead, he'd been gently but inescapably herded into a conversational trap. He shifted back a step, ears twitching, tail stiff behind him.

"Ah... What do you mean by that?" Ash leaned away. There was a slight annoyed edge to his voice.

"Oh, you know exactly what I mean." She waved her goblet in a lazy arc, wine sloshing dangerously close to the rim. "Is he a secret softie? A gentle giant? Or is he always fire and brimstone? The great almighty death at all times?"

The air behind his skull prickled, like cold fingers brushing his thoughts. He clenched his jaw. "He's... fine," he said after a moment. "I guess."

The big silver cat's ears perked, her eyes glistening with amusement, her cheetah friend adorned in a black embroidered robe giggled beside her.

"*Fine,*" the cheetah repeated. "Fine as in tolerable, or fine as in—" she gestured vaguely at Ash's face and body, "*—fine?*"

Ash frowned; a deep, amused chuckle, not his own, curled in the back of his mind. "I don't understand what you're implying," he said flatly.

"Oh, don't play coy," the cheetah groaned. "We've known Thanatos since before he came into his true power. Even then, despite constantly being involved with his creations, teaching them the ways of healing and nature magic, not once—*not once*—has he kept the private company of anyone who wasn't a reaper. You're... unprecedented." Her eyes flicked over him with open curiosity. "We just want to know what he's like when no one's watching. What does he *do* on his own?"

Ash shook his head quickly, his hand coming up to rub the skull markings on his face. "I don't know. I keep to my room."

"Well, that's dreadfully dull," the cheetah sighed, sipping her wine. "If I were here with our lord day in and day out, I'd be on his tail constantly. He is *quite* dashing, even more now than in the old days."

Ash's brows knitted together. "The... old days?"

The cheetah's smile widened. "Oh. So, you *don't* know."

"I know plenty," Ash said too fast, hoping to cut the conversation short before it slid somewhere worse. *I've heard this before.* A soft, knowing *hmm* brushed the back of his thoughts.

"Do you truly? Then you know everything about what happened before this became Thanatos' domain?"

The snow leopard's ears twitched with renewed interest. "Long before the reapers and death gods," she said, swirling her wine. "When Nullhymm was known as Everthem."

A tall lion stepped into their circle, his robe heavy with silver filigree instead of bone. His voice was calm, reverent. "This city was alive once," he said. "A thriving university. Mages. Healers. Druids. Scholars. We came from across the world to study here."

Ash looked around the red-illuminated cathedral. He couldn't picture it any other way, honestly. It's frigid, cold, and miserable. He felt the cold in the back of his mind slip away.

Out of the corner of his eye, he noticed Thanatos gazing into the crowd, reclining on his throne with his chin resting on his hand, seemingly lost in thought. Leroy stood beside him, also watching the crowd.

The lion continued. "Thanatos taught them. Walked among them freely. Not as a ruler. Not as a god. But, as a guide."

The cheetah smiled wistfully. "He refused worship, you know. Said it made creation dishonest; he wanted to walk side by side with his creations."

Yeah, I know what happens next. His whiskers twitched.

"But they didn't value that gift," the snow leopard said, her tone sharpening just slightly, swirling her wine again.

"They begged him," the lion murmured. "To change it. To let things end. They were going mad with immortality. They had made up that there was a realm beyond life—they were obsessed with finding a way to it. They deemed the only way to get there was to be killed or be allowed to die by their Creator." He scoffed, "They'd rather cease existing entirely than *possibly* go to this *fairytale afterlife* than be in the presence of the Creator of Life himself."

Ash exhaled through his nose. "And he refused."

"He *loved* them," the cheetah said softly. "How could he condemn them to death?"

For a moment, the noise of the celebration seemed distant: muted laughter, the clink of goblets, the low hum of divine conversation. Within their circle, the silence pressed in.

Finally, the snow leopard spoke. "So, they forced him to kill. One afternoon, during a gathering, a fox and some caracals showed up. One of the cats had retrieved a pair of bone-carved blades, an enchanted weapon created by those who opposed our lord, to present to Thanatos. He thought by giving the blades to Thanatos he could lock them away to dissuade the extremists. But, just as our lord bowed his head in thanks... one of the lunatics shoved the cat onto his antlers with such force that he became impaled."

The cheetah sighed dramatically. "Oh, it was a bloodbath. They screamed that our lord drew first blood, so they all massacred each other."

"From then Thanatos claimed that if his creations couldn't live with his gift, that if they no longer loved him, he would take *everything* from them... just as they took *everything* from him." The lion smiled slyly.

Ash swallowed, attempting to hide the panicked look on his face. *That's... a little different from what Nikolas told us.*

"Us loyalists were promoted to gods of his newest creation—death. Unlike your family, who forced themselves in. I'm still surprised he picked from an... unoriginal group of 'gods,'" she scoffed softly.

Ash's ears went back at the comment, and he couldn't help but growl under his breath. He exhaled slowly through his nose, forcing his claws to relax at his sides. If he stayed here any longer, he was going to say something he couldn't take back. "I think," he said carefully, voice clipped, "that's enough history for one evening."

The cheetah blinked, clearly disappointed. "Oh, don't be like that. We were just getting to the interesting part."

"I'm sure," Ash replied flatly.

He took a step back, then another, easing out of their loose circle before anyone could stop him. The snow leopard opened her mouth, whether to tease, pry, or prod him further, he didn't know—but Ash was already gone, slipping sideways into the tide of bodies that filled the cathedral floor.

The noise swallowed him whole. Laughter brushed his ears. Glasses clinked. Names he didn't recognize floated past him in fragments. He nodded where politeness demanded it, ducked when someone reached for his arm, ignored a few lingering glances that felt too appraising to be accidental. His chest felt tight; his pulse was too loud.

His head was on a swivel. From across the room, he could see Mercy stood radiant beneath the red light, her posture immaculate, her expression sharpened into something triumphant as she spoke with two other gods. Hawthorne hovered at her side, nodding along, warm smile firmly in place. They hadn't noticed Ash yet.

Good. Stay there.

He turned sharply away, heart hammering as if he'd narrowly avoided something far worse than a conversation.

"Running already? No longer want to be social?" came the familiar murmur in the back of his mind, smooth as velvet.

Ash stiffened, but kept moving. *I'm not running.*

"That is a matter of perspective," Thanatos replied in his mind, amused.

Ash didn't answer. He threaded his way through the crowd, ascending the steps two at a time, until he made his way to the stairs and the familiar scent of myrrh filled his nostrils.

Thanatos hadn't moved from his spot. He lounged with his goblet balanced loosely in one hand, antlers casting long, branching shadows up the back of the throne. His gaze lifted the moment Ash approached.

"Finished mingling?" the stag asked aloud, voice loud enough to draw a few curious glances from below.

Ash moved to stand next to him once more, resuming his spot from earlier. "They all talk too much."

Thanatos hummed. "They always do."

<hr>

The cathedral was louder now, alive with chatter and clinking glasses. The reapers moved through the crowd as silent, spectral servants—refilling drinks, adjusting candlelight.

At first, no one noticed how they'd subtly changed their positions. The way they gravitated toward the edges of the room.

However, Ash noticed. His ears flattened. Something was wrong.

He stood beside Thanatos, who lounged on his throne, holding his scythe and sipping his fourth goblet of the night. Leroy stood on his other side, a patient soldier with his ever-present grin watching the crowd. Ash saw his eyes flicking among the group.

The reapers looked as if they were circling the edges of the room, much like a predator circling prey.

At the foot of the stairs, Mercy and Hawthorne were deep in conversation with a cluster of gods from another realm. Their smiles were polished and rehearsed. They didn't see the way the reapers' shadows stretched unnaturally long across the floor.

A cold feeling dragged down Ash's spine as he watched Thanatos rise from his throne with slow, deliberate grace, like a noose was lifting him up. The stag lifted his goblet, letting the red drip down his hand like fresh blood, and the entire hall fell into reverent silence.

"My beloved children, heralds of death," the stag said, his deep voice echoing through stone and bone. "Tonight marks the beginning of a long-awaited chapter. Tonight... destiny drinks with us."

Polite applause rose with cheers. They raised their glasses to him.

Thanatos' red eyes glimmered. "In regards to the Great Plan... we start again. The forces of life will fall. We start with the planet Earth and move back to the First Planet, where I have much unfinished business. The beings of life do not respect the gift I had given them thousands of years ago, and they shall have it no more! I will strip eternity to its bare bones, and Nullhymm will be the graveyard of all existence of what was."

The crowd cheered once more. Ash felt impossibly tense. His head hurt.

"My champion will accompany me, for he alone will stay at my side when all is said and done. We will be the last in this universe."

There was silence, a confused and pregnant pause from the crowd. A few turned to their neighbors to try to get clarity.

"So tonight," he continued, "marks a new beginning. As I feel the need to correct a mistake I made long ago."

Ash's breath hitched.

Leroy stiffened on Thanatos' opposite side, a smile frozen on his face. His hands drifted towards his bone blades, but his eyes focused on the door behind Ash.

What are you doing? Ash thought loudly, hoping to get the stag's attention.

Thanatos raised his goblet above his head.

"Cheers," a wicked grin crossed his face as he said loudly, "to fixing mistakes."

The temperature plummeted.

The candles flickered violently.

And then...

Silence snapped like bone.

With a horrifying unity that made the feline gods seem slow, almost mortal, every reaper in the room lunged at the group of gods in a cacophony of flesh tearing, blood-curdling screams, and divine blood splattering on stone.

One reaper plunged a spectral blade into the spine of the Maine Coon death goddess beside him; she gasped, magic flaring futilely as her body dissolved into drifting ash.

Another vaulted over a banquet table, bone sword sweeping in a wide arc that sliced three divine throats in a single motion. Blood—bright red—glimmered under the crimson orb above and spattered across the tablecloth like paint on canvas as they shattered into dust.

A tiger deity attempted to summon a protective ward; a reaper seized his jaw, forcing it shut before driving a knife through his eye.

A lioness goddess lashed out with fire, but shadows coiled up her legs, rooting her in place as a dozen blades pierced her chest.

Ash stumbled back, breath catching, vision swimming.

This wasn't a gathering.

It was an extermination.

Clean, absolute, rehearsed down to the breath.

Thanatos stood untouched, serene amidst carnage, swirling the wine in his goblet as bodies fell like marionettes with cut strings and combusted into dust. He watched his children die the way a sculptor might evaluate a piece of stone, appreciating its form even as he shattered it.

The snow leopard deity attempted to flee toward the exit, but the iron doors slammed shut, locking her inside the cathedral as a reaper's claws dragged her backward across stone, leaving a streak of wet ichor.

Another god tried to teleport; the instant his form blurred, half a dozen reapers plunged blades into the places his body would rematerialize. He appeared for a fraction of a second, long enough to scream before collapsing into a wet heap, then into ash.

The reapers annihilated, not with shouts, not with battle cries, but with the quiet, perfect unity of predators ambushing prey. Spectral weapons plunged into throats. Bone blades tore through divine flesh. Death gods gasped, choked, tried to summon magic, but alas, were too slow.

A tabby cat god at the center staggered back, clutching his chest as a reaper tore the heart from him in a fluid motion. His body collapsed into dust before it even hit the floor.

One hand gripped Ash's chest, the other covered his mouth as he gagged and dry-heaved, whipping away from the carnage. Images of the ritual room... His mother's frivolous slaughter and branding of Ash's skin... Flashed in his mind.

It was supposed to be a celebration.

Thanatos glanced down at him, almost pitying him.

"It is," he said, loud enough over the screams, "a celebration of endings and new beginnings! I am setting us *free!*"

Another god raised his staff, chanting a protective ward— only for Thanatos to curl his fingers. Shadows shot from the floor, wrapping around his body and yanking him downward. He fell to his knees, clawing at his throat as a bone-clad spectral guard crushed his windpipe with a boot.

My parents! The thought was strong enough to get Ash to spin around just in time to see Mercy grabbing Hawthorne's arm, pulling them both back toward the pillars, eyes sharp, frantic. Even she was stunned; even she had not seen this coming.

Ash's stomach twisted as something warm splattered across his cheek. He wiped it with trembling fingers.

Blood.

He didn't know whose.

Ash gasped and trembled, dry-retching as he stumbled back into the side of the throne. Thanatos reached an arm out to grab him, holding him steady, holding him in place to watch the slaughter.

The air vibrated with a pitch so high it nearly pierced his skull. Magic ruptured like overdrawn tendons. Bodies shriveled into dust or burst into cinders that blew away in the air. The floor gleamed with spilled divine ichor that reflected the red light above, making it seem as if the cathedral itself bled.

"Ash!"

He turned his head sharply. Tears streamed down his face.

Hawthorne stood in the chaos, one arm wrapped protectively around Mercy, both bloodied and coughing but unmistakably alive. His father's eyes widened with desperate urgency.

"Ash, do something! Stop this!"

A reaper collided with Hawthorne's side, slicing open his ribs before he shoved them back with a green burst of necrotic magic. Mercy snarled, grabbing the feline reaper's jaw and snapping its neck with brutal, practiced ease, spiraling the reaper into their own pile of dust.

"Ash!" she barked, eyes ablaze. "Move!"

Ash took a step toward them.

Thanatos shoved him back into the seat of the throne.

Then he descended the steps.

His hooves struck the stone with the weight of a falling empire. Shadows rippled outward from him, devouring candlelight, drinking the color from the air. The reapers froze mid-kill, parting like a tide as their lord approached.

"Ash," the stag called gently, the way one might call a pet back from danger. "Do not look away." Thanatos didn't lift a finger. He *willed it*, and the surrounding darkness responded like something alive.

Tendrils erupted from the floor beneath Mercy and Hawthorne, wrapping around their legs, dragging them down with brutal force. Hawthorne slashed downward, necromantic magic crackling from his claws, but the shadows only swallowed the energy greedily, tightening their grip.

"No!" Ash's voice tore from him, raw and broken. "Let them go!"

Mercy's composure cracked. *"Ash! Run—"*

Her command strangled into a gasp as one tendril whipped across her torso, opening her from hip to rib in a clean, slicing arc. Bright red blood, shimmering in the light, spilled down her black robe, pooling on the floor like a waterfall.

"Mercy!" Hawthorne lunged toward her, but the tendril moved to wrap around his throat, yanking him upright, choking off his breath. His legs kicked uselessly as he clawed at the constricting darkness.

Ash stumbled from the throne onto the frigid stone floor, crawling towards the steps. "Stop—*stop—please—*"

Thanatos watched him with a serene stillness; his now wildly glowing eyes mimicked the orb of his staff.

"They were proud of you," he murmured, almost conversationally. "This is what they raised you for, is it not? To bring death and destruction? To beat you into submission for *their* desires?"

"Leave them!" Ash's claws scraped against the floor, a futile attempt to get closer. His body was numb; everything shook. The air was colder than it had ever been, making his tears burn as they ran down the skull-like markings on his face. He could only watch.

Mercy collapsed to her knees, one hand pressed desperately to her open wound. She lifted her face, and her eyes met Ash's.

Her expression was not anger.

Not disappointment.

Not even fear.

It was regret.

"Ash," she mouthed. "I'm…"

Thanatos brought his scythe through her back and out her chest in a single, terrible motion.

Her body sagged. Her head fell. She crumbled into dust.

"Mother—" The scream came from deep within Ash's soul, tearing from him as if part of his heart was ripped out with her.

Hawthorne's roar shook the very pillars of the cathedral. Grief eclipsed the pain in his throat, his magic bursting outward in a final, wild surge. It struck the tendrils, burning them away in flashes of green fire.

He fell to the ground, coughing, scrambling toward where his wife had been—

With a slow, almost bored gesture, the Creator of Death raised one hand.

Hawthorne froze mid-crawl, body twisting unnaturally by the shadow tendrils that encapsulated him, as if someone had seized hold of his very spine. His limbs jerked once. Twice. A choked sound escaped him, like a sob caught in his throat.

"Your father was strong," Thanatos said softly, almost admiringly. "But even strength rots."

Hawthorne's chest caved inward. Bones cracked, sharp, wet noises echoing through the cathedral. His eyes widened, breathless, disbelieving, and then, with a final shudder, his form collapsed into ash that scattered across the blood-slicked floor.

The silence afterward was worse than the screams.

Ash stared from his position on the floor in front of the throne.

Something inside him broke.

He sank lower until his head was on the floor, one hand hitting the ground as his breath came in short, violent gasps. His vision blurred. His ears rang. The world tilted.

"No... no, no, no, no..." His voice fractured, cracked into pieces between heaving sobs. "They were right there—they were supposed to live. You *killed them!*"

Thanatos stepped up the stairs towards him, slow, calculated, like approaching a feral animal. "Ash," he said gently, as though soothing a frightened child. "Look at me."

Ash didn't. Couldn't. His fingers dug into the stone, claws scraping helplessly. His chest felt sliced open. This was worse than his skin being carved.

"You see now," Thanatos murmured, kneeling beside him. "This is the truth you were never given. The truth they sheltered you from. Cruelty. Futility. The world takes everything you love... But... You have me now."

A warm, clawed hand lifted Ash's chin.

The intense scent of myrrh filled his nostrils

He couldn't fight. He could barely breathe.

All he could do was stare into the red, unrelenting orbs that locked onto him.

"My chosen one," Thanatos whispered, leaning until his forehead rested on his. "You will never be alone anymore. I am all that is left of your past now. I promised I would set us free; I have upheld my promise. I erased my mistakes along with yours. Now we will rebuild this universe anew. I am your future. You are my eternal companion."

Ash's breath shook violently; tears mingled with the blood that splattered his face. "I didn't... I didn't want this—"

"I know." Thanatos' thumb brushed his cheek, wiping away the tears and simultaneously smearing the blood. "Destiny is merciless. Now... I repaid our past for what it had done to us. We can rebuild free of their ideocracy. They will not use us anymore. They will no longer put us on a pedestal as patrons to their sins. Don't you see? We are *one and the same*. We have been forced to cater to their will. We have experienced the same betrayal from those we love. Now, we will never feel it again; we have each other."

"Get... get *away* from *me*!" The words burst through him like a tear in fabric. His arm flew up, and a burst of bright, necromantic fire rushed through the air in an arch in front of him, steaming the frigid air.

The blow sent the stag flying backward from the stairs. He tumbled down them until he landed on his back at the bottom. His head knocked into the blood-soaked stone with a *thwack* and *crack* as the tip of one of his antlers snapped on impact.

Reapers who were nearby fell backward. The armor-clad guards fell back like broken statues.

Ash's chest heaved, and he pulled himself to his feet. His whole body trembled. Blood of the other gods dripped from his face. A guttural, feral cry erupted from his lungs before he collapsed again in front of the throne.

A single thought echoed in his mind as his consciousness gave way.

This is my fault.

I set him free.

530 Years Ago, Val-Tirath

The light from the window beside Ash's bed caused him to squint. His mouth felt dry, his head was swimming, and every muscle felt weak. He lifted his hand to block the light from his face, feeling his bones creak with the stiffness of his joints.

"Ash?" a voice asked softly from beside him.

Ash turned his head, moving slowly as he fought through the lingering haze. He blinked several times, forcing his vision into focus. When his eyes adjusted to the light, he saw the concerned expression of his twin brother staring back. He opened his mouth to speak, but nothing came out; his throat was too dry.

Auburn quickly grabbed a glass off the nightstand and held it to his brother's lips, holding it while he sipped. Ash wiped his mouth after a few big gulps of water and cleared his throat. "What happened? My head is killing me..."

"You don't remember?" Auburn frowned, placing the cup down again.

"Remember what?" Ash's lips pursed in thought as he racked his mind for the last thing he remembered. *Oh, right... The ritual.* He remembered getting ready, his vague conversation with Oak, maybe seeing Auburn, then... nothing. "I remember getting ready for the ritual. That's the last thing I remember. What happened?"

His brother's ears flattened, and his eyes shifted to the floor. "You've been... asleep for a long, long time, Ash. After the ceremony, you fell into some sort of coma. Did you see anything in your dreams?"

Ash shook his head softly. "I... Just remember going to the talking with you and waking up here."

"Maybe the ritual was so powerful your body had to adapt all this time? Do you feel any different?"

The world felt sluggish; the light filtering through the window only made everything blurrier, pressing against his aching skull. However, nothing felt immediately different, he thought. Ash reached and pinched the bridge of his nose to ground himself. "I feel like I have a headache. How long has it been?"

The bone-adorned twin looked at his brother, cringing a bit before he spoke. "Ash... it's been a hundred and seventy years."

Ash's hand dropped from his face, his fingers curling weakly in the bedsheets. "A hundred and... *what?*" he rasped, sure he'd misheard.

Auburn's expression softened, but his eyes remained troubled. "A hundred and seventy years, Ash. We... we didn't know if you'd ever wake up."

The reality struck Ash with the weight of a brick hitting his chest. The room suddenly seemed foreign, despite looking exactly as he remembered. "What the hell did they do to me, Auburn?" He whispered, voice shaking.

The twin hesitated, ears folding lower, his fur bristling. "I wasn't there, Ash. I don't think we should dwell on it."

Memories fluttered at the edges of Ash's mind: the weeks before practicing with mother, dinner with his family, seeing the ritual doors... The images were fleeting; it felt like he only had bits and pieces. *Why can't I remember everything?*

He swallowed hard. "Why didn't I... why didn't I wake up sooner?"

Auburn shook his head. "We don't know. Mother assumed it was too much power at once." He paused, voice barely above a whisper. "I stayed by your side, Ash."

For a long moment, neither spoke. A bird sang outside the window, a sound so ordinary it made Ash question if it were real or not. Finally, he drew a shaky breath. "I need to get up."

"Yes, of course. Mother will want to see you for sure, father too." With his brother's steadying hands, Ash swung his legs off the bed slowly. His body felt strange. Underneath the ache, he could feel the essence of his magic stir in the pit of his stomach, but it felt different. Stronger? More alert? Ash wasn't sure; all he could tell was that it had preserved him after all this time. The world spun for a moment as his paws hit the wooden floor, then settled into sharp clarity.

"One step at a time," Auburn said softly, supporting Ash's weight as they made their way across the sun-dappled room. As they passed the mirror, a flash of white caught the corner of Ash's eye. "What is that?" Ash breathed, pulling his brother to a sudden stop, then backing a step to stare at the stranger staring back at him.

A large, white skull-like marking covered his face with small white triangles on his cheeks. Everything went still, even his heart felt as though it stopped beating. Ash pulled away from his brother, stumbling up to the mirror and grasping it on both sides to steady himself as he stared at the black and white cat that stared back.

"Auburn... Tell me you've been painting my face while I was asleep," he breathed.

In the reflection, he could see his brother's ears flatten once more, his tail tucked under his black robe. No words left his mouth.

Ash released one side of the mirror and reached up, half-expecting to feel the roughness of dried paint beneath his fingers, but all he felt was the softness of fur. His hand traced across his face, searching for any shift in texture, but there was none. The white fur was real, softer and a bit thinner than his usual black coat, with faint traces of pink, slightly scarred skin visible underneath. His breath caught in his throat, unsolicited tears welled up in the corners of his eyes.

"What... did she do to me?"

"It's just permanent ritual paint, is all."

"Permanent ritual paint, *that's all*?" Ash breathed a sarcastic chuckle, stifling a sniffle. His eyes scanned over his face once more, then noted his hair was cut as well. "*And* she cut my braid off?"

"Well... You know how she is. New beginnings and all."

"*New beginnings*," Ash said sarcastically, turning to look over his shoulder at his brother. "I've been *maimed!*"

Auburn's ears couldn't go any flatter; the tip of his tail flicked under his robe. "I think you look nice. You look the image of our lord."

"What are you talking about?" Ash spat.

"Our lord?" Auburn tilted his head worriedly. "The one true god of death? The Corrupted One?"

Ash simply stared, racking his brain for any ounce of recognition, but came up blank. "I don't know what you're talking about."

"How about we get some food into you? Come now." Auburn came over and took his brother's arm, gently guiding him away from the mirror. Ash begrudgingly complied, allowing himself to be led from the room and down the stairs. The staircase creaked under their combined weight, each step sounding louder in Ash's ears than he remembered from his entire life being here. The house was quiet, eerily so, as though every sound was holding its breath for him. Pictures still lined the walls—oil paintings of the family together, other family members, and some of the landscapes of the island. The scent of incense and firewood lingered in the air. He felt like he was walking through a dream. It was all surreal.

In the dining room, the morning sun cast golden patches onto the long, old wooden table. Auburn guided Ash into a chair. "I'll be right back. Don't move," he said as he scurried off into the kitchen beside the room. Ash's fingers fidgeted on the tabletop, tracing invisible patterns as he tried to anchor himself in the present, but his reflection made his stomach hurt.

"You want honey with it?" Auburn called, his tone too casual, too careful.

Ash simply shrugged, not trusting his voice. He could hear his twin huff from the kitchen from the lack of an answer.

Auburn set a plate of toast with honey in front of Ash and sat across from him. For a moment, he ate in silence. The only sounds were the soft chewing of bread and the distant sound of the birds outside.

Finally, Ash broke the quiet, his voice hoarse. "You never answered me. Did she do this to me during the ceremony?" He said sternly, searching Auburn's face for answers.

Auburn looked away, fiddling with his sleeve. "Mother said it was an honor. She said you'd been chosen. I don't know more than that, Ash, I swear. She wouldn't let any of the siblings into the room." His tail flicked nervously under the table.

Ash swallowed, staring into his plate with two more pieces of toast on it. The food tasted bland, but he forced himself to keep eating; the honey coated his throat.

"I'm going to go get mother now, ok? Just keep eating, please." Auburn stood quickly and then exited the room without another word.

He watched Auburn leave; the silence settling around him like a heavy blanket. Ash's eyes wandered over the dining room. It felt emptier than before. Hollow. He tried to steady his breath, taking a small bite of toast, but something about it all still felt unreal.

After a few minutes, soft footsteps echoed from the hallway. Mercy entered before Auburn. She paused near the threshold, her gaze lingering on Ash before she came over to him quickly, pulling him into a tight embrace, causing Ash to stiffen and stop chewing. He held as still as a statue while she gently petted his hair, then pulled back to inspect his face.

"Perhaps you do look a little older."

Ash swallowed. The question burned inside him, and he couldn't hold it back anymore. "What did you do to me?" His voice trembled, torn between accusation and confusion.

Mercy's eyes narrowed with something unreadable—a flicker of annoyance, maybe pity. "What did I do to you?" she said, her tone flat. Before Auburn could interject from the doorway, Mercy raised a hand, silencing him. "I made you even more powerful than before. Your brother says you're experiencing some memory loss. What exactly do you remember?"

"He didn't know who Than—"

Mercy's hand shot up once more to silence Auburn. "Let your brother speak."

Ash's ears flattened against his skull, his chest felt heavy staring at his mother. He could feel something just at the edge of his memory; something about her eyes made his head hurt. "I remember getting ready, seeing Oak and Auburn... And that's it."

"Do you remember the name of our lord?"

He averted his eyes. It felt as though there was a gaping hole in his mind. No matter how hard he thought, nothing came up. "No."

"Interesting." She straightened her posture before glancing at Auburn. "I believe he willed this. He must want your devotion to be true, without his name. Perhaps it is so that when the end comes, your devotion to him will be pure. So be it."

"The end?" Ash repeated.

She leaned forward, her voice dropping almost to a whisper. "Yes, the end. Allow me to remind you of your destiny. You were chosen, Ash, to save us all. To change the fate the universe may have set for this family. We will live during the Great Plan because of you." Her words hung in the air, heavy, causing him to press back against the backrest of his seat. "You are the one who will bring the end, but not here, on another world. Our future is tied to you. The cycle must begin: the dead must rise so we have sufficient followers, an army for our lord. You bear the symbols of our lord, symbols on your body and pentagrams on your tools. You replicate his signs perfectly; you're now in his image."

Ash felt cold. The honey on his tongue tasted bitter now. He looked at Mercy, searching her face for any sign that this was a cruel joke. She just watched him as if she saw something far beyond this moment.

"For now, you will rest." She sank into the chair next to him and pushed his plate closer to him. "When the time comes, you will proceed to the chosen world and live your legacy in the name of our lord. This is your *destiny*, Ash."

Monday Morning, Present Day

All Ash could hear was his heartbeat in his head. His eyes felt crusted over. Every muscle, joint, and hair on his body hurt. He woke up only an hour ago, or was it two? Yet, he couldn't bring himself to open his eyes. Last night played on repeat in his head.

It was just supposed to be the zombie apocalypse.

A knock came at the door. Once. Then again, softer.

Ash didn't answer. He pulled the blanket tighter. He didn't want to see anyone. Not anymore, not ever.

The door opened anyway. The creak of the hinges rang in his ears, forcing his eyes to open. Ash gritted his teeth, his green eyes started to blaze as he opened them.

"Go *away!*" he snapped loudly, sitting up straight and throwing the blanket off his head. The motion made him dizzy.

Leroy stood in front of the now-closed door. No cigarette. No grin. No lazy swagger. His hands were shoved into the pockets of his priest's garb, ears low, eyes guarded. He looked... wrong. Unarmed.

"Hey," he said simply, softly. Too softly.

"What do you *want?*" Ash spat, his claws digging into the blanket. His palms were hot; he could feel his energy stir.

"They're gone," he said quietly. "Your parents."

Something inside Ash snapped. He surged to his feet so fast, the room spun. "*No*," he said, voice rising. "No—don't say it like that. Don't say it like it just *happened*! Like it's just another fucking day!"

Leroy's jaw tightened.

"*You* did this," Ash hissed, stepping closer. His claws were out now, ready to strike. "*You* dragged us there. You *lied* to me about *everything*. You betrayed me, betrayed Lunette. *You* made me set him free. If you hadn't—" His voice cracked hard. "If you hadn't, they'd still be here!"

Leroy's ears flattened as he looked away. "Careful."

"No," Ash shot back, shaking. "You don't get to tell me to be careful. You used me. You used me for *nine years* and now they're dead!" Tears welled up in his eyes. He didn't bother wiping them away.

Leroy looked at Ash, his mouth twitched. Then his expression hardened.

"They were awful to you," he snapped.

Ash recoiled as if he were struck. "Don't you *dare*."

"They were," Leroy pressed. "I saw it. The way they talked to you. Treated you like you were nothing more than an errand. Like a failed experiment. You think that pride they wore last night erased centuries of that? Erased the hundreds of calls I heard you on with them in the basement when they belittled everything you are constantly? Who was there for you during all of that? *Me!*"

"That doesn't mean they deserved to die!" Ash shouted, stepping forward almost into Leroy. His voice echoed off the stone. His chest heaved. "They were my parents!"

The silence that followed stung like pouring alcohol on an open wound. Leroy looked away first, dragging a hand through his hair.

"I know," he said, quieter. "And I'm not saying it didn't matter. I just..." He swallowed, taking a moment to consider his words. A rare occurrence for the caracal. "It wasn't on you. Or me, for that matter."

Ash laughed, a broken, hollow sound. "You're really good at telling yourself that."

Leroy didn't argue; his ears stayed folded back.

"You weren't there," Ash said suddenly, his voice dropping. "When it started. I saw you looking at the door, then you were gone."

Leroy exhaled slowly. "Yeah."

"So, where were you?"

"I left."

Ash stared at him. "You ran. You left me there. Betrayal after betrayal!" he shouted. Every muscle in his body was taut. Leroy thought he might hit him.

"I slipped out," Leroy corrected, irritation flaring. "There's a difference."

"Why?" Ash demanded.

Leroy hesitated. For once, the answer didn't come easy. "Because staying wouldn't have saved anyone."

Ash's shoulders shuddered, his rage giving in to the heaviness in his body. He turned away, hands shaking, ears flattened.

"I *hate* you," he whispered.

Leroy's voice softened with a sigh, not much, but enough. "Yeah. That tracks too." After a moment, Leroy cleared his throat. "Get dressed," he said quietly. "Drink some water. And... don't do anything you'll regret. Sih will be here to take you to breakfast."

"I am *not* going near him," Ash spat.

"You and I both know you don't have a choice."

Ash didn't respond.

Leroy turned back towards the door, his paw resting on the handle. "For what it's worth," he started, not turning around, "I never wanted it to end like this. But... it'll all be over soon. For all of us."

"What the fuck does that mean?" Ash whipped around to face him, but Leroy was already out the door, the sounds of his paw pads descending the long corridor.

Ash sat at the table, staring at the unappetizing meal before him. His eyes hurt. He could feel his bones under his skin and every fiber of the chair he sat on. Sih stood nearby, staring. He ignored her; he couldn't look at any of the reapers anymore. The only sound in the room was the flickering flame of a wall torch, and it made him nauseous.

The sound of hoofbeats jarred him from his dissociation.

He didn't dare look up. The potent scent of myrrh filled his nostrils as the rustle of fabric and weight replaced the sound, thumping down into the chair beside him. Sih moved and filled the wine goblet quickly.

Ash could feel the stag's eyes boring into him as he sipped his wine.

"You did not sleep well," Thanatos said mildly.

Ash's jaw tightened. He didn't answer. He kept his eyes fixated on the steaming meal in front of him.

Thanatos hummed softly, as if this were a casual conversation between old acquaintances rather than the morning after a massacre. He set the goblet down, the metal clicking once against the wood. "That is understandable. Loss has a way of... lingering."

Ash's claws dug into the table's edge. "You *killed* them." He spoke through gritted teeth.

Thanatos did not bristle. Did not deny it. He merely tilted his head. "Yes. I set you *free*, as promised."

The words landed heavier than any excuse could have, causing Ash's ears to flatten.

"They were proud of you," the stag continued, voice low and even. "They believed in what you could become. That matters, even at the end."

Ash let out a shaky breath that bordered on a laugh. "You don't get to say that."

"Do I not?"

Ash finally looked at him. Thanatos looked… more unkempt than on the other mornings. His braids were frayed, his long black hair lay in tangled waves unbrushed, his eyes looked tired. The tip of one of his antlers was missing. Did it break when he fell?

Ash's fur bristled. *I struck him down.*

Thanatos looked away, seemingly ignoring the thought. He picked up his goblet again, his sleeve slipped ever so slightly to reveal his usual bandages. They weren't as neat as before, as if they were hastily wrapped before coming here.

"You… paraded me in front of them. You let them think…" His voice cracked. He swallowed hard. "You let them think I'd finally done something right."

Thanatos regarded him for a long moment, studying him. "And did you not?"

Ash said nothing.

Sih shifted uncomfortably nearby. Thanatos lifted one clawed finger without looking at her. She stilled immediately.

"You see cruelty where I see inevitability. I never lied in what I said I would do with you. Your parents understood that. They accepted their role in the Great Plan long before you were born."

"They did it so that they would *live*. So, they would be spared. They didn't deserve that kind of death," Ash said hoarsely.

"No," Thanatos agreed. "Death is seldom deserved."

"Don't *you* have control over that?" Ash spat.

Silence stretched. The torch flame on the wall fluttered, flaring too brightly, then settling again.

Thanatos leaned back in his chair. "You may hate me, you may blame me. That is permitted. Grief is normal when change happens; however, you will get over it. You will move on, and we will continue to build our future. I am all you have left of your past."

Ash's shoulders trembled despite his effort to still them.

"But do not confuse grief with guilt," the stag added. "This was *not* punishment. This was progression."

Ash's breath stuttered. "You *planned* it."

"Yes," the stag said, matter-of-factly.

"You *planned* for me to watch."

Thanatos' gaze softened—dangerously so. "I planned for you to *understand*. I planned for you to feel... relief from past notions. Much like I felt being rid of those... other gods. I wanted you to see how similar we are, how we both have suffered from destiny being forced upon us."

"*Relief?*"

Ash pushed back from the table so abruptly that the chair legs scraped loudly before clattering backwards onto the floor. He stood, shaking. "I don't want your food. I don't want your fake 'freedom.' I don't want your *fake* companionship or your stupid explanations. I want Lunette and me to go *home!*"

For the first time, Thanatos' lips twitched into a frown.

"You will eat," he said—not loudly, but with an edge that made the air tighten. "You will not wither away in my house. I did not choose you for that."

Ash laughed again, sharp and bitter. "*You* didn't choose me. My parents chose me for you."

Thanatos rose slowly to his full height, placing the goblet down with force. He loomed over the table, nearly toppling over Ash. "They *offered*," he corrected. "I *accepted*. I saw what they were doing to you. How they *forced* you to bend to their will. Their idiotic scrabbles at life to *possibly* be spared in death." He leaned closer to Ash, the warmth of him stark against the cold room. "And now, *Ash Darkscream*, you belong to me."

Ash's vision blurred. He looked away, jaw clenched so tightly it hurt.

"Well, I didn't *choose* you. I'm not your fucking charity case. I won't be your fucking 'companion.'" His eyes met the stag's again, blazing in defiance.

Thanatos gritted his teeth and straightened. "Finish your meal," he said calmly. "Afterward, you may grieve in whatever way suits you—so long as you remain alive."

Ash flipped his plate at Thanatos, causing his wine goblet to clatter onto the floor from the table, sending the red liquid and food everywhere.

"*Eat thi*s."

Thanatos didn't move a muscle, only his eyes narrowed. Sih flinched from where she stood, then moved quickly to attempt to clean up, but Thanatos raised a hand at her to still her.

"I am losing my patience." He said slowly.

"Lose it some more. I'm going to find Lunette and we're *out* of here." Ash turned quickly, rounding behind Thanatos' chair to head for the door.

"Lunette *isn't even here!*" Thanatos snapped, turning to face Ash.

Ash stopped in his tracks, turning quickly to look at the stag, his tail lashing like a whip. *"What?"*

"They escaped. They haven't been here for some time." Thanatos said slowly, keeping an edge to his voice. Ash noticed his shoulders trembling ever so slightly with contained rage.

"Where did they go then? Did you kill them too?" Ash stepped forward, the palms of his paws white-hot with necromantic power that flared under his skin.

"No. I did not." Thanatos spat. "I don't *know* where they ran off to."

Ash gritted his teeth and shook his head. *I'm alone out here then? They left me?* The feeling pressed down on his chest. He felt as if he might suffocate.

Thanatos watched him, then ever so slowly raised a hand to touch Ash's face. His sleeve slipping down to his elbow, revealing poorly wrapped fresh wraps around his wrist in their entirety, patches along them seemed lighter than the rest.

Ash slapped his hand away, causing the stag to recoil, balling his hand into a fist.

Without another word, Ash stormed out, power-walking down the hall, wiping his eyes with the back of his paw. The armored guards and a few reapers stared as he pushed past them. He shoved into his room and slammed the door, grabbing the map Leroy had made, he looked it over again with blurred eyes.

I need to get out of here. I need them.

Monday Late Morning, Present Day

After a somewhat restful night, devoid of strange dreams, Lunette and Oak stood outside the church in New Bedford that held the portal back to Antarctica. Lunette stood sword in hand, staring at the door to the basement on the side of the building. The morning felt heavy and silent. The two didn't talk much after Lunette had met with Nikolas privately. Lunette had gone to bed in the guest room, falling asleep staring at the sword as if they were worried it would get up and walk away. Now, this morning, the weight of their promise to Nikolas, and what possibly lay ahead of them, weighed heavily on their mind.

"What exactly did he ask you for? I've been curious." Oak said softly, adjusting his coat as he stared at the door.

"He didn't want me to tell anyone."

"Suspicious. But I understand he is a private individual." Oak looked at Lunette, his tail flicking from underneath his coat. "I can't go with you to Nullhymm."

Lunette turned to him abruptly. "What? Why?"

Oak hesitated, his green eyes flicking away from Lunette's searching gaze. "I can't go with you, not past this point," he murmured, voice thick with an emotion Lunette couldn't quite name. "I can't bring myself to see Thanatos after what our parents put us through. I resisted all of my parents' teachings before Ash came along, but I fear that I won't be strong enough if I'm right in front of him. I don't want to hesitate and be responsible for Ash getting hurt again." The words hung between them, heavy, the sword's glow pulsing with Lunette's increasing heart rate.

For a moment, neither spoke. Finally, Oak placed a steadying hand on Lunette's shoulder, his touch warm through the chill. "If there is anyone who can do this, I believe it is you. When I saw Ash with you in that room when he summoned me, I saw the way he looked at you. He might not show it, but he cares for you, and I see you care for him. I know you will do right by him. I'm sorry for doubting you at Nikolas's."

Lunette looked up at the tall cat, their bright blue eyes meeting his. "I forgive you. And... thank you. I hope I'll see you when this is all over. Maybe the three of us can get a pizza or something."

He nodded once. "I would enjoy that. But now you should go. I'll take my leave." Oak then stepped back, turning away and walking off until he disappeared into the morning mist.

Lunette turned their focus to the path ahead.

Then they shoved open the door.

Monday Afternoon, Present Day

Ash threw open the door to his room. He had studied the map with raw, blurred eyes for a while now and determined the front door was the only way in or out of this cathedral. At this point, he didn't give a damn whether anyone tried to stop him or not. Thanatos did say he had full reign to go outside—so all he had to do was walk out, cross the bridge, and just leave, right?

The slap of his paw pads resonated against the cold stone. The cathedral was eerily empty, its tall, arched windows filtering in strips of red light. Shadows clung to the corners, and the air held that ever-present chill that had seeped into his bones, though he barely felt it anymore. The guards only watched him as he walked.

Ash turned sharply into the fountain room; his claws dug into his palms as he rehearsed what he would say if anyone got in his way: He was *not* a prisoner. Not anymore, anyway. Especially not if Thanatos was true to his original word. Which was... Questionable at this point. Ash was rolling with it, though.

As he approached the main hall, heat of necromantic power under his skin reminded him he wasn't defenseless. Especially after what he had done to Thanatos last night. *I struck him down; I could do it again.*

Inside the barren throne room, he could practically feel the tension in the air, as if the cathedral itself was holding its breath. Or maybe it was him? Despite the massacre that took place, the room was spotless. As if nothing had ever happened. Ash swallowed, tears stinging the corners of his eyes while his gaze swept the room.

Just stay focused. Don't stare at it.

The double doors loomed ahead. All he had to do was cross the room and open them. He kept his head down, his chin practically touching his chest as he power-walked across the room, ignoring the red glow above and the increasing tension in his chest.

For a moment, doubt flickered. Was he really doing this? *What if they come after me? Kill me?*

He shook his head, jaw set.

No, no, this is the right move. I need to get out of here.

His face still stung.

Why does it feel wrong then?

Ash's paw gripped the door handle; he stared at his hand and rasped his fingers along the metal. Taking a deep breath to steel himself, he tensed his arm to yank the door open.

"What do you think you're doing?" a voice echoed across the throne room.

Every muscle went rigid, cold spread across his chest as he jolted from the sound. Ash turned his head slowly. Leroy stood atop the stairs next to the throne, tail flicking at his feet.

"*I said*: where do you think you're going?"

Ash swallowed, rolling his shoulders and pinning his ears back. "I'm *leaving*, Leroy. I am not his prisoner, and I'm sure as fuck not yours." Despite the venom in his tone, his voice still trembled, earning an ear flick from the caracal.

"Oh," Leroy scoffed, "you're not going anywhere."

"Yes, I am. I'm here at the door, aren't I?"

"Sure," Leroy slowly descended the steps, his paws shoved in his pockets and bone daggers jostling at his sides in their sheathes. "Then why haven't you opened it?"

"Because that's what—I'm literally in the process of that!" Ash gestured to the door with his hand still on it with a hiss.

"Really? And what exactly do you plan to do once you're outside that door, hmm?" The reaper stopped in the center of the room, pulling a cigarette from his pocket and lighting it.

"I'm going to *leave*. That's what I said, are you even listening? No one listens to me around here!"

"Where the hell are you going to go, Ash?"

"I'm going *home*."

"Back to New Beige?" He paused to take a puff of his cigarette and shook his head. "We'll find you there."

"Then I'll go somewhere else!"

"Like London? Japan? The Caribbean? California? Montana—"

"*Shut up!*" Ash shouted, dropping his hand from the door and fully facing the caracal, necromantic fire flaring to life in his palms.

"Oh, I'm sorry, do you mean Michigan? Illinois? Or maybe good-ole Kent, Connecticut?"

"Shut it!" Ash jolted his arm out in front of him, casting the flame at Leroy.

A shadow shot out from under the reaper's feet in front of him, blocking the blow before it could touch him as he took another drag from his cigarette.

"Are we really doing this right now?"

Ash's chest heaved, the embers flickering in his palms as he glared at Leroy. "This is your fault! All of this! They wouldn't all be gone if it weren't for you! You just *had* to let him go!" he spat through the break in his voice.

Leroy looked away, the smoke from his cigarette curling around his face. "You know I can't just let you walk out."

"Well, you're not going to stop me."

The reaper let out a low, almost disappointed sigh. "You really want to fight me right now? You do realize you're not the only one who's lost people because of him, right?"

Ash hesitated, his breathing ragged as the pain in his chest flared. "Only if you get in my way. I'm done being trapped here."

A tense silence hung between them. The cathedral's vast emptiness seemed to press in from all sides—the only sounds were the soft crackle of fire and the wind whipping outside. Leroy sighed through his nose, exhaling smoke as he did before he spoke.

"I really, really don't want to hurt you, Ash."

Without warning, Ash launched forward, his paw slicing through the air with a wave of green fire. Leroy moved with practiced ease, dodging the strike.

"You're making a huge mistake, Darkscream!"

Ash lunged at the reaper again with a yell, claws and fire slicing the air as Leroy dodged at the last second. Shadow tendrils flicked out of the ground and knocked Ash off balance, causing him to nearly fall.

"Just go back to your room like a good boy!"

Ash righted himself and struck at Leroy once more. This time, Leroy unsheathed his bone daggers, holding them in an X-shape in front of his chest where Ash's engulfed hands crashed into the bases of the blades. The blue gems in their pommels shimmered under the green glow of Ash's green fire, conflicting with the red light above them.

The two cats' eyes locked, both staring with gritted teeth as they pushed against each other equally.

"I fucking warned you, Darkscream."

In a flash, Leroy swept his blades apart and darted sideways, leaving Ash off balance as the resistance vanished. Ash lurched forward, nearly hitting the ground. He barely steadied himself before pivoting and preparing to attack again, but the split second he had to react had already slipped away.

"It's the only way we'll get rid of him *for good!*"

Leroy's shout echoed through the chamber; all Ash could see was the dagger's pommel crashing down toward his head, followed by the icy stone floor rushing up to meet him.

Monday Evening, Present Day

Lunette stepped through the icy portal into Nullhymm and was greeted by the ever-present chilling air, causing them to shiver. They could see the city in the distance. Thanatos' cathedral stood over it with the brightly glowing orb, casting a red glow that mingled with the orange ring in the sky. They gripped the sword more firmly, mind racing with possible outcomes and scenarios of what might unfold.

Would they bust open the door, cut down the reapers, and get to Thanatos? Would Thanatos just be waiting for them in that throne room? Would he threaten to hurt Ash and force them to back down? Maybe they could sneak in another way? Or have the reapers already noted their arrival?

Lunette's fur stood up on end, their heart raced.

I have to do this. I have to save Ash, save everyone. This is bigger than I am.

The feeling of something brushing against their shoulder jerked them from their thoughts.

They whipped around toward the feeling, facing the small bit of dead land behind the portal where it dropped down to a smaller cliff, then dropped off entirely. The rift to Earth sat in the distance, barely shrouded in the fog.

Nothing was there.

However, they couldn't deny that something had just touched them.

I have to stay focused.

They turned back towards the city, took a step forward, and immediately were stopped by the feeling again. With a huff, they turned around again to face the dead landscape behind the portal.

The surrounding fog swallowed everything. They could only see a bit ahead where the cliff dipped down to where the start of a rope bridge remained, suspended between this land mass and who knew where.

Lunette stared down the slope to where it started. They could see better now that where was a wooden barricade in front of the swaying structure, as if someone was trying to deter anyone from walking across it.

Then they felt that pull again. Something gently nudged their shoulder, causing a familiar tightness in their chest.

Without another thought, their hooves scraped the stone as they slid down toward the barricade. The wind bit at their skin, the tips of their ears were going numb, and it arguably felt worse near the foggy drop-off.

I should turn back. I need to get to Ash.

That would be the logical thing to do, right? Who knows what Ash was going through right now? However, the pull in their chest only intensified, insistent, like a hand guiding them forward. Something was beyond that bridge. It swayed violently in the wind, ropes creaking, planks knocking together like bones. A few boards dangled loosely, swinging into the mist.

What would Ash say?

They exhaled, breath clouding white. "This is stupid," they said aloud, before proceeding to vault the barrier anyway, hooves landing on trembling wood. The bridge lurched and groaned beneath them.

"Don't look down," they whispered, gripping the ropes tight enough with their free hand for rope splinters to prick their palm. They used the weight of the sword in the other hand to balance. Step by step, they moved forward. The pull guided them, dragging them deeper into the fog until the end came into view. More icy, dead landscape encased in mist, they couldn't see beyond it.

As they stepped onto the dead grass, the pull vanished.

Lunette turned in circles, their breath hitched.

Was that it? Did I just risk my life for—

"Lunette?"

The voice came from just beyond their sight, deep and rough-edged with disbelief. It sent a jolt through them—something primal, something *familiar.*

"Who's there?"

"Lunette... it's you."

The fog shifted as a shape moved toward them. Dense footsteps echoed against the frozen dirt. Out of the mist stepped a wolf—massive, gray and white, his armor glinting faintly beneath layers of age and wear. The silver plates shone as they reflected the land's strange ring-like sun.

He stopped a few paces away, staring at them as if afraid to blink. His brows were furrowed, then relaxed. "Oh, Lunette..."

Before Lunette could react, his large arms were around them, pulling them into his chest. The metal was cold, but beneath it his body radiated with something colder—it made the energy under their skin recoil a little. They froze, every instinct fluctuating between fear and an ache they couldn't name. Their arms hung at their sides, their fingers locked around the sword's handle.

"Despite all that has happened," he murmured, leaning back just enough to look at them. "You're still here. You're alive and well."

Lunette's throat closed. The way he said their name...

What is this?

Their chest ached so hard it hurt to breathe.

"I don't..." Their voice cracked.

Lunette searched his face. There was a scar across his neck, and despite his gruff appearance, there was a softness about him. Their heart twisted painfully, an echo of something they couldn't reach.

"Who..." Their voice was barely a whisper. "Who are you?"

The wolf's smile faltered just a bit; his claws flexed on their shoulders. "It's me, Lunette. It's Alastair."

"Alastair," they repeated, familiar and foreign at the same time. "That name. I've heard that name is my dreams. You look... So familiar."

Alastair tilted his head; his paws rubbed their shoulders. "You are warm. You're alive. That is what matters."

"I lost my memory. I keep getting pieces here and there... I just... don't remember much. I'm sorry."

"I see," the wolf nodded thoughtfully, yet there was a hint of sadness in his eyes.

"Are you... dead? You're cold, Alastair." Their body tensed, looking him over. Their eyes lingered on the scar on his neck. Tears, unbidden, welled in the corners of their eyes.

I couldn't save you... Could I? What if I can't save Ash?

Their heart raced, their grip loosened on the sword.

"Lunette... It's alright, especially now that I see you're alive. I was worried after I fell that he would have killed you."

Lunette's brows knit in confusion; they wiped their eyes quickly with the back of their hand. "What do you mean? Who would have killed me?"

"Thanatos."

"Thanatos... tried to kill me? You were there?" They reached into the depths of their memory, yet came up with nothing. This all felt so familiar...

Why can't I just remember?

"When we attacked Nullhymm. We performed a ritual with Valdis to open a gateway from Astravir to here so we could attack Thanatos at the source, to stop our world from becoming another victim of his rage. We led the Valdarr through the portal and attacked. It seems we succeeded; Thanatos was imprisoned by the Creators once more."

Lunette's ears drooped. "At the cost of all their lives..." The words left their mouth before they realized what they had said.

Do I remember? Will this happen again?

Alastair rubbed Lunette's shoulders once more. "Yes. But we accomplished our task. It was a sacrifice that we all were willing to make. I just never knew what had happened to you after."

Lunette's lips trembled. "Alastair... their sacrifice was in vain. Thanatos lives. He walks among Nullhymm, he's planning to destroy Earth; he has my... my friend!"

Alastair frowned slightly. "It was not in vain. Our world lived because of our sacrifices. I am sure Astravir lives today."

"You don't *understand,* Thanatos is free *now!* I must kill him or else!" Tears welled up in their eyes again. "Or else Ash will die too. Your lives were sacrificed for nothing! I can't... I can't let that happen again. What if I can't save Ash?"

"No, not nothing." He raised his paw to gently wipe away Lunette's tears. "For hundreds of years planets were able to live on, mortals and gods alike lived without fear of Thanatos' Great Plan. You will stop him again. I'm not sure who your friend is, but your feelings for him are strong; therefore, I know you can do this. When your feelings are strong, you are too stubborn to let there be any other outcome." He chuckled softly under his breath. "You're the strongest being I know."

Lunette tilted their head up to meet the wolf's bright yellow eyes. Their grip tightened on the sword. For once... they didn't know what to say. The words resonated in their mind, it eased a fraction of their anxiety, but they still felt worried.

Alastair's head tilted to look at the sword in their grip. "You have Valdis' sword. Do you remember him? Do you remember what he said to you? To us?"

"Yes, he's who I see in my dreams."

The wolf nodded softly. "Well, let me remind you. Valdis loved you, as do I. He always told us that no matter what, we are never what others force us to be, and only we are in control of the outcome. You are in control of this outcome. You will stop him again."

Lunette stared at the wolf, their eyes softened at the words. "Where is Valdis? Could he help me? I really need him right now."

Alastair's ears drooped, his expression turned sullen. "I don't know... I haven't been able to find him since I got here."

Lunette opened their mouth to speak, but was cut off by something—rather someone—clearing their throat behind them.

"You should not be here. The barrier is up for a reason." A low, smooth voice said softly.

Lunette turned quickly to see a short, cloaked figure standing behind them. They wore a black robe over what looked like a priest's garb, a hood pulled over their head, and a tall—taller than they were—carved wooden staff in their hand. The mysterious figure pulled down their hood, revealing a light tan and white fennec fox. Their dark brown facial markings and medium-length sandy hair shone in the orange light. Their tall ears perked as they stared up at Lunette.

Lunette blinked and tensed up, feeling the similar death energy as was in the cathedral radiating from them. They turned fully towards them and raised their sword in defense. "Who are you?"

"I am Fennigan. But you can call me Fen," she spoke, her long, bushy tail flicking behind her. "You do not need to be afraid. I am not like the other reapers. I don't follow Thanatos."

"But... You're a fox. Not a cat?" Lunette watched her confusedly.

"Observant, I see." Fen rolled her eyes. "No, I am not a cat like the others. One would think someone as observant as you would have noticed the barrier at the top of this bridge." She tapped her staff on the ground, ears flicking in irritation.

Lunette looked at her offendedly, then turned to look at Alastair... Who was gone. Their eyes widened, fur standing up on all ends.

"Do not be alarmed. This realm tricks you, plays with your thoughts, perceptions of reality, and tries all of your weaknesses."

Their ears drooped a bit, staring into the mist. "So... was he not real?"

"Oh, no, he was very real. That I can assure you. This realm was trying to get you to doubt yourself. It led him to you. I've been studying this place since I was condemned here."

Lunette turned back to the small reaper and lowered their sword. "What do you want then? You're not here to drag me to Thanatos or stop me, are you?"

"No, like I said, I don't follow Thanatos. I felt you wander this way and decided I should stop you before you got too far. Come with me." With that, Fen turned abruptly to the bridge and began to walk across it confidently.

Lunette's ears went back against their skull, observing the confidence she bore walking across the rickety structure. "Are you sure that can hold the two of us?"

"Yes, it is very stable. It purposefully looks scary to discourage people, but it is actually quite safe," the fox called back as she disappeared into the mist.

"Oh, ok," Lunette breathed.

Yeah, I don't really believe that.

They took one last look over their shoulder at the mist where Alastair came from. They swore they could see his outline in the fog, watching them leave. They released a shuddering breath, then turned and started to cross the bridge once more.

Eventually, they reached the other side where Fen stood, tapping her staff on the ground. "Glad you made it. So, you really think you can do it? Once and for all?" She gestured to the sword with his staff. "That's if I'm assuming correctly that you are here to do what I think you are."

"Yes. I'm here to kill Thanatos. I can do it."

Fen regarded Lunette for a moment longer, her amber eyes studying their determination. Then, with a quiet nod, she turned and led the way down a twisting path that led back up the rocky ledge that was off to the side. The bridge behind them creaked once before falling silent, swallowed again by the mist.

They stopped at the top of the ridge by the portal, where they could see the city again.

"I will take you to the city so that you are unnoticed. Once we get there, you're on your own. The reapers should be preoccupied for the most part. They had... a long night last night. You should be able to confront Thanatos before they rush to his aid... Hopefully." Fen nodded softly and began to walk towards the city.

Lunette tilted their head but followed.

She seems trustworthy enough...

"Why are you helping me?"

"Because I want this madness to be over just as much as anyone else. I was there when it started... I just want it to end."

"When it started? You mean when Thanatos started killing everyone?"

"You mean when *everyone* started killing *each other*. It's all chaos."

Lunette nodded softly. "Yeah, I guess. Well... I will save Ash and put an end to it all. For all of us."

"I sure hope you're right."

As they walked towards the city, the world around them grew quieter, the wind grew less intense, and only the occasional tap of Fen's staff broke the oppressive silence. Lunette gripped the sword tighter, the cold metal grounding them against the uncertainty. Their heart rate increased with every step towards the city.

After a while, the barren path that was carved in the dead grass turned to cobblestone, and they entered the city. Fen's staff tapped the stone as they made their way through the shattered, debris-riddled and torch-lit streets. Towering cathedrals and grotesque boney cat statues loomed over them as they walked. Specters of dead mortals of all different species hid around corners, watching from a distance as their hooves and paws tapped their way down the center.

Lunette looked around warily. "This place... It's so creepy. Are the people scared of us?"

"They fear me. They fear all reapers, so they will not bother us. I also doubt they've seen anyone who's alive since they were alive themselves. They are the citizens of this lost city."

Lunette's eyes wandered over some of the spectral faces before they disappeared around corners. Pity tugged at their chest.

In the distance, there was a loud *crash*.

Fen's ears perked. "Something is happening."

Then another crash and roaring of yelling in the distance that could be heard even this far from the cathedral.

Fen looked at Lunette quickly. "You must go. Hurry! Something is happening."

"Come with me!" Lunette urged, stepping ahead and gripping their sword.

"I can't move fast enough, just go!"

"What? Why not?"

"I-I just can't!" Fen stumbled forward as the ground shook with another crash. Lunette caught her arm to steady her. With a growl, she yanked her arm from Lunette to jerk up the bottom of her cloak and readjust a wooden prosthetic that attached to her hock. "*Go!* Get your friend and *end this!*"

Lunette stared at the fox for a brief moment before turning on their heels and sprinting towards the cathedral.

520 Years Ago, Val-Tirath

Ash stood in his room, studying the stranger in the mirror. The stark white markings on his face, and the two triangles on each shoulder, still were foreign to him, even ten years later. He looked away from the reflection to adjust the satchel on his belt, then pulled the long, old black cloak over his body.

"Are you prepared?" a low voice asked from the doorway.

Ash glanced at his twin brother, who was doing a very poor job of concealing the sadness across his face. "As I will ever be."

"How long do you think it will take?"

"Not long," Ash pulled the hood over his ears, "I plan to arrive on the new planet, plant the plague immediately and get this over with as soon as possible."

"Do you... think we'll see each other again?"

"Of course we will, Auburn. From what Mother says as soon as we have enough followers, we will be united with the Corrupted One as a family during the Great Plan. Everything will return to normal."

"You're positive mother won't let me accompany you?"

"Yes. I already asked, and you know how she feels when I ask questions." He turned to look at his brother fully, who was looking at the ground. Ash sighed through his nose. "It will be fine, Auburn. This is what I'm meant for."

"I know. I just..."

"Dwelling on it won't make it any easier." Ash said quickly, crossing the room to stand in front of him. "While I'm gone, you will promise me that you'll keep practicing as you're supposed to."

Auburn nodded once. "I promise, Ash. When you get back, I will be fifty times more powerful than you. I'll be the next god of necromancy." A playful smile crossed his lips, but the gloom lingered in his eyes.

Ash snorted softly, patting his brother's head. "I don't doubt it. Now, come, mother awaits."

"Juni would like to see you before you go too; she's in her room."

Ash nodded once. Gently pushing past his brother, he stepped out of his room and went up the hall two doors to Juniper's room. The door was slightly ajar; he could just barely see her sitting on her bed, watching out the window. Her long black hair was braided down to the base of her tail, and she wore a simple black robe. Ash still couldn't believe how much older she got while he was asleep; he still looked at her and saw the little grinning kitten swaying at the table.

He knocked softly. "Juniper? Can I come in?"

"Yes, come in, please." She didn't turn around when Ash slipped into the room. Her amber eyes stayed fixated outside.

"Auburn said you wanted to see me before I went down, so…"

The younger black cat turned to face him. Tears welled up in the corners of her eyes. Silently, she stood and wrapped her arms tightly around her brother. Ash relaxed in the embrace and squeezed her back, sighing shakily as he did. "I'm going to miss you," he whispered, petting her gently.

"I'm going to miss you too. I don't know what I'm going to do without you and Oak." She sniffled and leaned back to wipe her eyes with the back of her paw.

"You're going to have to convince Auburn to play games with you now."

Juniper scoffed and shook her head. "He's no fun, he's so... rigid about everything. Practicing constantly, only wants to read scripture... The only time I can get him to have some fun is when I hide his practice bones in the graveyard and he has to reanimate them to find them." A small, playful smile graced her lips, causing Ash to scoff softly.

"Give him a break, he goes through a lot with mother. I'm sure with just the two of you, you'll bond more."

"Yeah, but he's not you. Or Oak. Do you think Oak will come back this time?"

"I doubt it. He and Mother had that big fight when I woke up... He said he was finally done with 'all of this.'" Ash gestured to his skull markings, causing Juniper to frown.

"It was for good, though. He has to understand that."

"I don't think he ever will, Juni."

The young cat's shoulders drooped with her sigh. "I'm just going to miss you. Do you promise you'll come back?"

Ash nodded once. "I'm going to do my best."

She nodded back, giving him one more quick hug. "Then you shouldn't keep Mother waiting."

With that, Ash walked down the hall onto the second-story landing. He glanced down to see his mother standing by the front door, his father beside her. She looked up at Ash expectantly and gestured for him to come down. Ash descended the stairs, footsteps echoing softly in the quiet foyer. When he reached the bottom step, his mother reached out, brushing a strand of hair from his face with a touch that was tender but firm.

"Remember what we've taught you," she murmured, gaze lingering on him.

Ash nodded, the weight of what was about to happen was setting in.

"You were made for this. You have one mission. When the Corrupted One is released, we will be at his side because of you. When you get there, you speak to *no one;* we can't risk any of the other gods learning our plan. They'll steal it or report it to our lord's opposers."

"I understand, Mother," Ash said firmly, glancing away.

She grabbed the fur of his chin with her claws and jerked his head to make eye contact with him again. "No. One. Not a single soul. Who knows what lingers on that world? They could attack you, kill you, so always be on guard. Do not stay in one place for too long and keep moving."

Ash grunted and pulled his head away. "My intention is to start the apocalypse as soon as I get there. The sooner the better."

"Good. Do not think about us here. Focus on your job."

Ash nodded once and looked at his father, who smiled softly at his son. "Be swift, be careful," his father said quietly, voice low, almost as if he was holding back tears. "And don't look back.

Once you're there, you won't be able to get back here... Well, not easily. But it will be ok, Ash, I promise, especially if you complete your purpose. Check in with us often with the ritual your mother taught you."

Ash swallowed, glancing at them one last time. He could hear Auburn and Juni's footsteps behind him, pausing at the top of the stairs, watching. For a moment, the world seemed to stand still—a family suspended in the doorway between what was and what would be.

"Right, well..." Mercy broke the silence, patting Ash's arm. "You had better go before the boat leaves without you. The mage who is making your portal will be waiting at the docks when you get to the mainland."

He nodded again, taking a steady breath while looking between all of his family. Studying their faces for what might be the last time. "Yes, Mother. Goodbye, then."

With a final breath, Ash stepped forward, his hand trembling as he gripped the door handle. When he opened it, a wave of cool air rushed over him, flowing through his cloak and ruffling his fur. The early morning was quiet, so quiet that his own footsteps sounded unnaturally loud against the path that led to their home. Every chimney was bare, the usual wisps of smoke absent. The only light, besides the rising sun, was the bone lanterns that lit the path.

Ash pressed forward, passing through the gates with barely a glance, his mind racing with memories of his family and the life he was leaving behind. As he reached the edge of the island, the horizon opened before him. There in the distance, docked at the water's edge, was the small outline of a boat, its silhouette barely visible in the dim morning light. The salty tang of the sea filled his lungs as he approached, each step feeling heavier than the last.

Ash stopped one last time, letting himself absorb the scene: the gentle waves lapping against the dock, the crisp air wrapping around him, and the fathomless quiet of the world before dawn. He inhaled deeply, the cool salty air stinging his nostrils and filling him with a sense of finality.

This was the moment he had been waiting for, the point of no return. Every lesson, every trial, every hardship he endured had brought him to this single instant, and now, with the fate of his family's lives resting on his shoulders, he was about to step into the unknown.

To start the zombie apocalypse in a world he didn't even know the name of.

He let the memory of his family's faces linger in his mind one last time. His mother's fierce instructions, his father's quiet encouragement, Oak's absence, and the silent presence of Auburn and Juni watching from the shadows. The weight of their expectations pressed against him, but he pushed it aside.

This is it. I know what I must do.

Without daring to cast a glance over his shoulder, Ash took another deep breath and set out along the path leading to the dock, his expression steeled even as his heart fluttered with uncertainty.

This is my destiny, he continued to convince himself, *and when the Corrupted One is released... It will finally be over.*

Life will return to normal, just like they said.

Monday Midnight, Present Day

Ash jerked out of his restless sleep when a sudden bang nearly jolted him from the bed, followed by a thunderous rumble so loud it could have been some kind of bomb.

Where's Leroy?

His head throbbed as another wave rattled through the cathedral walls like a hurricane that was attempting to sweep up the entire building in one go. The torch by his bed flared violently, its flame stretching sideways before snapping back into place. Ash bolted upright, heart slamming against his ribs.

What the hell was that? Did Leroy bring me here? Where the hell did he go?

A second impact followed, closer this time. Stone groaned. Somewhere down the hall, the sound of metal hinges being torn from a wall reverberated down the walls.

Ash swung his legs off the bed and staggered to the door just as a shockwave rippled through the floor, nearly sending him sprawling. The sound that followed was unmistakable: an echoing *crack* like reality itself splitting under pressure.

Then came the yelling. His heart was in his throat. *Please… No more killing.*

With a breath, Ash yanked the door open.

The hallway was chaos.

A familiar black, inky goo seeped through the floor at the end of the hall. Several twisted, serpent-like figures dripping with the black, oily substance poured out of the open doorway at the end of the corridor. They tackled the guards nearby, practically eating them alive and tearing them to shreds with their claws.

Ash's breath hitched. He backed up against his door.

Reapers scrambled through the hallway in panicked disarray, some clamored into their rooms—robes whipping around their legs as they ran, not toward the disturbance, but *away* from it. Others unsheathed their blades and began slashing at the creatures, the weapons barely did any damage to most of them and the more they cut down the more appeared out of the wave of black goo that now poured from the doorway like a dam that had broken.

More creatures tore down the hallway, grabbing at any reaper they could get their grimy claws on, slamming them down and tearing them into shreds that dissolved into ash.

"What's *happening?*" Ash shouted at no one in particular.

Another detonation shook the cathedral, this one violent enough to tear cracks through the stone ceiling. Dust rained down in clouds as a pulse of cosmic energy tore through the hall, cold and burning all at once.

From below the doorway, at the bottom of the stairs, a voice thundered upward through the stone. "You... *pathetic* piece of *roadkill!*"

Ash's blood turned to ice.

Teramir's claws scraped the doorframe as he gripped and pulled himself through, huffing and shaking the metal chains from his wrists. His eyes blazed a fiery purple; the light rolled over his cheeks and reflected off the red windows beside him. His snake-like body slithered through the goo with ease, almost as if he was floating on top of it, his amethyst scales reflecting off the surface.

A reaper launched at him with a bone blade, but he grabbed them by the throat and tossed them through the stained glass beside him. Other reapers scrambled away from him in fear. The inky snakes slithered up beside him, forming a line on either side.

Teramir's eyes locked with Ash's at the end of the hall as his clawed hand came up to point at him.

"*You*. This is *your* fault. Do you have *any* inkling of what you have *done?*"

The serpent Creator began slithering towards Ash at an alarming pace.

Ash gasped and reached for his door handle, but black vine-like goo that launched from underneath Teramir struck him, forcing him back. The floor around his paws became saturated in the oily substance. The hallway looked like a black river. Tendrils came out of them and wrapped around his legs, holding him in place. Ash struggled against them, breath coming in panicked huffs.

As the serpent passed the halfway point of the fountain, the creatures lurched ahead of him and started scrambling towards Ash, teeth gnashing.

Ash raised his hands, and just as the necromantic power surged and created a flame between his paw pads—the floor beneath him tilted, pitching him forward, but the tendrils tightened, gripping him in place. The creatures stopped just short of him before whipping around to face their Creator.

The sound of their collision was deafening.

Thanatos collided with Teramir in the hall, smashing him back into the windows where the two Creators toppled out with an earthquake-like *slam* into the ground below.

The creatures receded almost immediately, the goo as well.

Ash shook himself free as the tendrils retreated and sprinted to the broken window. He grabbed the edge, careful of the shattered glass, to peer below.

Thanatos and Teramir were nowhere to be seen; only the deafening sound of combat could be heard from somewhere around the cathedral. Roars of anger, tears of fabric, and sounds of claws on flesh echoed in the frozen wasteland.

There was a guttural roar that rang out.

A feral, angry sound that shook the walls again.

This place is going to come toppling down, Ash thought, his heart hammering in his chest.

Then... there was silence.

He paused for a moment, waiting for the violence to return, but it didn't.

Ash turned quickly and ran down the hall, through the fountain room, into the throne room, and down the steps. He made for the iron doors, his tail lashing behind him. He could hear reapers following him now.

Just as he crossed under the red orb above, the doors flew open with a gust of frigid wind.

In the doorway stood Teramir.

The serpent's chest heaved, golden blood painting his face from the scratches on his snout and chest. His waist wrap was tattered and torn by clawed hands. Scales around his torso were torn out in chunks.

Where's Thanatos? Ash's heart thundered in his chest. He took a few steps back.

The reapers recoiled. They all scrambled back, fighting to get through the small doorway at the back of the throne, tearing the curtain down in the process.

"*You.*" The naga pointed at Ash and slowly slithered towards him. "I'm not finished with you *yet*."

Ash scrambled backwards, his paw pads losing traction on the frosted stone floor, causing him to slip.

An oily tendril shot out from under Teramir, wrapping around the length of Ash's body, burning his skin, causing him to yelp. He struggled against the bind, kicking and attempting to summon necromantic power in his hands, but the ink snuffed it out.

"Let me *go!*"

"In your dreams. I need you," the Creator huffed. His blazing galaxy eyes shifted to look behind him at the throne.

"Where is it?"

From the corner of Ash's vision, he saw the crowd of reapers who were still there part, and someone stumbled out. Leroy staggered to the throne, clutching his ribs. His hair was a mess and robes torn by claws.

"Thirty-five miles from my old home," Leroy coughed and winced in pain, "Cape Cod Canal. It's a man-made structure, dug so deep part of it is exposed. You'll want to go there."

Ash's brows furrowed watching. "What the fuck are you doing, Leroy?"

Leroy watched him, his eyes looked... full of pity.

Why is he telling him *where it is?*

The serpent huffed and rolled his shoulders back. "Excellent. He should be up in a little bit. Good luck when he gets up." He scoffed and tightened his grip on Ash.

Ash winced and struggled more. *Why does it always have to be tentacles? Can it be anything else?*

Teramir turned and raised a hand, a portal tearing through the frigid air that seemed to open back... Home. Back to Earth.

Ash's eyes widened at the sight.

"Don't get too excited, *cat*. It is the beginning of the end; it will all finally be over."

"What are you going to do? What the fuck is your plan here?"

"Oh," he laughed, a snickering, evil laugh, "what would be the fun in that? Let's just say we're going to get rid of that *helminth* once and for all."

Ash's ears flattened against his skull. With a smirk, the serpent turned and slithered through the portal. The tentacles pulled Ash along, but not before he could get one last glimpse at Leroy—who stood watching with his ears flat and a smile absent from his face.

Monday Midnight, Present Day

Lunette slid in the wide-open cathedral doors, their hooves skidding on the frost.

"Where *is he?*" They shouted, looking around frantically before locking eyes on Leroy who was slumped over in Thanatos' throne holding his ribs.

"You're going to have to be more specific." Leroy grimaced, but smiled, anyway. He sat up a little straighter then flopped back into the backrest of the oversized throne.

"You know damn well who I'm talking about." Lunette marched to the bottom of the stairs. "Where is Ash?"

"Just missed him. Slimy took him."

Lunette's breath hitched. "*Teramir* took him?"

"Yeah, not even five minutes ago." Leroy waved his hand nonchalantly, looking away from the faun.

"*Where* did he take him?"

"Do I look like I fucking know?" Leroy scoffed, rubbing his face.

Lunette marched up the stairs and grabbed him by the front of his robe, roughly yanking him forward inches from their snout.

"Damn, ok we're doing this now?" Leroy laughed with a smirk, wincing as he did.

"Shut *up*. Tell me where he is."

Leroy stared, smile faltering at the corners of his mouth, but he remained silent.

Lunette shook him roughly.

"Ow! Ow! Hey! You told me to shut up!"

"Now you decide to do what you're told? Tell me where he is!"

"Alright! Alright!" Leroy put his hands up in mock surrender as Lunette released his robe from their grip.

"Where is he?"

"He took him to the canal."

"*Which* canal? There are literally hundreds!"

Leroy shook his head fast. "The one at home. Cape Cod Canal. The one with the bridges."

Lunette's brow furrowed in confusion. "What? Why? Why on Earth would he take him there?"

"For a vacation?" Leroy shrugged.

Lunette reached to grab him once more, but he flinched away from their hand with a yelp.

"The vein! There's a vein there. One of the ones that leads to the heart of the Earth. Thanatos needs one of those to destroy the world. He cuts it open, so he has direct access to the soul of the planet so he can just suck it into Nullhymm."

"*Why* would Teramir go there? Isn't that what Thanatos wants? That's like leading a kid to a candy bowl!"

Leroy stared at them and raised his eyebrows.

Lunette's eyes widened. "He's planning something, isn't he?"

"If you want to live, I'd suggest staying here." The caracal crossed his arms, leaning away from them.

"What are you even talking about?"

"It's the only way to finally *kill him!*" Leroy shouted, his smile fully vanished now, his chest heaving. "The only way to kill Thanatos is to have him blow up with that planet!"

Lunette studied his face for a moment, their expression agog. "You... You wanted that all along... Didn't you?"

The caracal's ears flattened as he grimaced and turned away.

With a quick swipe of their hand, Lunette grabbed the reaper by the front of his robe once more and yanked him to his feet so he was nearly towering over them, attempting to pull away with a yelp.

"*What are you doing?*"

"*You* got us into this stupid mess, now you're gonna help me get us out of it!"

Leroy let out a hiss and struggled against their grip while they proceeded to drag him down the stairs. As they got halfway across the barren, frozen room, a figure stumbled into the doorway.

Lunette stopped short, still gripping Leroy.

Their breath hitched in their throat.

In the doorway stood Thanatos.

The stag's chest heaved, golden blood painting his face from scratches that littered his snout and chest. His robe was tattered so much that his chest was bare and streaked with more golden blood. Neither of them was sure if it was all his or Teramir's.

Thanatos' breath fogged the air as he stood holding the doors wider with both hands. His eyes blazed a crimson so bright it made the orb above appear dull.

All Lunette and Leroy could do was stare at the disheveled Creator. A large pink scar that crossed his chest was now scratched ever so slightly open. Lunette's heart stopped as they stared at it. Then their eyes met his.

The sword in Lunette's hand glowed more in their grip. Pain stung the back of their head, causing their eyes to narrow.

"Where... *is he*?" he roared; the pillars of the room vibrated with the bass of his voice. "*Answer me!*" he screamed once more; the feral howl reverberated in Lunette's ribcage.

Lunette gritted their teeth and took a step forward, gripping their sword.

Leroy yanked them back to him with a swift pull.

"He went to the vein." He breathed out, gripping Lunette's arm. "He overhead it; one of the reapers reported it to me this morning in the prison while I was with him."

"What the fuck? Don't tell him that!" Lunette snapped, whacking Leroy in the chest with the hand that was holding onto him.

"Where is it?" Thanatos hissed, stepping into the room more.

Lunette flicked their attention back to the Creator, raising their sword in defense.

"You are *not* going to get near him."

Thanatos let out a dry laugh, his breath coming in a few ragged gasps. "Do you want him to *live* or not?"

Lunette's ears flattened, their teeth bared slightly.

Leroy moved between them.

"Thirty-five miles from my old home," Leroy coughed and raised his hands in surrender. "Cape Cod Canal. It's a man-made structure, dug so deep part of it is exposed. That's where he's going."

Thanatos' chest continued to heave. His eyes flicked from Lunette to Leroy, then back to Lunette. One hand lifted, and his scythe materialized in his hand.

Without another word the stag whipped away from them back out the door, his hooves echoing off the barren landscape as he vanished into mist.

"*What the fuck are you doing?*" Lunette shouted at Leroy, grabbing him by the robe again and shaking him roughly.

"You can't expect *us* of all beings to *kill* a Creator, can you? He needs to just explode!" He snapped back, his ears flattened against his skull, but a grimacing smile was still present on his lips.

Lunette raised their sword and gestured wildly at it.

"I didn't go all the way home to grab this thing again for *nothing!*"

Leroy stared at the sword and growled. "Well… all this arguing isn't saving Ash right now, is it?" Leroy hissed through his teeth.

Lunette paused, baring their teeth more and letting out a frustrated groan. "Shut *up!* We need to get to the canal. Now!"

They turned away from Leroy, letting him go and closing their eyes, exhaling. *I can do this. Just… conjure a portal. It can't be that hard, right? I've done it a few times already.*

They reached their hand out, their eyes squeezing more shut in concentration. They could feel the energy stirring under their skin, the neutral energy shifting and coming to life.

"What the hell are you doing? You look constipated."

Lunette opened their eyes and glared over their shoulder at Leroy.

"Are you serious right now? I'm *trying* to open a portal. Remember when that happened in New York?"

"Alright. If you say so…"

Lunette huffed and turned back to focus. They closed their eyes and outstretched their hand. The energy rose through their chest, the lukewarm neutral power flowed down their arms, feeling hotter and more hectic as it traveled.

With the blink of an eye, chaotic energy enveloped them.

Tuesday Early Morning, Present Day

Teramir hovered in the air, positioned precisely between the overarching Bourne Bridge and train bridge that connected the island to the mainland. A wide canal ran beneath them, creating a pathway for barges and boats from the ocean, that ran directly through what was once a solid mass of land. His tail curled beneath him, providing balance through an invisible force of energy that allowed him to float. He extended his hands, channeling his power to manipulate the water. The sea responded to his command, parting dramatically to either side and sending the excess water rushing underneath both bridges before flowing back out to the ocean.

Beside him, being held hostage in the air by a black, oily tentacle that formed from a puddle of the substance on the seafloor, was Ash. He didn't dare struggle this far up in the air. He had no intention of taking the chance of falling to his death. Nausea overwhelmed him; he couldn't bring himself to look down.

"What the hell are you looking to accomplish here?" Ash shouted, peeking one eye open from squeezing them shut.

"Be *quiet*. I'm focusing!" Teramir snapped, not looking at him.

Ash growled under his breath. *Gods, he's a dick.*

He leaned just a smidge to peek down at the seafloor below; a faint shimmer caught his eye before he immediately was slapped by vertigo and nausea. Ash looked at the sky and squeezed his eyes shut again, attempting to make the feeling go away.

This is so much worse than an airplane.

"What is your plan here?" Ash gritted his teeth and kept his eyes closed. "Why did Leroy tell you this? Is he in on whatever the hell you're attempting?"

"Originally, no," the serpent scoffed. "I wanted nothing to do with that tall-eared *freak*. I had my own plans. However... he made some interesting points."

Ash opened one eye to look at Teramir. "You're an idiot for believing *anything* he says."

"That is so comical coming from the one who has been practically groveling at Thanatos' feet for the last week."

"I've literally been a *prisoner* this entire time!"

"Were you in a cage?" The serpent looked at him quickly, an eyebrow raised. Ash said nothing, his mouth open as if he were about to say something but couldn't find the words. The naga scoffed, flicking his forked tongue out as he did.

"That is what I thought. You catered to his will. You did not even *attempt* escape."

"I *couldn't!*" Ash snapped.

"You *chose* not to." Teramir rebutted with a shake of his head. "You have been disgustingly complacent with that *roadkill.*"

"I had no choice—"

"No, perhaps not. After all, it was *your* destiny. But I have my own destiny to uphold... And that is making sure both of you don't make it any farther. You were meant to be dead last week, and *he* was never supposed to walk free. Now you're both going to die."

Ash opened his other eye and stared at the Creator, his ears flattened. "What do you mean, both of us?"

"You and that pathetic stag. Who else? Perhaps I'll mount his antlers somewhere, *if* there's anything left of him."

Ash swallowed hard. "He kicked your ass before. What makes this any different?"

Teramir turned his attention back to the growing shimmering gold in the sand below that glistened in the rising sun. A smirk crossed his lips; the golden glow reflected in his fangs. "Because this time... I have you."

Ash stared at him, eyes wide. Panic spread in his chest, and he couldn't help but feel his breaths starting to come in ragged gasps. His tail was rigid beneath the oily tentacle that gripped him and caused his skin to burn.

This can't happen. Where is Lunette? His thoughts began racing through his head until the Creator's voice interrupted.

"He was always *weak*, you know. He probably was spending his days of freedom loafing around that stupid cathedral, acting melancholy as if he wasn't the one who condemned himself to it in the first place, while the reapers did all the work down here."

Weak.

The word rang like a clarion call in Ash's head. Thanatos' words echoed in his head. *We are one and the same, forced to cater to their will. We have experienced the same betrayal from those we love.*

Despite the anxiety that bubbled in his chest, he felt his lips curl into a snarl. Rage began to override fear. "He was *forced* to do it." Ash couldn't stop himself; the words rolled off his tongue before he even realized what he was saying. Was he really defending this... monster?

The serpent's eyes snapped to meet his. "It was his *destiny*. What is meant to happen, *always* happens. Thanatos was always *meant* to die; such was prophesied when he turned on his creations!"

"What are you even talking about?" Ash hissed.

"The *Great Plan?* Do you not remember? I knew cult members were idiots, but you are on an entirely new level!" The Creator flicked his forked tongue with a hiss, causing Ash to recoil against the tendrils.

"*The Great Plan.* When Thanatos turned on all of us, we believed it was a sign from *our* Creator that we were meant to destroy all that was *evil*. That Thanatos himself brought darkness to our glorious creations, and *we* would be the ones to snuff him out and restore *order* as she intended! Thanatos seeks to destroy *all* of *our* hard work!"

Ash stared at the Creator with wide eyes as he shouted, his ears flat against his skull.

"Do you not *understand?*" the Creator shouted, moving closer to Ash, his eyes blazing like dying stars.

"He does not seek to eradicate all *life*; he seeks to eradicate *everything!*"

Something twisted in Ash's chest. Rage? Anxiety? Fear? He couldn't put a label on it, but his muscles began to shake. He kept his gaze fixed on the Creator. His teeth ground so hard it felt like they were about to shoot out of his skull. "His *followers* turned on him."

"He did not maintain *order!* Our creations are meant to *obey their Creators!*" A single clawed hand reached out to grip the front of Ash's robe, yanking him closer to Teramir's bared teeth. "He is, and always will be, *weak.*"

Ash's green eyes blazed, every muscle shook.

As he was about to respond, a sudden scream drew both his and Teramir's attention. They quickly looked back toward Bourne Bridge, where a commotion was erupting.

From the bridge, cars were stopped; mortals scrambled at all angles to get out of their vehicles and flee from the bridge. Screams rang out all around them. Standing in the middle of the road, behind the bars of the bridge, was Thanatos. His tattered robe and long obsidian hair fluttered in the wind, hand gripped around his glowing scythe, and his eyes blazed like twin flames staring up at the serpent.

Teramir smirked and flicked his tongue. "A timely arrival."

The world seemed to recoil around the stag. Screaming mortals scattered instinctively, bodies pressed against guardrails, abandoning vehicles mid-bridge as if fleeing a wildfire. His presence alone bent the air—heavy, suffocating, oppressive—it was the cave all over again.

It was pure *rage*.

Ash's breath caught in his throat. Memories of the shattered world from his dreams flashed in his mind. The scythe in

Thanatos' grip pulsed brighter, its red core flaring like a heart pushed too far.

Teramir laughed softly.

"Oh, look at you," the serpent cooed, drifting higher as if savoring the sight. "Our *oblivion incarnate*. No cathedral. No throne. No reapers to do your work. Just you, exposed among the very mortals you claim to despise."

Thanatos' gaze wasn't on Teramir, though.

It was on Ash.

The inky tendril tightened around his torso in response to the new crushing energy, pinning his arms tighter to his sides. Ash gasped, breath tearing from his lungs as he growled.

Thanatos' eyes narrowed. His jaw clenched, his ears back.

"Bring. Him. To. Me," he commanded. His voice carried effortlessly through the barrel canal, over the roar of wind and water and clamoring mortals, rendering them silent. It vibrated every structure, every being, even the bridges themselves.

Ash felt his stomach drop when the tentacle holding him abruptly lowered him as Teramir adjusted his hovering to meet the stag's gaze at eye level. He slowly began moving backward towards the train bridge. More of the inky substance rose from the sea floor, holding the water away from the exposed gold like a dam on both sides under the bridges.

"Oh," the serpent snickered. "You're going to have to try harder than that."

Fighting back the urge to hurl, Ash's eyes flicked down to the now brightly glowing structure that was now fully exposed at the base of the canal. *That's a long way down...* The sand had fully exposed what looked precisely like, well, a large vein. No different from what you would see on a medical model. Smaller branches broke off its sides, descending deeper into the Earth. The thickest part, about as wide as a sunken barge, lay exposed in the sand, golden liquid visibly flowing and moving through the planet's crust.

Ash's eyes widened at the sight. He shifted to glance at Teramir, who was still backing them away toward the train bridge, then back at Thanatos. His energy thickened in the air, staining it like coffee on a white sheet. Shadows extended from under his hooves, lifting him from the asphalt with an unsettling ease. He rose above the bridge, then the shadows began guiding him towards Teramir. He took his scythe in both hands.

"Drop. Him!" the stag's voice boomed. The bass in his voice caused Ash's bones to vibrate under his skin.

"You want me to *drop* him?" Teramir smirked playfully, tilting his head.

Thanatos' eyes widened slightly.

Ash's heart dropped.

The tendrils that encircled his body loosened ever so slightly, causing Ash to gasp. His claws scraped against them.

"*Stop!*"

A familiar voice echoed from behind the serpent.

The trio turned their attention to the train bridge, where Lunette stood atop the beams of the arch. Sword gripped in hand, trembling ever so slightly. Their snowy white hair glowed like a halo around their horns from the sunrise in front of them, eyes blazing with determination despite their visible struggle to maintain their stance. Next to them, Leroy clung to a beam with all his limbs, struggling to pull himself up next to Lunette.

"Lunette," Ash uttered quietly, unable to look away from the sight before him.

Teramir tilted his head the other way in thought. "Well, isn't this *fun?* This is turning into quite a party. However," he turned his attention back to the stag whose eyes were still locked onto Ash, "I'd like to move this along. I'm not one for doing exactly what I'm told, but... you did tell me to drop him."

Just as Ash whipped around to look at Teramir the tendrils that held him hostage vanished. It was like time held still for just a moment as he hovered in the air... then plummeted.

Ash could barely register Lunette's scream over his own as he clawed at the air, yelling as he plunged rapidly towards the exposed seafloor of the canal. He squeezed his eyes shut, feeling the rush of cold fall air, preparing for inevitable contact with the ground.

Yet something else struck him—a wave of warm energy hit hard, gripping him tightly. He sensed a gust of wind, followed by sudden calm, before he was sent rolling into the damp sand. Ash's claws dug into the pressure that grasped him as they tumbled in the drenched, salty sand.

They came to a halt, Ash flopping on top of whatever it was that grasped him so firmly. Breathing in ragged gasps, he opened his eyes just a fraction, trembling all over. Staring up at him were two big, blue doe-like eyes.

"Fancy meeting you here." Lunette breathed through gasping breaths, a smile crossing their lips. They were covered in sand; the side of their face was illuminated by the golden glow of the vein that was now only a few yards away from them.

"Lunette." Ash stared at them, dumbfounded. He took a moment to study their face to ground himself. Maybe he really did die?

"How did you do that?"

"I can make portals better now, aren't you proud of me?"

"You *jumped* off a bridge!"

A loud *ting* rang out right beside them as Lunette's sword lodged into the ground beside them. Ash flinched away from the blade with a gasp, but Lunette firmly held onto his arms to hold him in place, so he didn't get struck. "Easy!"

Ash brought his attention back to them, shaking his head and still gasping for breath. "You're here. You're alive."

"Yeah, I am." They shared a brief, breathless laugh before their gaze drifted to something behind Ash. *"Move!"*

With a swift motion, he was hurled off Lunette, landing hard as sand exploded into the air right next to them. Ash tumbled, rolling in the seaweed-covered muck, before pushing himself up onto his hands and knees, shaking some kelp from his ears. He surveyed the scene. The glistening vein that flowed in the center of the canal was massive. Exposed above the sand now, the liquid flowed through it like molten metal. It pulsed like a heartbeat from this close, causing the ground to shudder faintly with each beat.

In the newly formed crater near it, Thanatos was pinning Teramir down with the snath of his scythe, using both hands to push it closer to his neck as the serpent struggled to push it away. With a yell, the naga threw Thanatos back. The stag rolled but landed on his hooves, skidding with the scythe in his grip. Within seconds he charged at the serpent again, swinging his scythe, but Teramir dodged each strike with trained precision.

"You're out of practice!" he hissed, throwing Thanatos back once more, this time with an ethereal, bright purple arcane blast.

The stag fell backwards, skidding back almost against the black, inky dam under the train bridge.

Using his scythe for support, he pushed himself upright, grim determination etched across his face as he gritted his teeth. He steadied himself, forcing his body forward.

Without warning, an oily tendril snaked out from the dam, twisting rapidly through the air. It coiled tightly around the wrist with which he gripped his scythe, halting his advance and threatening to wrench the weapon from his grasp. A snarl ripped through his teeth as he pulled against it. Another tentacle lurched from the dam and twisted around his other leg. Teramir watched, eyes radiating, a sharp, toothy grin spread across his face.

"The prison was a fluke! You're out of touch, out of shape after all these years of having other beings do your dirty—"

A strike across the face that sent Teramir hurtling into the raised golden vein beside them cut his monologue short. Lunette stood nearby with the sword in their grasp. They shook their fist out from the punch, shakily moving towards Teramir. "I don't think you get to talk about 'other beings' doing the work for you."

Teramir hissed at the faun, righting himself against the vein. "*You!* Decided to crawl your way back to save your *lover* despite his betrayal?"

Lunette struck at the Creator with their sword, but he dodged; their blade nearly collided with the vein before they stopped themselves. Teramir whipped around, his tail swiping their hooves out from under them, causing them to fall back with a dense *thud.*

"You have no idea what you're dealing with here! I will not be touched by ravel such as you!" The naga hissed.

Thanatos yanked himself free from the tendrils, rolling his shoulders back and adjusting the grip on his scythe. He lunged at Teramir once more from behind, throwing his arms over the serpent's head to lock him against his body, snath pinned to his throat. Teramir grabbed at the stag's hands and whipped him back and forth, attempting to unsteady his hooves in the sand.

Ash hurried over to Lunette, who was almost standing, and helped both of them get to their feet. He gripped their arm and yanked them away from the Creators' struggle. "Come on!" he shouted.

"What?"

"We need to get out of here; they're going to end up killing us!"

"Ash, there's a bigger problem here than us—"

"*Coward!*" Teramir's voice cut through the air.

Ash barely had time to register movement before Teramir slammed his full weight into Thanatos.

The impact sent the stag skidding backward into the exposed vein, hooves scraping uselessly against the slick sand. Thanatos hit hard, the breath tearing from his lungs with an animalistic snarl as his back struck the glowing life force behind him. The ground trembled, the vein pulsing violently under the sudden pressure.

Teramir moved with brutal precision.

He slipped out from under the scythe before the stag could recover. The naga's clawed hands crashed down on the snath, forcing it flat against Thanatos' throat. The impact rattled Ash's bones from where he stood.

Thanatos snarled, baring blood-streaked teeth as golden ichor ran down his muzzle. The scar on his chest split wider with the movement of him pushing back hard against Teramir, weeping blood that stained his tattered red robe.

"I am ending this," Teramir hissed, looming over him. "You will not crawl back to your realm. It all ends here."

Thanatos opened his mouth to shout back but halted mid-breath. Something *shifted*. Something else soaked the arm sleeve of his robe.

He turned his head and froze.

The blade of his own scythe had sunk deep into the vein beneath him, its tip buried in the glowing structure. Brilliant gold spilled down the curve of the metal, coating Thanatos' arm and side. The crimson orb at the staff's peak flared, the red light surged as black shadows emitted from it flowed down the blade into the open wound, threading into the exposed life force like dye into water.

Teramir leaned back, eyes alight, grin unhinged.

Lunette's breath caught.

Ash's ears flattened as dread clenched his chest. "What... what is happening?" he whispered.

The answer came violently.

Black ink erupted from the stone beneath Teramir, tendrils snapping upward like living things. One coiled tight around Thanatos' throat, crushing down until his head was yanked back so far, his antlers pierced the structure too. Another wrapped his legs, anchoring him helplessly against the glowing vein.

Teramir wrenched the scythe free, causing the golden liquid and black death magic to gush from the exposed wound. Thanatos braced against the tendrils; he outstretched his hand at Teramir to summon the scythe back to him—

The sound was sickening.

Violent energy tore from the stag's body in a shockwave, shadows lashing around his hooves wildly as if trying to claw their way to Teramir. Golden blood poured down his torso, splattering the seafloor from Teramir slashing his chest wound wide open. He drug the blade across it, splitting his hide apart like an overstuffed coat busting open.

Ash's feet moved without thought, but Lunette grabbed him and held him back. "*Stop!*" he screamed, his voice breaking.

Teramir didn't look at Ash. Instead, he reeled back, the scythe above his head, and drove the blade downward in an arching motion into the vein again, splitting it further, causing the gold liquid to spurt out from around it. The life force pulsed erratically now, light flaring and dimming in panicked bursts. The ground beneath them shook.

"This will be the last world to perish," Teramir snarled. "And you with it."

"*No!*"

Lunette surged forward, jumping in front of Ash, their sword slashing wildly as they screamed. Their strike never landed.

A blast of magic caught them mid-step and hurled them aside like a broken doll. They hit the ground hard, skidding across sand back against the dam.

Ash's vision went white.

"*Lunette!*"

Magic tore through his veins as he lashed out on pure instinct—but the attack shattered against a rising wall of black. Tendrils snapped up, wrapping around his wrists and yanking him off his feet, slamming him into the ground with enough force to knock the air from his lungs. He gasped, struggling uselessly as the ink burned against his skin.

"Don't you understand?" Teramir shouted over the chaos. "That reaper was right. This is the only way it ends. Thanatos will die with this world, engulfed in its implosion! The Great Plan will finally be over!"

The scythe embedded beside Thanatos began to hiss; the orb glowing brighter and brighter. The light surged, light exploding outward as its death magic was forcibly injected into the Earth, corrupting the golden flow. The life force convulsed violently—then erupted.

A beam of blinding light tore skyward, black magic spiraling around it. The clouds split apart, the rift to Nullhymm yawning open above as the beam connected with it, a bridge of light and ruin.

The very lifeforce of the Earth. The ichor that coursed beneath the surface and connected to its core… Was now being drained into Nullhymm. The sky darkened. The trees and grass along the sides of the canal started to droop.

Ash and Lunette stared at the sight, agog. The light from the bleeding vein and beam spilled across the sand like molten gold, casting eerie reflections on the inky dam holding back either side of the canal, and reflecting in the tears welling up in Lunette's eyes.

Did we… just start the end of the world?

Ash looked over at Lunette.

His chest hurt.

Every hair on his body, every cell in his being, felt heavy.

Lunette simply stared up at the sky from where they lay on the ground. He shifted his eyes to Thanatos, who also stared at the sky. His chest heaved, his eyes no longer glowed, his energy dull. Golden blood coated his face and body. The great, violent rage Ash felt radiating from him before had vanished.

"Yes. We did," his voice whispered in the back of Ash's mind. His eyes drifted closed.

"Well, my work here is finished. My task is done." Teramir looked over the broken beings scattered about him; he let go of the scythe and brushed back his iridescent hair. "The Great Plan is no more. Evil is vanquished from the universe, thanks to *me*. Too bad the others couldn't be here to watch you explode into dust, Thanatos." He grabbed Thanatos' chin with a clawed hand, jerking it up to look at him, yanking his antlers free from being lodged in the vein, forcing Thanatos' eyes to open slightly. "You are defeated."

Teramir's hand dropped from the stag. He waved it in front of him, tearing open a portal to who-knows-where. "This has been fun, absolutely riveting. I will be taking my leave. Enjoy the end!"

With that, he slithered through the portal, the inky tendrils receding from around Ash and Thanatos, and the dams falling. The water did not move , the energy radiating from the open wound kept the water away, leaving it exposed.

Ash scrambled to his feet, darting to Thanatos who now sat slumped against the gushing, open vein. He kneeled down beside the stag and looked over the gaping wound in his chest.

Thanatos' breathing was shallow, each exhale trembling with the effort it took to keep going. The rage was gone. The oppressive magic that made the world around him bend was completely absent. He felt nearly mortal. Ash pressed his paws against his golden-stained gray fur, desperate to staunch the flow, but the wound pulsed endlessly.

His mind raced with images of his parents, their gaping wounds, their screams, everyone in that room he couldn't save.

I'm not letting someone else die. I can't.

Ash's eyes met the Creator's, his whole body shook.

You're all I have left of the past.

The world seemed to hold its breath, the silence after Teramir's departure stretching out, heavy and suffocating. The pulse and hum of the life force being drawn into the rift was muffled in Ash's ears.

The stag's eyes opened slightly to stare at Ash, who sat frozen, unsure what to do.

"We have to stop this. This can't happen." Ash breathed shakily, still pressing his paws to the wound. "If anyone can fix this, it's you." His green eyes looked up at the stag, whose lips were pursed.

"I cannot... fix this. It is already done," he whispered.

"You *have to*! You—"

Ash was interrupted by something bright appearing in the corner of his vision. The feeling of overbearing neutral energy surrounded him. He turned his head to see the tip of a sword pointed directly at Thanatos... At the end of it stood Lunette, towering over them, arm shaking.

"Ash. I don't want you to see this," they said, eyes locked on the stag.

"What are you doing, Lunette?" Ash spat, eyes wide.

"Ash, you know what he's done. Everyone he's killed. He did this! We need to kill him and find a way to fix this!" They gestured to the open rift in the sky. "You have no idea the damage he's already done, Ash! He doesn't deserve to live!" Their voice cracked on the last word.

Ash's ears flattened. "Lunette, I know firsthand everything he has done. But *Teramir* did *this*. He started the end."

"*This* time! Thanatos was also planning this himself; Teramir only sped up the process! And what about all the other times? I must finish what I started! I have to clean up my own mess!"

Ash flinched at the words. The words he had spoken in Connecticut lingered in his mind. *Do you just stumble through life waiting for someone to come along and clean up your messes?*

"Lunette... What did you do?"

They stared at Ash, tears welling up in the corners of their eyes. Something unreadable was behind them. Something Ash didn't recognize. Their grip on the sword tightened, their breath shaking as the conflict raged across their face.

"This... This is my mess. Every cycle, every life Thanatos took, and I couldn't stop him. I've carried this burden too long, Ash. For gods' sake, it was my hand that released him. This is *my* mess I've dragged you and everyone else I've ever known into yet again. And if I don't end it now, it will never end."

In a sudden movement, Ash stood. He positioned himself between Lunette and the wounded stag. His posture was rigid. The tip of the sword just barely grazed his chest. His skull markings nearly glowed in the golden light. Jaw clenched. Claws curling into his palms.

"Lunette," he said firmly, yet desperation snuck in, "I know what he has done. I don't really know what you're talking about, but... I mean, for fuck's sake, he killed my parents." Lunette flinched at the words, their teeth bared slightly before Ash continued.

"But... I can't let you kill him. He's all that's left of them."

For a moment, Lunette faltered, shoulders sagging from the weight of old memories and new pain, the sword trembling in their grip as the tip barely grazed Ash. Images of Alastair flickered in their mind. The feeling of Valdis' wet fur in their hands as they clutched his lifeless form.

"Ash... I don't want to hurt you." Their voice trembled; their pleading eyes locked on him. "Please... move. Let me finish this by myself. Let me clean up my mess."

"I'm not moving, Lunette," he breathed, despite the firmness behind his eyes... He still couldn't believe he was standing up for this... This *monster*. Was he doing the right thing? Is this wrong? "I won't let you kill him."

The corners of Lunette's lips trembled. Their eyes flicked from the broken Creator, who stared at them numbly, to Ash.

Ash stood firm. He did not summon magic. He did not flinch away. "If you want to kill him, you're going to have to kill me first." He felt like he was watching the scene from afar. The words left his mouth. While he meant every word, it felt... foreign. "I won't let anyone else get killed."

"Ash—I... I can't—"

"*Wait!*" a voice cut through the tension. Lunette and Ash whipped their heads towards the train bridge to see Leroy running over breathlessly. He stopped and bent over coughing and holding his chest. His brown and blue hair stuck out in all directions, his robe askew on his body, and the bone daggers on his hips looked as if they might fall off his belt at any moment.

"If you kill him," he stifled a cough and sat up to look at the two, "we're all going to fucking die here."

"What do you mean?" Lunette pressed, their ears flattened.

"Because without him we can't get back to Nullhymm and avoid all this bullshit! We're sitting ducks down here while the world's life force is sucked through a straw there!"

"Why can't we just use the portal from before and get out of here?" Ash interjected.

"And let everyone on Earth die?" Lunette exclaimed, looking at Ash.

"Ah," Leroy tilted his head side to side, "someone... May have closed all the portals to Nullhymm. Except for that rift, obviously."

"You *what?*" Thanatos hissed softly from his spot slumped on the ground, through gritted teeth, causing Ash and Lunette to flinch.

"I didn't think I'd get trapped down here too!" Leroy shouted, gesturing wildly to the beam of light behind the stag. "I was supposed to be up there! I can't open a portal like this!" He gestured wildly to himself, stifling a cough.

"What happened to 'we perish together?' Your whole stoic speech?" Ash sneered.

"That was when I *knew* I wasn't going to die *again!*"

"Oh, yeah, before you betrayed us? You've betrayed us again *here!* All for your own fucking gain!"

"It was for the greater good! I knew the only way to stop—"

"Okay!" Lunette interrupted, shaking their head, raising their freehand toward Leroy, and scrunching their nose in annoyance. "I... can't open a portal either. Not... for a bit, anyways."

They sighed in exhaustion before looking back at the disheveled Creator on the ground.

Thanatos looked up at them wincing, his hand was now over his chest. "I cannot open... a portal in this condition." He breathed, looking up at the rift in the sky. "And we cannot go through that one."

"Then how do we stop all of this? We can't let everyone die!" Lunette shook the sword a bit as they spoke, causing Ash to tense up.

"Why not?" Leroy shouted.

"Because that would be *wrong!*"

"No one else is allowed to die!" Ash interrupted. His paw came up to pinch the bridge of his nose, then slid his hand down the markings on his face.

The trio stared at one another, then all simultaneously turned to look at Thanatos. He looked up at them, gritting his teeth while attempting to hold the wound on his chest closed.

"How do we stop this process?" Lunette said quickly, lowering the sword ever so slightly.

"We cannot. It's already started." Thanatos squeezed his eyes shut for a moment, then reopened them to look at Ash, a hint of something in his eyes. Was it remorse? "We're *all* doomed here."

"There *has* to be a way." Lunette looked at the gaping wound with the scythe still lodged inside it. "The blade is stifling some of the flow..." Their ears suddenly perked, their eyes widened as they looked at Ash quickly. "What if we healed it?"

"Healed what?"

"*That.*" Lunette pointed at the exposed vein that steadily was draining into Nullhymm. The hum of the flow vibrated the air as it steadily drained upwards.

Ash turned slightly to look down at Thanatos, whose brows were knitted together. "You would need a skilled healer. Beyond skilled. Possibly an army of them. Even then… I do not believe it is possible." The stag wheezed at the last word and stifled a cough.

"You *used* to be a healer." Leroy sneered, looking away from the group. He fished around in his pockets, extracting a single, bent cigarette.

Thanatos' eyes drifted down. Ash's ears flicked in thought before he looked at Lunette. "Teramir was saying Thanatos was going to destroy all of their 'hard work.' If the planets are all made from all the Creators… Could they be fixed the same way they were created?"

"Would that mean… We have to find all the Creators? All four of them?"

"Well," Ash gestured to Thanatos, "we've got one."

Lunette's brows knitted together in thought; they lowered their sword, and Ash visibly relaxed. "How would we even do that? They're probably all over the universe."

"There has to be a way." Ash pressed.

"Well, this is fun. You guys look like you have your hands full with that plan. I'm going to go try to find a way off this stupid floating rock." Leroy interjected, backing up slowly.

Lunette jerked the tip of their sword in his direction with a growl. "You're not going anywhere. You literally got us into this mess, you're going to help us fix it!"

Leroy put his hands up quickly, eyes widening at the sword tip that was mere inches from his stomach. *"Fine!"* He used his finger to, ever so carefully, push the blade away from himself. "So we either heal the planet... or explode into a million pieces?"

"Pretty much."

"Where the hell are we going to start then?"

"I don't know," Ash turned to stare up at the gaping hole in the sky. The glittering light reflected in his green eyes, the vibration subtly rattling his bones. Mortals were stopped along the sides of the canal to gawk, news helicopters appeared overhead to survey the scene. "I hate all of this."

Lunette moved to stand beside him, also gazing up at the abyss consuming the planet little by little.

"That's how we know we're on the right track."

Ash, Lunette, Leroy, and Thanatos will return.
Lesser Gods: Revival
Coming soon.

About the Author

"A huge nerd."

Alex Frey is an author, illustrator, and full-time daydreamer with an insatiable love for fantasy, sci-fi, and horror. Fueled by coffee and spite, they've been crafting the *Lesser Gods* saga since 2017.

As an autistic, LGBTQ+ creative, Alex is on a mission to bring more representation to the genres they adore. They hope to encourage people that anyone can blaze their own trail with enough determination, passion, and audacity. When they're not writing or sketching their favorite characters, you can probably find them in a movie theatre, gaming, or plotting their next adventure.

Follow the Alex and the *Lesser Gods* Journey!

Join the Newsletter & Check Out Their Blog
www.lessergodsofficial.com